ZANDER

HEROES AT HEART

MARYANN JORDAN

Cover Design by: Becky McGraw

Editor: Shannon Brandee Eversoll

Proofreader: Myckel Anne Phillips

ISBN print 978-1-947214-09-5

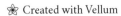 Created with Vellum

As a adolescent counselor for over twenty-five years, I had the opportunity to work with many young people. One young man, upset over a poor choice he had made, came to me. As I listened to his story and his confession, I told him that the true measure of a man was not in the mistakes he made, but in how he handled those mistakes. I remember the look on his face when I told him I was sure he was going to be a good man.

So this book is dedicated to all the students over the years who allowed me to be a part of their lives.

ACKNOWLEDGMENTS

First and foremost, I have to thank my husband, Michael. Always believing in me and wanting me to pursue my dreams, this book would not be possible without his support. To my daughters, MaryBeth and Nicole, I taught you to follow your dreams and now it is time for me to take my own advice. You two are my inspiration.

My best friend, Tammie, who for over twenty years has been with me through thick and thin. You've filled the role of confidant, supporter, and sister.

My other best friend, Myckel Anne, who keeps me on track, keeps me grounded, and most of all – keeps my secrets. Thank you for not only being my proof-reader and my Marketing PA, but friend. I do not know what I would do without you in my life.

My beta readers kept me sane, cheered me on, found all my silly errors, and often helped me understand my characters through their eyes. A huge thank you to

Denise, Sandi, Barbara, Jennifer, Danielle, Tracey, Lynn, Stracey, and Jamila for being my beta girls who love alphas!

Shannon Brandee Eversoll as my editor and Myckel Anne Phillips as my proofreader gave their time and talents to making all my books as well written as it can be.

My street team, Jordan Jewels, you all are amazing! You volunteer your time to promote my books and I cannot thank you enough! I hope you will stay with me, because I have lots more stories inside, just waiting to be written!

My Personal Assistant Barbara Martoncik keeps me going when I feel overwhelmed and I am so grateful for not only her assistance, but her friendship.

Most importantly, thank you readers. You allow me into your home for a few hours as you disappear into my characters and you support me as I follow my indie author dreams.

AUTHOR INFORMATION

I am an avid reader of romance novels, often joking that I cut my teeth on the historical romances. I have been reading and reviewing for years. In 2013, I finally gave into the characters in my head, screaming for their story to be told. From these musings, my first novel, Emma's Home, The Fairfield Series was born.

I was a high school counselor having worked in education for thirty years. I live in Virginia, having also lived in four states and two foreign countries. I have been married to a wonderfully patient man for thirty-six years. When writing, my dog or one of my four cats can generally be found in the same room if not on my lap.

Please take the time to leave a review of this book.

Feel free to contact me, especially if you enjoyed my book. I love to hear from readers!

Facebook

Email
Website

Author's Note

I have lived in numerous states as well as overseas, but for the last twenty years have called Virginia my home. All my stories take place in this wonderful commonwealth, but I choose to use fictional city names with some geographical accuracies.

These fictionally named cities allow me to use my creativity and not feel constricted by attempting to accurately portray the areas.

It is my hope that my readers will allow me this creative license and understand my fictional world.

I also do quite a bit of research on my books and try to write on subjects with accuracy. There will always be points where creative license will be used to create scenes or plots.

Hanging onto the windowsill, his grip slipping, the thought entered twelve-year-old Zander's mind that perhaps he should have thought the adventure—or rather misadventure—through more carefully. *I'm the oldest...I'm the leader...I can't back out now.*

His foot found a limb on the old, gnarled tree next to the house and he slowly let go of the windowsill with one hand, listening for sounds of cracking. Luckily, the only sounds that met his ears were the wind blowing through the bare branches and the gasps from the two boys peering down at him from the open window, their eyes wide with fright.

Sliding to the limb on his knees, he grasped its rough bark, wincing slightly as it abraded his palms. Looking upward, he spied two pale faces, eyes wide and mouths hanging open. "I got it now," he claimed in a whisper, his words braver than he felt. "Hang on and I'll get the ladder."

Miss Ethel's bedroom was on the first floor, right at the bottom of the stairs, and Zander surreptitiously looked in that direction. He was not sure, but he often thought she had supernatural powers because she seemed to know when they were up to something even before they did it.

Shimmying along the branch, its sturdiness increasing as he neared the trunk, his confidence grew. Reaching the thick truck, he climbed down the rest of the way, landing on the soft ground with a thump. The moon was hidden behind a cloud, but he knew his way. The yard was neat, Miss Ethel making sure he and the others picked up their toys each evening. Same with the inside rooms. *An orderly house helps create an orderly mind.* Miss Ethel's words rang in his head and he stifled a grin.

A ladder was lying on the ground, left there by the man who had been hired to clean the gutters. As soon as he saw it, a plan formed in his mind. A way for them to escape without Miss Ethel finding out.

The ladder was heavier than he thought and, as it bumped against the side of the house twice, he winced at the clanging. Leaning it against the windowsill, he held it steady as the two other boys scrambled down. Rafe and Cael, both eleven, looked at him, ready to follow his lead. Watching as he plastered himself against the brick, not breathing, they then did the same, listening to see if Miss Ethel was stirring. All was quiet.

"Come on," he said, waving for the others to follow, the sound of dogs barking in the distance causing them all to hurry.

Slipping through the gate at the back of the yard, they ran down the alley between the properties. The streetlight's ineffective illumination concealed them as they skirted between trash cans and puddles in the broken concrete.

"Are we going to get in trouble?" Cael asked, his brow creased with worry as he hustled to keep up with the others.

"Shh," Rafe hushed him, not wanting Zander to know he, too, was worried.

The three made their way to the small store a few blocks from their house. Zander had been inside the Five n' Dime the prior week and that was when the idea had been born. He had tagged along as Miss Ethel shopped for a few items, carefully pricing them as she searched the store. With six boys in the house to feed and care for, he had watched her count out her change in the stores long enough to know that there was precious little money to take care of all their needs. As they passed a counter with dime store jewelry, he observed as her pace slowed and her eyes cut over to the necklaces. She appeared taken with a shiny gold one in the shape of a heart. With a sigh, she had passed on by, but Zander had stopped and stared at the pretty piece.

"Come on, Alexander," she had called. "Don't dawdle."

He had rushed to catch up to her in line, waiting as she carefully counted out her money for their purchases.

Now, in the dark, the store loomed large in front of

them, the poor lights ineffectively stabbing at the shadows the boys stayed in. Zander led them to the alley where they halted outside the back door. The smell of garbage hit him and he wrinkled his nose.

"How we gonna get inside?" Cael asked. "Ain't it locked?"

"Nah. I heard Mr. Timms on the phone complaining to someone that they needed to come fix the lock. That's why I figured we could get in before it gets fixed."

Rafe and Cael stood still, watching as Zander lifted a shaking hand to the doorknob. Giving it a hard turn, he felt the doorknob shift in his hand. With his heart in his throat, he pulled and as the door opened, he felt his breath leave his body in a whoosh.

"Come on," he ordered.

Slipping in first, he led the trio through the back hall to the store. The narrow aisles were lined with racks of clothing and pillows, the shelves filled with dishes and cups. Zander passed them all, his eyes on the prize, moving directly to the jewelry.

"Oh, my God," Rafe exclaimed, staring at the candy bars. "Look at all this stuff. We could take anything we want and they'd never know."

Cael, a grin spreading across his face, looked at the toy trains. "Zander...can we take something?"

"No," came the harsh whisper. "We ain't here to steal nothing."

"What do you mean? Ain't we gonna steal that?" Rafe accused, pointing to what was now in Zander's hand.

"Yeah, but this is for a good cause," Zander defended.

Rafe and Cael walked over and stared down at what

4

he was holding. The shiny, gold, heart necklace lay in his palm, barely glistening in the slim light coming from the front window.

"We got what we came for," he said, "now let's go." Sticking the necklace into his pocket, he headed toward the back door knowing the others would follow, slipping out as silently as they had entered.

"Surprise!" the boys all cried, rushing into the house after school, surrounding Miss Ethel as she sat in her rocking chair knitting. Immediately bursting into a round of "Happy Birthday to You", the six boys currently living with her laughed at her shocked expression followed by her huge smile. Her grey hair was twisted into a bun at the back of her head, her glasses perched on her nose. Wearing a shirtdress, neatly belted at the waist, stockings, and comfortable black shoes, she always looked the same to Zander—comfortable, loving, safe.

He once overheard one of the social workers from school, who always came to check on him and the others, tell his teacher that Miss Ethel was the best foster parent they knew and any child she took in was lucky. Zander did not need to hear that because he already knew it. He had been around long enough to know there were some foster parents who should not have kids, no matter how bad things were where the kid came from. But Miss Ethel was…home.

The room was comfortably furnished with a dark

green sofa, colorful throw pillows against the back. The wooden end tables were covered in white, crocheted lace. A thick rug covered the center of the wooden floor. Two, deep cushioned chairs sat facing the sofa, one always used by Miss Ethel, her knitting bag at her feet. The walls on either side of the fireplace held bookshelves filled with children's books.

"Oh, my stars!" she exclaimed, drawing Zander's attention back to their celebration. She tossed her knitting needles to the floor and, standing, hugged each boy. "How did you know?"

"Duh," Rafe said. "You got it written in your Bible. You know, in the back with the other birthdays."

"Well, aren't you clever," she pronounced.

Rafe, Cael, Jaxon, Jayden, and Asher settled on the rug, sitting cross-legged in a circle, while Zander stood behind them, watching as she accepted the presents they had for her.

Asher, nine years old, was the youngest. His snaggle-toothed grin lit his face as he held up a rock painted with her name surrounded by pink and red hearts. "It can hold open your cookbook when you're making us cookies."

Tears filled her eyes as she exclaimed it to be the best paperweight she ever saw.

The ten-year-old twins, Jaxon and Jayden, gave her a picture frame they made from painted popsicle sticks. "As soon as we get a picture of us, we're gonna put it in there," Jax announced, Jayden nodding enthusiastically.

"Well, boys, I declare, I've never had such a good birthday," she smiled.

Rafe and Cael bounced up and down on their knees, enthusiasm spilling over. "We've got something too! Zander's got it!"

Just as Zander stuck his hand in his pocket, a strange feeling hit his gut, as though one of the other boys had punched him. Pushing the emotion down, he pulled out the paper towel wrapped gift and handed it to her.

"Oh, my, what can this be?" she wondered aloud. Her fingers shook as she opened the present and she gasped at the heart necklace laying in her palm.

Her eyes darted quickly to him and he swore he saw a flash of doubt in them, but she only smiled and said, "It's beautiful."

Standing, she gathered her gifts and asked, "Well, I guess it's a good thing I made a cake today while you were in school. Who wants some?"

"Me, me," they shouted, trailing her like ducklings as she moved into the kitchen.

That night, Zander lay in bed reading aloud to the other boys while they played with their trucks on the floor. He loved reading and was thankful Miss Ethel had not given up on him when he came to live with her four years ago. Now reading beyond his age, he devoured every book he could get his hands on.

Miss Ethel came upstairs, first taking Jaxon, Jayden, and Asher into their room, tucking them in after their prayers. When she walked into their room, she sat down on Zander's bed, a warm smile on her face.

"Boys, we need to talk about the necklace you gave me," she began.

Cael and Rafe's eyes widened, shooting their glances over to Zander. He sat very still, his gut hurting even while he forced a blank expression on his face. The same one he used to wear when the other students teased him about his dirty, worn clothes.

"I know you don't have any money," she began, her voice warm and soft.

"We helped Mr. Timms and he let us have it as payment," he lied, each word stabbing his stomach even more. Cael and Rafe's eyes now bugged, their mouths hanging open wide.

She lifted her brow at the same time as she lifted her hand, interrupting him. "Zander, do you remember what I told you boys about words? Words are so important…they can hurt or they can heal. A person needs to choose their words wisely. That's what I need you to do right now. Talk to me, honey, but don't tell me what you think I want to hear. Tell me what I need to know."

The lump in his throat made it hard to swallow, the sting of tears hitting his eyes causing him to blink rapidly. His voice barely above a whisper, he confessed, "I took it."

She lifted her hand to his head, smoothing his hair back. "Can you tell me why?"

"I saw you looking at it and it was so pretty. You should have something pretty." A tear slid down his cheek and he glanced at the others, seeing Cael and Rafe crying too.

"It wasn't just him, Miss Ethel," Rafe said. "We helped."

"I don't want to go to jail," Cael cried.

"Shhh, now. No one is going to jail. But what do you think we need to do about this?" she asked, peering closely at each boy.

"I'll take it back...tomorrow morning. I'll tell Mr. Timms what I did," Zander said, the words jerking from his quivering chest.

"We'll go together," she said. "Now y'all climb into bed." Bending to kiss Cael and Rafe, she moved back to Zander's bed. "Do you know what your name means, Alexander?"

Wrapping his arm around his middle, he shook his head.

"Alexander. That's a Greek name. A very important name. It means defender of men." She chuckled, adding, "Well, defender of women, as well." She reached over, her hand gentle on his arm. "You've always been such a leader. I remember when you first came to live with me. The social worker was afraid you were so behind in school that you'd be lost. But I knew how smart you were. Smart and good. Such a good boy. And, you've helped me so much with the others."

His mouth tightened into a straight line, but her soothing touch made his stomach hurt a little less.

"And now look at you, reading books that are so much above your age. So smart...and so good. I know why you took the necklace and it touches my heart that you cared to get me something. But Zander, all I ever want is for you boys to be safe, happy, and as good as you can be. That's the only present I need."

"You deserve to have something pretty," he said, his heart heavy.

"Sweetie, my something pretty is seeing you boys smile every day. It's seeing the sunset or a pretty flower."

"I'm sorry, Miss Ethel," he said, another tear sliding down his cheek. He hated the feeling of disappointing her. He remembered what life was like before he landed on her doorstep. His mom being gone for days strung out on drugs, looking for her next fix, leaving him with no food. He had been in two other foster homes for only a few months until Miss Ethel took him in. Now he had clean clothes that fit. Food in his belly. School every day. And books. She made sure he could go to the library any time he wanted.

"Oh, Zander," she smiled, leaning over to kiss his forehead. "The measure of a man isn't in the mistakes he makes. The true measure of a man is in how he handles those mistakes."

The next day, he tried to hide the quivers as he stood in front of Mr. Timms and confessed the theft. Miss Ethel was stunned at the lengths the boys had gone to in order to get the present for her and made them vow to never climb out of the window again. Mr. Timms peered over his glasses at the three of them, his face severe.

"Well, I suggest that you three boys come over every day after school next week and work for me until suppertime," he said, his deep voice reverberating through them. "That'll work off the necklace, which I agree, Miss Ethel should have."

Zander's breath left him in a whoosh, a grin snaking across his face as the pain in his stomach eased. Casting his gaze up to Miss Ethel, she smiled back at him. Walking home, she put her hand on his shoulder and said, "I always knew it, Zander. You'll make a good man."

2

SIXTEEN YEARS LATER

Friday night. Zander King was already tired and the night was still young. He walked from the back office of Grimm's Bar and cast a wary eye over the crowd. As owner, he should be excited about the business, but he knew the combination of alcohol, loud music, and crowds could be explosive.

He much preferred the days when the bar, at the edge of town, only held a small group of regulars. Faces he knew. People he could talk to…listen to. It had been easy to keep an eye on who was drinking and how much. Plus, he had had no problem cutting them off and ordering a cab for them, though that was still the same. And, yet, his customers always came back. He had made enough money to pay the bills, which was fine for him.

But, with the resurgence of development in the area, more white-collar workers had discovered the bar and word got around that it was a good place to gather after work. So, now, it was packed with bodies, all vying for the bartender's attention and trying to catch the eye of their next dance partner or, more likely, the partner for the night.

As he cast his gaze around the interior, he remembered the hard work that went into Grimm's. When he bought the property it was a wreck inside, but the bones of the building were solid. With the help of his close friends, they turned it into a place he was proud of.

The bar ran along the left side of the long room, ending at the hall leading to the bathrooms, office, and stockroom toward the back. Mismatched bar stools lined the old, wooden bar counter. He thought about polishing it, but somehow the rustic look appealed to him. And, it seemed, to others as well.

Round wooden tables filled most of the space, sturdy wooden chairs circling each one. The walls held little adornment. He figured people came to Grimm's to drink and socialize, not look at decorations. The sound of clinking bottles against glass caused him to turn to his right, watching as his two bartenders worked efficiently, filling orders as the three waitresses hustled to keep up with the demand. Laughter filled the room, mixed with the music from the jukebox.

Lynn, one of the servers, passed him, her fingers linked through multiple long-neck beer bottles, smiling her greeting. A young mother, she worked evenings while her husband watched the kids. She was a hard worker, though her smile gained her extra tips. Zander made sure his servers dressed in jeans and t-shirts, nothing too revealing. He was not desperate enough for money to use sex to sell drinks and was determined to keep the assholes who wanted to hit on waitresses out of his bar.

Catching Joe's eye, one of the bartenders, he lifted his brow in silent question, gaining a quick nod, letting him know everything was under control.

"God, you still look like a grumpy bugger."

The words paired with a clap on the shoulder had him quickly turning around, his gaze landing on a tall man standing behind him. "Rafe! Good to see you, man. When did you get back?"

"Got in this morning. Figured I'd come here first and see you."

The two men hugged, fists thumping each other's backs. Pulling away, Zander stared into the face of his best friend. He did not have to look around the room to know every woman's eyes were pinned on him. Rafe had always been blessed with good looks. Pair that with the serious bodybuilding he had worked on while in the Army, the boyish charm that seemed to come naturally to him and Zander knew women flung themselves at him.

"What?" Rafe asked, placing his hands on his hips. "You're staring at me as though trying to figure me out."

"Nah, just wondering why you haven't got some groupie hanging on your arm—ow! Hell, man. You don't gotta punch me," Zander groused, rubbing his shoulder.

Rafe laughed, drawing more glances his way and ignoring them, as usual. Sliding his gaze over the bar, he said, "Place looks really good. Damn, business is good too. You got people in here drinking and dancing and spending their money."

A jukebox stood in the corner, the music blaring for a group dancing in the back. Scowling, Zander recalled how he had initially balked at purchasing the contraption, but Rafe had insisted people wanted music in a bar.

"Yeah, maybe too good," he grumbled.

"Oh, come on, Zander. This is great. You're doing what you like and making money at the same time."

"And you're not?" Zander watched as a speck of doubt flew through Rafe's eyes, quickly replaced by the ever-present twinkle.

"Sure. What's not to love about having my picture taken and getting paid ridiculous sums of money for it?"

"Ever sorry you did that calendar?" Once more, Zander watched the twinkle dim in Rafe's eyes, this time lasting longer. Two years ago, the Hunks in the Army Calendar featured Rafe as July and as soon as he was discharged modeling contracts rolled in.

Shrugging, he replied, "Nah. Listen, I'm beat from my flight. I'm checking into the hotel—"

"Like hell you are. You still got the keys, so go crash at my place."

"I didn't want to impose in case you were with someone."

Now it was Zander's turn to throw his fists onto his

hips, a glower on his face. "First of all, if I was with someone, don't you think you'd know it? Secondly, I sure as hell don't have time to date and God knows, I'm not hooking up with someone I meet here. Fuck, man. Just head to the apartment and I'll see you tomorrow."

With another back-slapping hug, Zander watched as Rafe weaved through the crowd toward the door. Seeing Zeke, his bouncer, open the door to let Rafe out, he walked past the bar. He inwardly smiled at the sight of the huge, antique pub mirror and cabinet on the wall behind the counter. When he and his friends had first entered the dirty, ramshackle building, his gaze was immediately drawn to the wall behind the bar. While the actual building was falling apart, it held a full length, floor to ceiling, wooden pub cabinet, with a massive mirror, still intact. Running his hand over the dusty oak, he knew the antique alone was worth the price of the building.

Making his way to the door, he greeted Zeke. "How's it going?"

"Good, good, boss. Crowds are pouring in. I've got Roscoe keeping an eye on the numbers so the fire marshall ain't got no reason to complain."

"See any potential problems?"

"Nah, not so far. Roscoe's in the back, but reported all's good."

"Thanks." With a chin lift, he made his way back to the bar. Pulling out his phone, he sent a quick group text. **Rafe's in. Meet tomorrow on schedule. 11am.** Hitting send, he allowed himself a small smile, thinking of tomorrow's activity. A body slammed into the back of him, immediately wiping the smile off his face.

Turning, he glared as a young man, eyes slightly glassy, mumbled, "Sorry, dude."

Dude? Seriously?

"Not your dude, man. I'm the owner and guess who just decided you've had enough." Looking up, he called out, "Roscoe!"

A large, dark-skin man hustled over, a huge smile on his face. Looking at the young man attempting—and failing—to match Zander's glower, he placed his hand on his shoulder. "Time for this one to go, Mr. King?"

Nodding, Zander ordered, "Show him the door, but call a cab."

Roscoe's fingers dug into the young man's shoulder as he maneuvered him toward the door, his phone already at his ear with a cab company on speed dial. Watching to make sure the man was not causing a problem, he walked behind the bar. Seeing Charlene serving drinks with flair, her t-shirt skin tight, he rolled his eyes.

"You servin' drinks or being the show?"

"Aw, boss. You know a girl's got to get her tips where she can," Charlene laughed.

"Just make sure you let us know if anyone gives you a problem."

Winking, she finished pouring tequila shots for one of the servers, and said, "Got it covered, but thanks."

Hearing a rousing cheer go up from the back, he looked over to see the cause. *Bachelor party. Fucking hell.*

Bunch of idiots, taking out a man before his wedding, and plying him with liquor and tales of the ball and chain.

"You okay, Zander?" Joe asked, a grin curving his lips. "You look even more sour than usual."

"You wanna keep this job?" Zander shot back, only barely kidding.

Joe chuckled, shaking his head. Tossing a bottle in the air before pouring the contents into three glasses to the cheers of the crowd around him, he replied, "Admit it. You need me to keep 'em coming back."

From the looks the women were shooting at the hotshot bartender, Zander knew Joe wasn't entirely off the mark with that comment. Blowing out a deep breath, he moved back to the stockroom, escaping the crowd and the noise.

Zander lay in bed scrubbing his hand over his face, having just looked at the clock. Three a.m. When the bar closed, the crew cleaned while he counted the till before locking the money into the safe, seeing everyone out, and setting the security. His apartment was only a ten-minute drive and he was home by two o'clock. With the second bedroom door shut, he assumed Rafe was sound asleep. Showering, he had climbed into bed a few minutes later, only to lay there, his mind on the past.

Rolling over, he punched his pillow a few times before forcing his mind to clear. Giving up on sleep, he sat up and leaned against the headboard after turning on the lamp on the nightstand. Opening the book lying on top of the pile, he began to read, his mind taking flight with the words.

An hour later, he turned out the light, willing sleep to come. Memories of childhood stories full of princes, kingdoms, fairies, and princesses came to mind. Sighing heavily, he knew there was no such thing as a happily-ever-after in real life.

3

Zander drove down the street, the homes on either side seeming much smaller than when he was younger.

"Looks different, doesn't it?" Rafe asked from the passenger seat, his face turned toward his window. "I know you've been around often, but I haven't been back since last year. Some of the houses look a little better than they used to."

"Some of them have been bought by younger couples trying to do the house-flip shit that's on TV. You know, buy a run-down house, put a fuck-ton of money into it, and hope to sell it for a profit."

"Well, they look pretty good."

Turning at the next corner, Zander noticed Rafe lean forward, his gaze now focused on the house at the end of the street. Quiet, neither spoke for a moment, the comfortable silence passing between them.

"Do you ever wonder what would have happened if

we hadn't ended up here?" Rafe asked, his voice strangely hoarse.

"Every damn day," he replied. Pulling to a stop on the street, he parked his truck, but neither made a move to get out.

"She saved my life."

Zander shot a glance at Rafe, wondering what was going through his mind, but did not ask. If he wanted to talk, he would. "I reckon she saved all our lives."

With that, he opened his door, the gift in his hand, meeting Rafe on the sidewalk. A roar of motorcycles came down the street, halting behind them, and they watched as Jayden and Jaxon climbed off. The two pulled off their helmets in sync, shaking out their dark hair, hooking them on the handlebars before turning their wide smiles toward the house. When they moved as one like that, it was hard to remember that they weren't identical twins. Greeting the twins, Zander and Rafe moved forward, hugging the pair.

An SUV was the last to arrive, Cael at the wheel and Asher in the passenger seat. Asher slid out first in the lithe way of his, followed by Cael, the sun catching on his light hair. Both stopped and stared at the house as well. More greetings filled the air before the six of them moved to the front door of the house.

They made the trip every year, sometimes joined by a few of the other boys Miss Ethel raised in the large home she opened whenever social services called. But this year it was just them, all having been taken in at about the same time that came to remember.

Using his key, Zander opened the door and stepped

in, immediately greeted with the smell of Miss Ethel's rosewater perfume, the gentle scent having permeated the walls. Walking into the front hall, the others at his back, he stopped, assaulted by the memories. Miss Ethel greeting them after school with a platter of homemade cookies, dinner around the old, wooden table in the dining room, always finding room for another chair whenever their ranks increased with a visit from another social worker. When times were lean, they had soup and sandwiches. Other times, she would cook a large chicken or roast. When the kitchen was filled with the scent of pies or cookies baking the boys knew after-school snacks would be a treat. All served with love.

Some boys stayed a few weeks, some for longer. And then some, like Zander, stayed until they were eighteen.

Walking past the dining room on the right, he turned toward the living room, once more his mind filled with memories...the holiday decorations and the tree she would have in the corner.

"Well, my goodness, boys. Come in, come in," came the call from the corner chair, next to the floor lamp. Knitting needles now resting on her footstool, Miss Ethel pushed herself upright as Zander hurried to assist.

"Miss Ethel, you know we'd never forget your birthday," he assured her, moving in for a hug, feeling her feeble hands pat his back. "We haven't missed one yet, have we?"

Stepping back to allow the others their chance with her, he stood to the side, watching the annual tradition unfold. Her hair, still in its bun, was now snow white. Cael, last to greet her, assisted her back into her chair and she adjusted her wire-framed glasses after wiping her eyes.

"Sit, sit," she ordered with a smile. "It hurts my neck to look so high up to see your faces. I never get over seeing what good-looking men my boys turned out to be."

Zander sat on the end of the worn, but clean, sofa, Rafe and Cael settling next to him. Jaxon and Jayden headed to the dining room to bring in two more chairs while Asher took the wing-back chair matching the one Miss Ethel used.

"So, tell me all," she said, clasping her wrinkled hands in her lap. Not waiting for one of them to speak, she turned to Rafe. "I haven't heard from you in a couple of months. Are you still a hot-shot model?"

The others laughed as Rafe blushed bright red and dropped his chin, shaking his head. "Yes, ma'am." Shrugging, he said, "It pays the bills and I figure I'll do something else when this gets old."

Holding his gaze with her watery, blue eyes, she nodded. "I have a feeling it'll get old before too long. But you'll know when the time is right." Looking over at Cael, she said, "How's your family?"

One of the few boys with a family outside their group, Cael had been reunited with his sister, who was now married and with a little girl of her own. He had enthusiastically welcomed being an uncle. Grinning, he said, "Family's good, Miss Ethel. My niece is a whirl of motion and I can see why you only took boys. She's got so many dolls and fairy costumes and, even though she's only six, play makeup."

Clapping her hands, Miss Ethel cackled. "Oh, I would have loved taking in little girls as well, but I never wanted to have both. So, when boys started being brought to me, I decided that I would just keep boys." Settling back in her chair, she said, "I remember every boy ever brought to me, including the ones who did not get to stay long."

"But we were your favorites, weren't we?" Jaxon asked, his easy laugh causing the others to grin again.

"Oh, you two were rascals. Always trying to mix me up," she said, pointing her finger at Jayden and Jaxon. "You were the only twins I ever got and I knew you apart from the first night you were here." Smiling, she leaned forward and patted Jaxon's knee. "When are you going to stop breaking hearts and find someone special?"

"Aw, Miss Ethel, there's just too much of me to go around to settle with just one woman for now."

"Don't you sass me, boy," she laughed.

"No, ma'am," Jaxon nodded. "Honestly, the garage keeps me busy. I've got more business than I can handle, so it's all good."

"Jayden, how's the rescuing people going?"

"I passed the EMT training, so I still work at the fire station, but now drive the ambulance," he replied.

Beaming her pride, she turned her attention toward Asher. "And you? You taking care of yourself?"

"For now, I'm good. I'm working at the homeless shelter."

"You've always had such a good heart." Finally, she

turned her eyes warmly upon Zander. "How's your bar?"

"Not much to tell since I last saw you, Miss Ethel," he said. Her gaze pierced his and he shifted in his seat under her deep perusal.

"But are you happy?"

"Happy?" She had not asked the others if they were happy. Shrugging, he said, "The bar is a lot of work. That's kind of my life right now."

"Oh, my dear, boy. You always were so serious. Do you still take time to read?"

Chuckling, he nodded. "Every chance I get. Just re-read a few of the classics in between some new mysteries."

Smiling widely, she said, "Oh, I should get them on audiobook, unless you think they have too much sex in them for this old lady!" Laughing, she threw her head back, slapping her hand on her lap.

Zander loved the sound of her laughter, hearing it so often as he grew up. As a child, it seemed natural, but as an adult, he often wondered how she found so much enjoyment raising a group of rowdy boys, all needing love and structure.

Standing, he walked to the door where he had set her gift. After picking up the large bouquet of flowers, he walked back into the room, presenting them to her. She always said she did not need presents, but still she exclaimed over the flowers they brought.

Bringing the blossoms to her face, she sniffed in appreciation. "Some people say they don't like cut flowers, 'cause they'll just die. But, I've always loved all flowers. After all, that's life, isn't it? We live and then we die. But just like these flowers, life is to be enjoyed while we have it."

As the others smiled, Zander felt the strange prick of tears hitting the back of his eyes. *What the hell is wrong with me?* "I'll get a vase," he said, leaving the room and heading to the kitchen. Reaching inside one of the cabinets, he took down a glass vase, holding it under the tap, letting the water fill the bottom.

His gaze roamed around the room, still neat and clean. He took care of the household repairs during his weekly visits, usually in the mornings since the bar was not open at that time. He knew that Rafe paid to have someone come clean once a week and a neighbor brought over food so that Miss Ethel did not have to cook every day. She was determined to maintain her independence for as long as she could.

Blinking rapidly, clearing out the cobwebs, he walked back into the living room and placed the flowers in the vase before setting it on the table next to her. The others were hugging her goodbye and, when it was Zander's turn, she patted his back while whispering, "You take care, Alexander. I sense you need more than the bar to make you happy."

Giving her a squeeze, he smiled, wondering if she were right.

Piling the pillows behind his back, Zander settled into bed, heaving a sigh. The evening rush had been especially taxing with one server out sick, two customers taking swings at each other after too many drinks, another rowdy bachelor party, and Joe dropping two bottles of whiskey as he spent more time trying to impress the female customers than pouring drinks. At the moment, Zander was trying to remember why he thought owning a bar would be a good thing.

Taking a large book off the nightstand he opened it to the bookmark. Eschewing eReaders, he preferred to feel the weight of the book in his hand, the paper underneath his fingertips and, if it was an old copy, the slightly musty smell from the old print.

Burying himself in the words of the classic, he felt his body relax, the cares of the day drifting away.

4

Music reverberated throughout the bar, even invading Zander's space in his office. Closing his eyes, he felt the base booming through his head. He was out on the floor earlier, but his employees had everything well in hand. Finishing the stock order, he looked up as Charlene walked in, her hands clutching one of the cash register drawers.

"Hey, boss. It's not too bad out there, but I wanted to get this to you now."

"Must be good if the till is already full," he responded, taking the metal drawer from her. Emptying the money into a money bag, he handed her the empty drawer and locked the money in the safe. "I'll be out in a minute," he said.

As soon as he left his office, he turned and locked the door, seeing three women just outside waiting for the ladies' room in the well-lit hall. All laughing and talking at once, he pressed against the wall as he passed.

Stopping at the end of the hall, he stood next to the bar, taking a practiced look around. As usual, Roscoe and Zeke appeared to have things under control at the door. Charlene was behind the bar with Joe, and the servers were moving between the tables.

The clink of glasses was drowned out by the dull roar of a multitude of voices filling the room all at the same time, each group vying for dominance. The game being played on all the TVs mounted on the wall brought cheers or groans in unison.

At six feet tall, Zander appreciated being able to see over most of the crowd. The women who had been behind him in the hall made their way back to a table near the side and he observed one with a plastic tiara and a tight, white t-shirt announcing her as the bride to be. *God, I hate bachelorette parties almost as much as bachelor parties.* While the men always seemed to be on the prowl, the groups of women just got loud and sloppy drunk.

Catching Lynn's arm as she passed by, he said, "Keep an eye on the bridal group over on the side. I don't want anyone stumbling outta my bar, puking their guts up."

"Sure thing, Zander," she grinned, a tray of beer and drinks in her hands.

Hearing another cheer roared from the back, he spied a few men eyeing the group of bridesmaids. Shaking his head, he leaned his shoulder against the wall, out of the way, but in a perfect position to keep an eye on things. The memory of Miss Ethel asking if he was happy floated through his mind. Sighing, he had to admit, he was not sure of the answer.

"Excuse me."

A soft voice from behind met his ears, jerking his thoughts back to the present. Turning, his attention snagged on a woman trying to squeeze past him as she returned from the restroom. She was petite, only coming to his chin. A mass of light blonde hair waved down her back and she swiped her bangs back from her forehead. As she leaned her head back, her light blue eyes captured his and a slight smile gently curved the corners of her mouth. Her pale complexion glowed with the mirrored reflection from the bar and he was suddenly reminded of a picture in a fairy tale book Miss Ethel used to read. Hair the color of corn silk, sky-blue eyes, and a light blush on her cheeks. Sleeping Beauty. He remembered the picture where the princess lay on her back, her long, light blue dress arranged perfectly, and her eyes closed.

As he continued to stare, she walked toward the back where the bridal group had gathered. He shook his head once more, this time trying to shake the feeling of wistfulness that descended as she walked past, and got back to work.

An hour later, he noticed the same woman sitting at the bar, ordering another drink. Just as he was walking toward her stool, a man stepped up behind her, placing his hand on her back as he leaned over her shoulder to throw some money down onto the bar. Zander watched wide-eyed surprise cross her face when she twisted her head to see who was there. She appeared shocked to see the man, but as he moved forward to intercede, she smiled shyly, ducking her head. Zander halted in his tracks at the blush rising from her neck up toward her cheeks. Swallowing hard his mouth tightened into a hard line and he forced his thoughts away from her.

Moving to the other side of the bar, he attempted to focus his attention on the customers in front of him, but was unable to keep his eyes from straying down the row to see the couple as they chatted.

"You okay, boss?" Joe asked, reaching past him to grab the vodka as he lined up shots for one of the servers to take to the bachelorette party.

"Fine," he groused, trying—and failing—not to notice that the woman had not rejoined her group, but instead continued to enjoy her drink at the bar. Watching as she tucked her hair behind her ear, "She's probably not fucking old enough to be drinking," he muttered.

"What are you grumbling about now?" Charlene asked, snagging money off the bar to put into the register.

"You check the ID of that girl down there?"

Charlene turned in the direction of his head jerk before looking back. "The bar's packed—who the hell are you talking about?"

"That blonde. The one that looks like..." his voice trailed off. If he said what he was thinking, that she looked like a princess, he knew he would never hear the end of it.

Charlene looked again and then speared Zander with a glare. "Seriously, boss? She wasn't in my section to begin with. She must have come up from one of the tables with her drink with her."

"So, the answer is *no*," he stated, sounding like an ass even to his own ears.

Charlene leaned in, an angry spark in her eyes, and said, "You want to check her ID to see if she's of age...be my guest!" With that, she stalked to the other end of the bar.

Keeping his eyes on the blonde, he noticed her body language as she moved slightly away from the man still towering over her. Her smile, less bright, appeared to be more from nerves than from enjoyment. He observed her shake her head several times and when the man put his hand on her arm, attempting to pull her from the bar stool, Zander had had enough.

"This man bothering you?"

Her blue eyes widened as she stared at Zander, her mouth opening and closing several times. "Uh..."

"I'm not bothering the pretty lady," the man said, his cheeks ruddy with alcohol and his body swaying slightly as he stood to his full height. "Me and her are just getting to know each other better, aren't we, sweet cheeks?"

"I...uh..." was her response, her eyes pleading toward Zander as she glanced at the man still standing next to her.

"Take your hand off her. Now," Zander ordered, his jaw tight and his fists clenched at his side.

"Who the hell do you think you—"

"I'm the owner but, more importantly, I'm the one warning you to get your hands off the lady right fuckin' now."

Looking down at the blonde, the man said, "You

don't have a problem with me, do you, sweet cheeks? Tell the man you and me are going to dance."

"Please, let me go," she said, wincing as his fingers tightened.

Roscoe, alerted by Charlene, walked up behind the man, clamping his large hand on the man's shoulder. "You want me to show him the door, Mr. King?"

"Hell, yeah. Show the *gentleman* to the door, and," staring the man straight in the eye, he added, "you don't come back."

Roscoe's fingers dug into the flesh just below the man's shoulders, causing him to curse as he let go of the blonde's arm.

Looking back down at her, he sneered, "So not worth it. Thought you'd be happy for a good time, but you're nothing but a cock tease."

"Shut the fuck up, man," Roscoe said, his wide smile still in place. "Listening to you is painful. Come on."

Watching Roscoe and the man disappear out the door, Zander dropped his gaze back to the beautiful woman sitting in front of him, her wide eyes now pinned on him, the nervousness appearing to morph into relief.

"Thank you," she said, her soft voice, caressing, as her tiny, pale fingers flitted across the bar, touching his arm. "Thank you so much. I had no idea what to—"

Pulling his arm back, the tingling from her touch feeling like a brand, he growled, "You shouldn't be here. You come into a place like this and expect, what? This is no place for someone like you. You would've been better off staying with your pack. Why the hell didn't you stay with your friends over there?" His chin jerked toward the back where the bachelorette party was still in full swing, their loud laughter drawing attention.

She twisted her head around to look in the direction he indicated. Turning back toward him, her brow now marred with a crease, she said, "I don't...uh...I'm not with—"

"You know what?" he said, "It doesn't matter. You come into a bar, you need to have some fucking sense of protection. You ain't got that, you don't have any business in my bar." Glancing down at her empty glass, he added, "As of now, you're cut off. Go back to your friends."

"I'm here alone...I'm not with them," she protested.

Rearing back, he blinked before leaning back in. "Then that makes it worse. You're not even here protected by friends. You come alone? You're setting yourself up for problems."

Her breath left her lungs in a rush as she continued to protest, "That's sexist." She cast her eyes around the bar before bringing them back to his face. "There're lots of single women here. You're not fussing at any of them."

He knew she was right, but the sight of the man with his hand squeezing her arm still had him seeing red, and as much as it made him an asshole, he continued to take his frustration out on her. He leaned closer, ignoring the subtle scent of her perfume, and said, "Maybe 'cause they all look like they know how to handle themselves instead of some little doll, too easily broken."

Pushing back, he watched as her eyes filled and she

blinked rapidly while swallowing. Guilt momentarily hit him and he dropped his chin to his chest, saying, "Look, I think it's better if you go."

"Fine," she agreed, stumbling on her heel as she slid off the tall stool.

"Hang on," he said, "I'll call a cab."

"I'm perfectly capable of taking care of—"

He walked around the end of the bar as he called a cab and, with his hand on her lower back, he moved her toward the door, ignoring the warmth that radiated from his fingertips to his arm. Irritated, he sucked in a quick breath through his nose, quickly realizing his mistake when her soft scent assaulted him once again.

I have no time in my life to be thinking of a beautiful woman to spend time with...especially not one that looks like a princess to my ogre. As that analogy flitted through this mind, he groaned. *Jesus, I've lost my fucking mind.*

"Roscoe. I've called a cab. Please see the lady safely outside."

If Roscoe questioned why he was escorting the beautiful woman out of the bar, he did not let on. "Sure thing, boss." Turning to the blonde, he smiled widely as he opened the door. "Follow me, miss."

At the door, she looked over her shoulder, tucking her long hair behind her ear as her blue eyes held his. Her shoulder hunched forward, an expression of sadness moving over her face. Just as he was about to call her back, she turned and walked out the door.

"Are you sure you did the right thing?" Lynn asked, coming up to stand next to him, her words laced with concern, eyes pinned on the now-closed door.

"No one's ever sure about anything," he said, already regretting his decision.

"She looked like some kind of little fairy," she added, patting him on the arm before taking her tray back to the bar for refills.

With his hands on his hips, his heart strangely empty, he whispered to no one, "Like a goddamn princess. But life's no fairytale, that's for sure."

Shouts rang out from the back, snagging his attention and he whirled around in time to see one man take a swing at another. Before the crowd broke into a melee, he bellowed for Zeke and Roscoe while he pushed people out of his way, trying to get to the fight quickly.

One man fell onto a table, knocking bottles and glasses crashing to the floor. Several women screamed while scrambling to get out of the way, tripping over each other. Zeke was already in the crowd, his arms around one of the men just as another man threw a punch, hitting the man Zeke was holding. Both men fell backward to the floor, causing more patrons to scramble out of the way.

"Shit," Zander cursed, ducking as another man attempted to hit him when he pushed by. "I'm the goddamn owner, so get the fuck out of the way." The man stumbled back, wide-eyed, allowing him to pass.

Roscoe, having rushed in from the door, his large body shoving people with no regard, grabbed another man attempting to throw a sucker punch, while Zeke scrambled to his feet. Zander and Roscoe managed to contain the final two men involved and, holding their arms tightly behind their backs, moved them to the door.

"Out!" Zander roared and the three troublemakers were pushed through the front door. "And don't let me see you here again!"

Hustling back in to make sure the remaining crowd was orderly, they stood inside the door for a moment. Looking at Zeke, Zander asked, "You okay?"

Scowling, he said, "Yeah. Can't believe the asshole got a punch on me." Taking the ice pack that Joe tossed to him, he nodded his thanks.

Looking at Roscoe, Zander asked, "Blondie get in the cab okay?"

The large bouncer wiped his face as he nodded. "It was just pulling into the parking lot when I heard you shout. I told her to get in and get home."

A sliver of doubt moved through him as he turned and stalked to the door, throwing it open wide, the cool air hitting his face, refreshing after the heat of the bar. Scanning the parking lot, he saw a cab just driving down the street. Sighing, he raised his eyes to the dark, night sky, feeling a strange tightening in his chest as he studied the stars for a moment. Suddenly, whirling around, he stomped back inside to his employees.

"We're closing an hour early tonight," he declared, adrenaline still pumping.

"You ain't gotta do that on my account, boss," Zeke protested.

"Nah. It's just been a helluva night and I'm ready for the crowd to leave." Turning to Lynn, he said, "You can pass the word around, bar closes at midnight."

She lifted her brow, but nodded as she moved to tell the other servers. As Zander moved behind the bar again, he wiped his brow, frustration causing his shoulders to tighten, thoughts of the blonde running through his mind. *Yeah...a helluva night.*

An hour later, sitting in his office, Zander leaned back in his chair, rubbing the tension out of the back of his neck. The money was tallied and locked in the safe. The books were balanced and ready for the next day. Leaving the office, he walked through the bar, satisfied with the way his staff cleaned every night. He recognized their hard work and paid them accordingly. They made good wages at Grimm's and he knew they were loyal.

Checking the locked door and security system, he moved to the back door, a small trash bag from his office in his hand. Pushing through, he double checked the lock before turning toward the dumpster. Hefting the bag into the air, he easily tossed it in. With a glance across the black pavement, water in the potholes shinning from the parking lot lights, the faint light shone down on something blue from the other side of the dumpster. Curious, he walked around, halting at the sight. Heart pounding, he stared in horror.

5

"Oh, Jesus, Jesus," Zander cried, rushing forward, dropping to his knees beside the still body lying in the dirt. Her clothes were torn, one shoe was missing, her purse dumped to the side, its contents strewn around. Bruises were already showing on her throat. Her long, blonde hair, now tangled and bloody, covered her face.

Reaching his shaking hand out, he brushed her hair back slightly, gasping at the extent of what he saw. Her face was battered and bruised to the point her eyes were swollen shut. The side of her head was caked in blood from a huge wound, still seeping. If it had not been for the sweater, he would have not recognized her.

"Oh, Jesus," he cried again, this time his hoarse voice barely above a whisper. With one hand, he pulled his phone from his pocket, dialing 9-1-1. He moved the other to her wrist, touching her, fear crawling up his spine. Cold. She was so cold. His heart leaped as he felt a pulse—weak, but still beating.

"Zander King. Owner of Grimm's Bar on Fifth and Washington. A woman's been attacked. Need an ambulance."

Leaning over her limp form, he placed his hand gently over hers. "Hey, princess. It's okay. It's gonna be okay. Help's on its way. Hang in there. Please." Choking on the last word, he swallowed deeply. Sucking in a breath, he repeated, "Hang on, princess. Hang on." Hearing a siren close by, he waved them over with his free hand and they pulled into the side of the parking lot.

Two EMTs rushed over, immediately beginning to assess her injuries. A police car pulled in next to the ambulance, an officer moving toward them as well.

"Who is she?" one of the EMTs asked.

"I have no idea," Zander replied, his hand still holding hers.

"Sir, you've got to let go."

Reluctantly, he let her fingers slip through his, missing her touch as soon as they were no longer connected.

"Can I see some ID?" the policeman asked as Zander stood, stepping back slightly to allow the medical team to see to her.

Pulling out his wallet, he showed the policeman his drivers' license as another officer parked nearby. Recognizing the newest arrival, he greeted him with a chin lift.

"Zander. What've you got?"

"I just left and found her out here, Pete. She was in the bar earlier. Had some problems with a male customer so he was ejected." Seeing the question in the officers' eyes, he shook his head. "Got no names for you...not for her and not for him."

Pete knelt at her purse and carefully looked inside. "Been cleaned out. No wallet. No phone. No ID."

Fear and disgust snaked through Zander's gut at the thought that she would probably be safe right now if he had not insisted she leave. *But I thought she left in a cab. Why didn't she?*

With an IV in place and her body strapped onto the gurney, the EMTs were ready to roll her to the ambulance. Halting them with his hand on the arm of the closest one, his eyes never leaving the woman's face, he asked, "Where are you taking her? Which hospital?"

"County General," came the reply, as they moved her into the ambulance.

Pete stood with the other officer, looking at Zander with a curious expression. "You sure you don't know anything about her?"

Rubbing his hand over his face, his heart in his throat, he shook his head with regret. "No...I have no idea who she is. I've never seen her here before."

As the officers walked toward the bar door, having asked for the security tapes from the cameras at the back of the bar, he watched the twirling red lights of the ambulance grow dimmer and whispered into the night, "But I wish I did. I wish I did know her."

Three hours later, Zander walked into his apartment,

seeing Rafe standing in the kitchen, a beer in his hand held out. Taking it gratefully, Zander took a long swig before setting it on the counter.

"I'm glad you called, man. I can cancel my flight... don't gotta leave today," Rafe said, his gaze pinned on him.

"Nah, no need. I mean, there's nothing that can be done and there's no sense in you changing your plans."

"What do you know? Anything else since you called?"

The two men walked into the living room, Zander sinking onto the sofa, his body more tired than he could remember in a long time. Rafe moved to the chair, sitting with his forearms resting on his knees.

"I talked to Roscoe, who feels like shit about it. Seems he walked the mysterious woman just outside the door and saw the headlights of a cab turning into the parking lot. Normally, he would have escorted her to the cab and seen her safely inside but, just then, all hell broke loose with a fight at the back of the bar. He said he pointed her toward the cab and told her to get in and then ran back inside without actually seeing her get in. I ran out and saw the cab leaving soon after. I assumed she was in it."

"Oh, shit."

He lifted his eyes to his friend and nodded slowly. "Yeah. That's about right." Sighing heavily, he said, "I should have never told her to leave—"

"Whoa, you can't start blaming yourself," Rafe interrupted. "You didn't attack her. You didn't cause this to happen. That blame lies right at the feet of the asshole who did this."

"If I hadn't insisted she leave, then—"

"And I'm telling you that going down that road, doesn't help anyone. It's just a set of circumstances that all added up to a fucked-up situation. But you're not responsible for her attack."

Zander knew Rafe's words made sense but the vision of her beaten body was in the forefront of his mind. Downing the rest of the beer, he sighed again, leaning his head against the back of the sofa. "God, I just keep seeing her lying in the dirt. That beautiful face battered and swollen. So much blood, so much…"

"That's it, I'm canceling my flight—"

"No," he halted him. "Seriously, Rafe. There's no need."

Rafe leaned back in his seat, his mouth tight. "I hope you don't mind, but I called Jayden and told him to let the others know. Just in case you needed anything."

"Nah, I don't mind," he replied, glad for his friends' support.

"You gonna go see her?"

Zander's eyes shot up to Rafe's. "Huh?"

Shaking his head, Rafe said, "Zander, you can't hide anything from me. There's something about this woman…something that's pulling you in."

Leaning forward, he replied, "I don't know. I swear I don't know. I see women every night…honest to God, Rafe, I'm so focused on work, they don't even register." Scrubbing his hand over his face, he added, "But I noticed her. She looked like...well, I noticed her. And now...fuck..."

Neither spoke for several minutes. Looking at his watch, Zander said, "Man, you gotta catch a flight in a few hours."

Standing, Rafe pulled him in for a hug. "I'll be gone when you wake up, but I expect a call. You gotta let me know how you're doing."

After Rafe headed back to the guest bedroom, Zander walked into his room, not stopping until he was standing in front of the mirror, his hands resting on the bathroom counter. His shirt had smears of blood, the red stark against the white material.

The image of her perfect face, large blue eyes staring at him and her brilliant smile, filled his mind. Dropping his head, he gripped the sink with white knuckles. *How I'm doing? Fuck, I'm not the one in the hospital.*

Sleep did not come easily and, when it did, his dreams turned into nightmares of her beautiful face looking up to his as she slowly disappeared into a fog.

6

Stepping out of the elevator, clutching a bouquet of flowers, Zander hesitated, uncertain which direction to go. The taupe walls covered in framed floral pictures contained signs, but he halted at the scent. It reminded him of waking up in a German hospital when he had been airlifted from Afghanistan after surviving an IED explosion. He had spent weeks in that hospital before being transported back to a VA hospital stateside. He knew he did not have it bad...he had all his limbs...just some added shrapnel in his leg and arm.

"Excuse me," a female's voice said, as she moved past him.

Jerking around, he sought the owner of the voice, remembering the blonde saying the same words to him last night. *Was it just last night? Jesus, it feels like ages since I first laid eyes on her.* Shaking his head, he muttered an apology to the nurse hurrying on down the hall. He stopped at the nurses' desk.

One of the nurses looked up, a tired smile on her face. "May I help you?"

"I'm here to see…uh…well…"

She tilted her head to the side, asking, "Do you know the name of the patient?"

"Actually, no. I came to see the woman brought in last night. The one who had been…uh…attacked."

Understanding immediately flooded the nurse's face. "Are you a relative? The police haven't been able to tell us who she is and we—"

"No, no," he said, shaking his head. "I'm sorry. I just…well, I'm not sure." Seeing her confusion, he added, "I found her. She was attacked outside my business. I'm not family, but I need to see her. Please."

"Well…" the nurse hesitated. "Let me check with the policeman who was just in with the doctor."

Zander nodded his thanks and watched her walk down the hall a few doors before moving inside. After a moment, she came back out, Pete at her side. Breathing a sigh of relief, Zander reached out to shake hands. "Good to see you, Pete. Any news?"

"I'm surprised to see you here," he replied, his gaze assessing, causing Zander to shift his stance. "But in answer to your question, no. The doctors have listed her injuries and, I probably don't have to tell you, they are significant. The biggest problem is the swelling of her brain and…ah, hell, he spouted a bunch of medical jargon, most of which I didn't understand. But, she's still in a coma, so, obviously, she can't tell us anything about the attack."

"Did you get anything from the security video?"

"We can see a man wearing dark clothing dragging her around the corner while she was still conscious. He kept his head down. After he hit her once, he dragged her behind the dumpster and we only have partial visual after that." Rubbing his hand over his eyes, he said, "It was brutal to watch."

Zander's gut clenched as though he had taken a punch himself. Sucking in a deep breath through his nose, he shook his head. "Can I see her?"

Pete's gaze dropped to the flowers in his hand before shooting back to his face. "She won't know you're there."

"I just want to sit with her for a few minutes. That's all." Unable to understand the connection he felt toward the woman, he had no way to explain it to anyone else.

Shrugging, Pete nodded. "Yeah, I guess it sucks to have someone attacked right outside your bar, and to see her like that. Let me tell the staff that you have permission to visit." Clapping him on the back, he walked to the nurses' station and spoke to the attending nurse.

After Pete left, the nurse walked back over, smiling. "It seems you are her first real visitor. Let me prepare you before you go in, okay?" Obtaining his nod, she continued, "She has a multitude of injuries and what you'll see initially will be the swelling and bruising on her face. There are a lot of lacerations and we need to be sure to keep down the possibility of infection, so always make sure to wash your hands when you go in and use anti-bacterial gel."

Following her into the dimly lit room, he was careful

to avoid looking at the bed, hearing the noises of machines filling the air. Instead, he observed the nurse as she showed him how to properly wash his hands at the sink by the door.

"I'm Chloe, by the way. If you need anything, you can call for me. I'll pull a chair up close, so you can sit with her for a while."

As Chloe moved the well-worn, metal chair over, Zander turned, taking his first look at the woman. His breath rushed from his lungs and as his knees buckled, so Chloe shoved the chair underneath him. She placed her hand on his shoulder.

"You okay?"

Nodding his head in jerks, she patted him.

"I know it's a lot to take in, but I promise you, she's in no pain." As she walked toward the door, she turned and said, "You should talk to her...there's a lot of research that suggests that she can hear you, even while unconscious."

"Oh...uh...sure..." he mumbled, barely aware of her as she left the room, his attention held by the woman lying in the bed. Seeing her in the dirt next to the dumpster had been horrifying, but in the light, even as dim as it was in the room, her injuries shook him to his core.

Blowing out a long, slow breath, he allowed his gaze to drift over her body. The blood that had caked her hair had been cleaned off, but there was now an area of her scalp, next to her forehead, that had been shaved. Stitches held the bloodied edges of skin together. The rest of her hair had been pulled back away from her face into a braid and he wondered if Chloe had taken care of that for her.

Her eyes were swollen shut, black bruises creating raccoon-circles underneath. Her nose had a bandage and he assumed it was broken. Bruises covered her neck, shoulders, and arms, all bare above the blanket. An IV was in her hand and as he followed the tube, his gaze moved to the various machines hooked up to her, beeping and chirping as they took care of their tasks. Another tube snaked from under the covers leading to a bag filled with what appeared to be bloody urine. Swallowing deeply, he lifted his gaze back to her face, willing his heartbeat to slow.

He wanted to touch her, but every inch appeared bruised or tender. Reaching through the rails of the bed, he placed his finger on her upturned palm. Expecting it to be cold, he was heartened to find her warm. Emboldened, he placed his whole hand on hers, not wanting to move her in any way, but wanting to be connected.

Remembering what Chloe had said, he leaned closer, resting his chin on the bed rail and said, "I know you don't know me, but I didn't want you to be alone. I…uh, well…I don't really know what to say. So, I guess I'll just say, hello. I'm uh…Zander."

His words sounded pathetic to his own ears, but he found himself tongue-tied. *What the hell do I say? You don't know me but you met me once and I was an asshole to you?* Standing suddenly, he felt the urge to flee, then shame slid over him. *I can flee if I want, but she's trapped here. Alone.*

Plopping back into the chair, he replaced his hand

over hers. "It probably seems scary here, doesn't it?" His eyes moved back to the machines humming and beeping around the head and side of her bed. "You've got that clip on your finger that tells the doctors something...maybe your heartbeat...and in your other hand there's a needle for the IV. I know the blood pressure cuff keeps going on, so it must be automatic. That's what you feel on your arm." He hesitated in his ramblings, wondering if his words caused more anxiety, if she could actually hear him.

Lifting his gaze around the room, he continued, "But the room is nice...well, for a hospital room. It's private and they've got the lights down low. There's a window to the side, but uh...the blinds are closed. And curtains cover the door so no one passing in the hall can just peek in."

She lay still, giving no indication she heard his voice. Inadequacy flooded his soul and he dropped his head, his chest squeezing. Sighing heavily, he said, "Oh, God, I'm sorry. So sorry. I guess I don't know what else to say to you, so I'll just sit here and hold your hand for now. Is that okay?"

Knowing no answer was forthcoming, he scooted the chair closer so he could rest more comfortably, his hand remaining on hers.

Jerking his head up, Zander realized he had fallen asleep and now was not alone. Looking over, bleary-eyed, he saw a doctor washing his hands before moving to the bed. Sitting back fully in his chair, he cracked his stiff neck and wondered if he had a sleep crease on his face.

"I understand you will be visiting her," the doctor said, a smile on his face. "Chloe has told me that you don't know her name, but have met her?"

"Yes," Zander said, reluctantly letting go of her hand. "I found her after she was attacked."

The doctor's forehead furrowed while he nodded. "That must have been quite a shock. I'm Dr. Calhoun, by the way. I'll be her hospitalist while she's here."

Feeling slightly foolish that the medical staff was speaking to him as though he were family, he simply nodded.

"As you can see, she has multiple lacerations, although the only one requiring stitches is the one on her head. Unfortunately, that injury to her head is the one that causes us the most concern. The broken bones and bruises will heal, but we don't know the extent of her any brain injury, at this time."

"Brain injury?" he repeated, numbly. "Broken bones?"

"Her nose is broken, as well as a couple of ribs. Given the contusions, which appear to have come from blunt trauma, she is lucky to not have more broken bones. We have done CT scans and there is some brain swelling. She's still in a coma, but breathing on her own, which is a good sign."

"When will she wake up?"

"There's no way of knowing. But, you should be prepared for her to have a long convalescence. I'm assuming you'll be visiting daily...or as often as you can?"

Blinking, Zander almost blurted that he was only here today to just check on her. But turning his gaze back down, seeing her lying perfectly still, he heard himself answer, "I'll be back every day."

An hour later Chloe returned, finding him still in the chair, his hand resting on the woman's. "Hey," she said softly. "When you come back tomorrow why don't you bring something to read to her. It will pass the time for you and she can hear you. It doesn't matter what you read...it can be a magazine...or...uh...whatever. But it'll be good for her to hear your voice."

As she walked back out, he looked down at his worn jeans, dark t-shirt, and the tats covering his arms. *She probably wonders if I can read.* Smiling, as though sharing a secret, he looked at the mystery woman, and said, "I'll be back tomorrow, princess. And we can read a story together. Okay?"

No response was given. None was expected.

7

Sitting at one of the large tables in the back room at Grimm's, the eerie silence of the empty space made the room feel larger. Zander faced his employees, all of whom had been questioned by the police that morning. While descriptions of the man who had been ejected were plentiful, no one knew who he was, had seen him before, saw him with anyone else, or could positively identify him as the assailant in the security video. And, as Pete reminded them, it might not have been that man who attacked her.

Pete and his partner left the group stunned, worried expressions on their faces as they stared at Zander.

"Boss, this ain't your fault," Roscoe began. "You did nothing wrong here."

Everyone quickly added their agreement, but Zander just threw up his hand for them to quiet. "My head gets it," he said, "but I still feel guilty. She was doing nothing wrong other than looking too innocent to be in a bar getting manhandled by some asshole. If I had just let her drink her drink and chat for a bit, she wouldn't be where she is now."

A somber mood hung over the Grimm employees, each silent, not knowing what to say or how to make the situation better.

Rubbing his hand over the back of his neck, squeezing the tense muscles, Zander continued. "I've called a friend to install security cameras inside the bar and I've already talked to Roscoe and Zeke. Our new policy is that if we call a cab, we get the cab's number and escort the person to the cab, no matter what."

"That's good, Zander," Lynn began. "You're taking something bad and making some changes that might help someone else in the future."

"Yeah…" he sighed, twisting his head back and forth to crack the kinks out of his neck. "Listen, I'm going to spend some time at the hospital with her—"

"Zander, you shouldn't feel obligated—" Charlene protested.

"No, it's not that," he defended. "But she's got no one and I…well, I'd like to keep her company. But I'll need some more help here."

Lynn smiled, saying, "My mother-in-law has been itching to spend more time with the kids, so I can easily come in a couple of hours early to help with whatever you need."

Joe grimaced, adding, "My part-time roofing job won't let me come in earlier during the week, but on weekends, I can."

Zeke leaned forward, his hands nervously rubbing

on his thighs. "Boss, I'd been wanting to talk to you about something, and I know the timing might not be good, nor doing it so publically, but I've wanted to take on more responsibilities around here. I know the pay won't go up," he rushed, "but I'd like to learn some of the managerial jobs that you do."

Nodding, he approved, "Sounds good. I've got no problem with you learning more about the business and now's as good a time as any." Looking at his watch, he stood. "I'm heading over there now and you all can go home. We're closed today anyway, so I'll see you tomorrow."

He watched as his employees headed out the door, their assistance welcome, but his heart was still heavy.

Stepping off the elevator, with less trepidation than the day before, Zander walked down the hall, nodding at a smiling Chloe as he walked toward the room. Walking inside, he immediately moved to the sink, carefully washing his hands, making sure to scrub with the astringent soap. Once dry, he picked up his book and turned around. Sighing, he saw little difference in her condition. The woman lying in the bed was just as bruised, just as still, hooked up to just as many wires and tubes. His gut clenched. He thought he was prepared, after all, he had seen her only yesterday.

Catching his breath, he let it out slowly, willing his nerves to hold. *I saw men in the war coming in with injuries worse than this. Missing limbs. Burns. Deadly injuries.* But, none of it had hit him like this. Maybe it was because she was so tiny. So innocent. All she had done was go out for a drink and now she was in a coma. *God knows for how long.*

"You can sit with her," Chloe said, startling him as she walked into the room. "I see you brought a book."

Clutching the large print book in his hand, he nodded in jerks. "Yeah. Uh...it's an old book I used to have as a kid. Someone special gave it to me years ago and I used to read it to my...uh...brothers."

"Well, I'm sure whatever you read will be fine. Remember what I said, research shows that she may be able to hear you even while comatose and it will bring her comfort."

His gaze slid to the whiteboard on the wall, seeing her name listed as **Jane Doe**. His heart hurt as he viewed the evidence that no one knew who she was.

Waiting until they were alone, he scooted the plastic chair across the tile floor to rest next to her bed. But, before he sat down, he reached over and placed his hand on her palm. His gaze moved over her swollen face, noting the reddened area where the dark stitches had pierced her skin. The bruises around her eyes had darkened even more, black and angry. The hospital gown was open at the neck, exposing the upper part of her chest and shoulders, those bruises deepening as well.

Bending low, he stared at her dry, cracked lips. Seeing a tube of lip balm on the tray, he squirted some on his forefinger, hesitating to touch her injuries before rubbing it lightly on her mouth. The flesh was pliant, warm, and his breath hitched as he realized how vulnerable she was.

Blowing out a breath, he whispered, "Hey, princess. It's Zander…uh…I'm Zander. I'm so sorry…so sorry. But, I want you…well, need you to get well."

He stared, hoping she might twitch, or blink, or indicate she could hear him. But she continued to sleep.

Sitting down in the chair, he said, "I brought a book to read. I don't know what you like to read, but this book was given to me years ago." His fingers moved along the worn cover, remembering when Miss Ethel gave it to him.

"Alexander, don't you let no one tell you you're too dumb to learn. You've got more intelligence than most and I know it's locked inside of you. Your teachers are going to go over the basics of reading, but that won't teach you to love the written word. You and me, son, are going to read through this book. It's got everything in it…classics…fairy tales…stories of bravery and strength. Stories of love. Stories of life."

Then she opened the book, flipping through the pages until she pressed her hand flat on a page, and I sat at her feet, listening as she opened my world.

"What do you say, princess? Ready to have me read to you?" Opening the book, he realized he had no idea where to begin. His brow creased as he tried to think of what she might like to hear. Rubbing his hand over his chin, he flipped to one of his favorites. "How about we start easy? Nothing too hard for you to concentrate on, right now." Glancing behind him to see if anyone was listening, he turned back to her, giving her all his attention.

Keeping one hand on hers and the other turned to Grimm's version of Sleeping Beauty, he began.

" 'In times past, there lived a King and Queen, who said to each other every day of their lives, "Would that we had a child!" and yet they had none. But it happened once that when the Queen was bathing, there came a frog out of the water, and he squatted on the ground, and said to her, "Thy wish shall be fulfilled; before a year has gone by, thou shalt bring a daughter into the world." And as the frog foretold, so it happened; and the Queen bore a daughter so beautiful that the King could not contain himself for joy, and he ordained a great feast.' "

As he continued to read, he glanced up occasionally, giving her hand a little squeeze. His voice, soft at first, grew stronger as he hoped she would be able to hear him. Not wanting to go too fast, he enunciated each word carefully. After a few minutes, he came to the description of the princess.

" 'The maiden grew up, adorned with all the gifts of the wise women; and she was so lovely, modest, sweet, and kind and clever, that no one who saw her could help loving her.' "

As soon as the words left his mouth, his gaze jerked up to hers. The truth was he had very little to go on as to her personality, but remembering her at the bar, he thought about the way she tried to be polite, first to the asshole bothering her and then to him...even when he was being a different kind of an asshole. He remembered the way she tucked her hair behind her ear, her head ducking slightly, having no idea how beautiful she was. Her voice had been soft, even when angry.

"This sounds a lot like you, princess." Giving her hand another squeeze, he continued the story. After another few minutes, he came to the line,

" '...**the beautiful sleeping Rosamond, for so was the Princess called...**' "

Sucking in a quick breath, his gaze shot back to her. "Rosamond. I know that's not your name, but I hate like hell for you to keep being called a Jane Doe. So, if you don't mind, can I call you Rosamond?" Shaking his head, he knew it was foolish to expect a sign from her. Looking down at her hand, he rubbed his calloused finger over her skin. Her arm was covered in abrasions from the gravel drive behind the bar. Grimacing, he forced the thoughts of her attack from his mind, focusing instead on the story.

As he came to the climax, he read,

" '**And when he saw her looking so lovely in her sleep, he could not turn away his eyes; and presently he stooped and kissed her, and she awaked, and opened her eyes, and looked very kindly on him.**' "

"Is that what you'll do with me, Rosamond? Look upon me kindly?"

A sound at the door interrupted his reading and, twisting his head around, he saw Pete walking into the room.

"Zander? Didn't expect to see you here."

Shrugging, he said, "Figure she's got no one. At least, not for now." Lifting his gaze up to Pete's face as he came nearer, he asked, "Anyone report her missing? Anyone looking for her?"

"No, and that's what's so damn frustrating. Her prints didn't come up in our system, but that's not unusual. What is unusual is for a woman that looks like her and dresses like her hasn't been reported by someone."

"What do you mean? Looks like her?"

"I just mean that there are times when we run into a Jane Doe in a sleazebag hotel, having shot up on whatever drug of choice they could get hold of. You don't exactly expect her to have people out there that will notice she's gone right away. But her," he nodded in Rosamund's direction, "she was well groomed, no drugs in her system...someone like her shouldn't remain a Jane Doe for long."

Sleazebag hotel...shooting up drug of choice...forgetting there was a child at home. Blinking, Zander forced his mind to move off his mother and back to what Pete was saying. "So, how do you usually identify someone like this?"

"Can't say I've had a case like this where someone did not come forward quickly. Family, neighbor, employer, friend. Someone. But, maybe if she was new to the area...it could take a little time for someone to miss her. We can hope."

Pete turned to leave the room but stopped at the door, looking back over his shoulder. "You gonna keep coming?"

Nodding, Zander said, "I hate the idea of her being alone."

Patting the doorframe, Pete grinned as he waved goodbye. Looking back over at Rosamond, he sighed at the thought of no one missing her, looking for her, wondering when she was coming home.

Squeezing her hand once more, he continued reading until coming to, " 'The End.' "

Floating...I must be floating...but why is it so dark? I hear words easing through the fog. The sound is deep...melodious... calming. Words moving through the air...chords of music... weaving around me. Lulling me back to sleep. Princess... prince...Rosamond...I want to look kindly on the one whose voice is so rich.

8

Standing at his kitchen counter, blinking the sleep out of his eyes, Zander sipped his coffee, willing the caffeine to kick in quickly. Startling at a knock on the door, he cursed as some of the hot brew splashed over his fingers.

Who the hell is here at this hour? Everyone knows I'm usually asleep.

Stalking over, he threw open the door and was pushed aside as Asher, Jayden, Jaxon, and Cael moved inside, all heading to the coffee maker.

"Well, come on in," he clipped, throwing the door shut behind them.

"Good morning to you, Sunshine," Jaxon grinned, taking the cup handed to him from Asher. "You're up early."

With his fists planted on his hips, he stared at the group, now lounging around the kitchen counter. "What's up with the early morning *welcome wagon*?" He observed the eye shifts between them and let out a heavy sigh. "Looks like this is going to be something I don't like much. Might as well get comfortable."

He picked up his cup and moved to the chair in the living room, watching as the others filed in behind him, the twins and Cael plopping down on the sofa and Asher taking the other chair.

"Hell, this looks like some kind of intervention. I swear I'm not on drugs, I'm not a hoarder, and I only drink occasionally. Anything else I can tell you?" he quipped, sarcasm dripping from his words.

"You want to cut to the chase, then here it is," Cael began. "You're visiting that woman at the hospital."

The widening of his eyes was his only blatant physical response, but his heart rate kicked up as he prepared for battle. "Seriously? That's what brought you out here in force at this ungodly hour—"

"You're up at this ungodly hour," Jayden interrupted.

"So what? A man can't get up early if he wants to?"

"Come on, Zander," Asher said, leaning forward, his eyes pinning him. "Tell us what's going on."

Lips pinched, he sucked in a deep breath before sighing once more. "Look guys, she's a customer who came in to have a good time and I fucked that up. I may not be the one who attacked her, but I sure as hell was the one who set it up so she could be attacked."

"So, you're doing this out of guilt?" Asher prodded.

"No...well, some. I mean, I do feel guilty but...I don't know. That's not all it is."

"Then explain it to us."

Leaning forward, cup in hand, he stared into the

depths of his coffee, his mind casting back to her hospital room. Bruised. Battered. Broken. His voice quiet, belying the emotions coursing through his veins, he began, "She's all alone. The police have no clues as to who she is. She's got no visitors…no one to even know she's been hurt." He moved his gaze to each of them, his jaw tight. "Come on…every one of us knows what it's like to be alone."

"You don't want her to wake up alone, do you?" Jaxon asked, his voice filled with concern.

Shaking his head, he answered, "No. No, I don't."

The group remained silent for several minutes, each lost in their own thoughts. Finally, he added, "She's still unconscious and the staff, while caring, can't sit with her. I just hate the idea that she's alone."

Cael asked, "So, you just go and sit?"

Shaking his head, he replied, "Nah. I read to her." Seeing their eyebrows lift in unison, he explained, "The nurse said that patients in comas can often hear," he lifted his great shoulders in a slight shrug, "so I read to her. I hold her hand, thinking maybe she can feel something and I talk to her and read."

Asher's eyes cut to the table next to the front door, a slow smile beginning to form as he spied the book. "The edited classics. You're reading those to her, aren't you?"

A slow nod began his reply. "Yeah…it gives me lots of stories to choose from."

"I remember when you used to read to us," Jaxon said, leaning back against the sofa cushions. "I loved that book."

The others smiled as well, fond memories sliding

across their faces. Zander, his forearms planted on his knees, said, "Look, I know you're worried. I'm not exactly Mr. Sociable, so this seems out of character—"

Jayden interrupted, "Actually it doesn't seem out of character at all. You were always the protector, Zander. The one who took charge and made sure we had what we needed. This is just an extension of your true self, you just don't see it."

"Like the way you take care of your staff," Cael added.

"And the way you still worry about Rafe," Asher said. "Hell, worry about all of us."

"But," Jayden added, "Zander, you gotta be careful."

"Careful about what?"

"Falling for a story."

Rearing back, he growled, "What the fuck do you mean by that?"

"Look, she's like a lost waif in one of the fairy tales. You know...like where the big bad wolf attacks and the prince comes to save the day."

Jaxon elbowed his twin and said, "Man, you got your tales all mixed up."

The others laughed, but Jaxon pressed on. "I'm serious, man. You know nothing about this woman. She could be married...a mom...engaged...on the run from the police...you have no idea. You keep seeing her, you could be setting yourself up for a world of hurt."

"I'm not falling in love with her, if that's what you mean," Zander bit out, knowing that he could not begin to explain his feelings for her and was not about to try.

Leaning back against the cushions, he sighed. "I'm just keeping an eye on a lonely patient, that's all."

"And when she wakes up? Remembers what happened…in your bar? What then?" Asher asked, his quiet voice cutting through the emotions in the room.

His gut clenched at the thought of her waking and looking at him in horror. Wiping that thought from his mind, he argued, "I'm just keeping her company. She wakes up, then she's no longer my responsibility." Looking at his watch, he said, "Hate to break up this little impromptu party, guys, but don't you have somewhere you need to be?"

Grins slipping out, they stood, moving to the sink to deposit their cups. Hugs and claps on the back ensued before he could close the door, alone once again. Scrubbing his hand over his face, he glanced down at the book on his table. "So, what's it gonna be today, princess?"

9

Stepping inside Rosamond's room, Zander halted, seeing the curtain closed. Unsure what to do, he cleared his throat loudly.

Chloe popped her head around the edge, her smile greeting him. "Oh, hi. I'm just giving her a lotion bath. She's modest, if you'd like to come around."

Nervously, he peeked around the curtain, seeing that she was still lying pale against the clean, blue hospital gown. Chloe was wiping her arms with a cloth, squeezing some white lotion from a bottle onto the cloth as she moved to her legs. Grateful the lotion was not antiseptic, he inhaled the cotton-fresh scent as it filled the room. Assuming Rosamond did not understand what was happening, he was glad to know someone was caring for her so gently.

"This is a cleansing lotion that both cleans and moisturizes at the same time," Chloe explained. "It's like giving her a bath, without the mess of soap and water."

Stepping forward, he nodded, but his eyes were stuck on her legs. Petite, but muscular. *A runner. I wonder if she's a runner.* A flash of her in running clothes, her long, blonde mane pulled back in a ponytail, and smiling up at him as they ran through a park filled his mind. Blinking, he looked out the window, rain beating against the glass, determined to keep his thoughts on something besides her smile.

"Okay, all finished," Chloe said, pulling the blanket up over her body, tucking her in tightly.

He noticed she left her arms out, one with the IV still attached and the other palm up. Wondering why she did this, he gave her a questioning look.

Offering an explanation as though she could hear his unasked question, Chloe said, "I saw you hold her hand the other day and thought the touch might be something she could feel."

Nodding his understanding, he asked, "Has the doctor said when he thinks she might wake up?"

A sad expression crossed her face as she shook her head. "No, but I'll let him know you're here. He might talk to you in the absence of any family since the police cleared you to visit."

"Thanks," he said, watching as she left the room. Turning back to the bed, he stared, trying to see any subtle differences in her condition. Her skin was still pale. Her hair was pushed back from her forehead and he assumed Chloe had used the wet washcloth to move it out of the way. The stitched skin appeared less raw. The bruises encircling her eyes were slightly more purplish than black. The same could be said for her arms and neck. The lesser ones were turning green and yellow, but the deeper ones were stark against her pale complexion. Her mouth was less swollen, and he noticed her lips were no longer cracked.

Smiling at the thought that he had made a tiny difference, he sought the lip balm again and reapplied it, less tentative this time. Once more expecting her skin to be cold, he was heartened to feel its warmth.

Satisfied he had done all he could physically, he pulled up the chair and settled in next to the side without the IV. Reaching through the sidebars, he took her hand in his, gently rubbing his thumb over her fingers.

"It's me...Zander. I thought we could read some more today." His gaze drifted to the window, hearing the sound of rain gently pecking against the glass. Unsure if she was able to identify other sounds, he explained, "It's raining outside today, princess. I looked out your window the other day and you've got a real nice view, so when you wake up, you can sit and see trees in the courtyard. Maybe when you're better, you'd like to go sit out there as well."

Opening the book with his free hand, he said, "Okay, Rosamond, what'll it be today? Another fairy tale or something more challenging? Of course, these aren't complete stories. Some are abridged so they're shorter, but I always loved them." Realizing he was talking to her as though she were an active participant, he chuckled. Turning a few more pages, he stopped on one. "Here, this will be what we tackle today.

" 'It was the best of times, it was the worst of

times, it was the age of wisdom, it was the age of foolishness, it was the epoch of belief, it was the epoch of incredulity, it was the season of light, it was the season of darkness, it was the spring of hope, it was the winter of despair.'

"Recognize this? I'm sure you read it in high school. It's A Tale of Two Cities by Charles Dickens. Gotta admit, the full version was hard to get through, but I love the story. And this version is shorter, so we can finish it today."

Holding her hand, he read for two hours, until Chloe came back in to check on her. Determined to not be stopped, he kept reading while Chloe adjusted the tubes and rehung a new IV bag. He nodded as she left, but continued the story.

The room's lights were dim and the blinds in the window were mostly closed. As the rain passed, the sun returned, casting light through the slits.

" 'And yet I have had the weakness, and have still the weakness, to wish you to know with what a sudden mastery you kindled me, heap of ashes that I am, into fire.' "

Lifting his head from the words on the page, he realized the slight beam of sunlight was lying across her head, catching the blonde strands of hair, making them appear as spun gold. He sat for a moment, mesmerized by her beauty, wondering about the sanity of his continued visits.

Was I lying to my friends when I just said I didn't want her to be alone? Or is there something about her that pulls me in...kindles my ashes into fire?

Giving his head a shake to clear his mind, he stood and lay the open book on the chair, walking over to the window. With the mostly closed blinds, the only real illumination came from the light behind her bed. Glancing out the window, he realized the clouds had passed completely and the sun was attempting to break through the constraints of the blinds. He twisted the bar, changing the angle of the blinds slightly, allowing light to pour into the room, wanting the feel of sunshine on his face and on hers. He looked over his shoulder, making sure it was not too bright on her but wanting more slices of warmth to be on her body. Satisfied, he returned to his chair, picking up the book again. But instead of focusing on the words, he watched her face. Still. Slumbering. The only sounds coming from the hissing and beeping of the machines.

Reaching over the sidebar, he held her hand, this time lacing his fingers through hers. Her hand appeared delicate next to his as he rubbed his thumb over her skin. On his first visit, he had been almost afraid to touch her, as though she would break into a million pieces. But now, he longed to make some connection that she might feel, willing his strength to seep into her.

Sighing, he continued to stroke her fingers as he looked back down at the page. As he neared the end of the story, he was once again struck by the quote,

" 'I wish you to know that you have been the last dream of my soul.' "

An audible gasp left his lips as he thought of the previous nights' dream—each night since the attack he had dreamed of her. Dreamed of her looking up at him in the bar with sky blue eyes, clear and shining. Dreamed of running his hand through her silken hair as he pulled her in for a kiss. Dreamed of tucking her next to him as he offered his protection when they left together.

Continuing to hold her hand, he lifted his free hand to his eyes, pinching them with his thumb and forefinger, quelling the stinging he felt. *I haven't cried in years... why now? Why her?*

Before he had time to ponder those questions, footsteps entered the room and the curtain was jerked back. Swinging his head around, he saw Dr. Calhoun, his business-like face breaking into a smile at the sight of Zander.

"I heard our mystery patient had a visitor," he said, his voice booming.

Zander winced as he glanced back down at Rosamond, afraid the doctor's voice would be frightening, but he observed no change in her sleeping.

The doctor's gaze drifted to the whiteboard, his brow furrowed in question. "Rosamond? You found out her identity?" he asked, his words laced with excitement.

"No, no," Zander hastened to reply, blushing as Chloe and a phlebotomist came in as well. She looked at the board as well and then turned her questioning gaze to him. "I just hated her being a Jane Doe. I picked a name from a book and thought it was better."

Chloe's face softened into a smile and she said, "The princess from Sleeping Beauty?"

"My daughter has that Disney movie," the phlebotomist said, her face scrunched in confusion. "The princess' name is Aurora."

"That's the Disney version," Chloe corrected, her eyes still pinned on Zander. "But in one of the Grimm versions, it was Rosamond. I think it's perfect."

He flashed her a grateful smile, but Dr. Calhoun interrupted.

"We cannot have a fake name on the board," he protested, taking the eraser in his hand. "It's not right."

"And Jane Doe is better?" Zander snapped, capturing their attention. "If her name's not Jane Doe, which I think we all agree it probably isn't, then having another name up there is no worse."

"But, Jane Doe is standard code for the fact that we don't know who she is. It's common knowledge that it isn't her real name."

Swinging his arm out toward the sleeping patient, Zander argued, "She's not a nobody. Calling her Jane Doe takes away who she might be. At least giving her a name until we find out her real name makes anyone who comes into this room see her as a real person."

"Now, see here. Everyone in this hospital treats all our patients as real people—"

"Dr. Calhoun," Chloe interrupted. "Is there a hospital policy that forces us to call her Jane Doe?"

His brow creased and, after a moment, he shook his head. "I suppose I will have to check with the legal department, but I don't know of one."

"On her official chart, it will still say Jane Doe, so legal and billing will know we don't know who she is.

But, perhaps, on the floor, we can leave her name as something pretty...like Rosamond."

Letting out a sigh, Dr. Calhoun nodded his head slowly. "I suppose there is no harm in it. It can't be any more confusing if she hears us call her that than to hear us call her Jane."

Zander's shoulders slumped in relief and, sparing another glance toward Rosamond, he smiled. Stepping back, he moved out of the way so the doctor could examine her. Looking toward Chloe, he said, "I'll be back. Gonna grab some coffee." As he walked out of the room, she patted his arm, and he knew the name Rosamond would stay on the board.

Walking down the hall toward the elevators, he heard familiar voices and turned to see who was sitting in the waiting area. There were Jayden and Cael, sitting with Miss Ethel.

She stood with Cael's assistance and opened her arms wide. "My boy, my sweet boy."

Without hesitation, he walked straight into her embrace, his eyes closing as her arms wrapped around him. For a moment, he felt the weight lift, just like when she hugged him as a child. Patting his back, she finally let go and he opened his eyes.

Smiling down at her, he asked, "I can see *how* you got here and assume these guys talked to you, but *why* are you here?"

"I didn't want to wait for you to come tell me what's going on, so once I heard, I made them bring me."

"Miss Ethel, I'm fine. There's no need to be concerned about me."

Her sharp gaze held his before a slight smile curved her lips. "Well, then, I came for her. No one should be alone." She eyed him carefully. "What are you reading her today?"

With a glance toward Cael and Jayden, he was unable to keep the blush from his cheeks as he admitted, "The abridged version of A Tale of Two Cities."

Her face softened and her eyes warmed as she said, "One of my favorite quotes is from that book. 'A day wasted on others is not wasted on one's self.' " She reached up and placed her hand on his cheek. "I've lived by that motto my whole life, and what you're doing for that girl is a good thing, Alexander."

The sting of tears hit the back of his eyes once more and as his gaze lifted from her to Jayden and Cael, he noted their raw expressions.

Sucking in a deep breath through his nose, he said, "We're all awfully glad you did, Miss Ethel." Pulling her in for a hug, he kissed the top of her head, deciding to change the subject. "The doctor's in there now," he explained. "I was just going to go get some coffee."

"Nonsense," she said, patting his hand. "Come on and sit down."

Looking at the table next to her chair, he saw a cooler. Dropping his chin, he grinned, shaking his head. Leave it to Miss Ethel to know what he needed.

Moving to the table, he assisted her to a seat, while shooting a pretend glare toward Jayden and Cael, ignoring their grins. Twenty minutes later, a full stomach of her chicken salad sandwiches, chips, a slice of her apple pie, and a large sweet tea, he looked over as

Chloe walked into the waiting room. Introducing her to his family, he breathed a sigh of relief when she said the doctor had left and they could visit Rosamond now.

Walking back down the hall, he hesitated at the door, worry creasing his brow as he glanced down at Miss Ethel.

"What is it, Zander?"

"Miss Ethel, she looks pretty bad—"

"Goodness gracious, boy. You think I haven't been in hospitals before? Now let's go in."

As he led the way, he moved to Rosamond's side, taking her hand as usual. Bending low, he whispered, "It's me…Zander again. I've brought some friends. More like my family. This is Jayden, Cael, and this is Miss Ethel." Looking over his shoulder, he understood the stunned expressions on Jayden and Cael's faces—her injuries were shocking when first seen. His gaze shot to Miss Ethel's face, soft and composed, as though this was an ordinary visit with a friend. He explained, "They say she might be able to hear us."

"Of course, she can," Miss Ethel agreed. "Her body's just healing and she's in a calm place letting it do that." Walking to the other side, she lay her hand on Rosamond's leg and said, "Sweet girl. You are strong. So strong. The Psalmist said, 'God is our refuge and strength, an ever-present help in trouble.' I pray that for you, sweet girl."

Feeling the sting of tears hit the back of his eyes, Zander blinked while swallowing deeply. Someone place a hand on his back and he knew one of his brothers was offering him strength. Lifting a hand, he swiped his eyes and nose, clearing his throat.

Looking over, he smiled at Miss Ethel. "Thank you," he said, his voice rough with emotion. "I'm sure she heard you."

Tall grass, filled with wildflowers blooming. The stems swish as I walk through a beautiful meadow. A breeze lifts my hair from my shoulders. The light feels warm on my face, but when I lift my head, I can't seem to see the sun. Darkness floats around me.

I hear deep melodious tones. It sounds so familiar...the words...best of times...worst of times. Last dream of my soul.

Words swirl about me like dust in a sunbeam. The sound is still soft...but higher. A prayer...a kind voice...God is my strength...so is my prince.

10

Zander lifted his chin toward Zeke, taking a look at the clipboard in his hand. "Looks good," he commented. "Real good." Zeke had completed the stock inventory and was ready for Zander to show him how to order what was needed.

After an hour, they hit send on the order and sat back in their chairs in the office. He noticed Zeke had opened his mouth several times, but nothing ever came out. "You got something on your mind?"

Looking down at his hands, Zeke finally said, "Some of us were wondering what happens if…well, if…"

"Spit it out, man."

Sucking in a quick breath, Zeke blurted, "What happens if she doesn't wake up? Or wakes up…not right?"

His breath left his lungs in a rush and he rubbed the back of his neck, feeling the tension radiating down his back. Used to moving around a lot, sitting for hours each day with his head down while reading had given him a stiff neck. *Nothing to complain about considering her injuries.*

Lifting his head back up, he stared at Zeke and shook his head. "Honestly, man. I got no plan with this. I don't want her to be alone. So, I'm just taking it one day at a time."

"I know you were almost graduated from high school by the time I got put with Miss Ethel," Zeke said. "She got me as a scrawny, scared, pissed off thirteen-year-old, but I remember you, Zander. You wouldn't let anyone fuck with me. Miss Ethel was the first time I felt love and you were the first time anyone ever stuck up for me. Protected me. So, I guess what I'm saying is…if you need something…anything, you just have to ask. You were there for me and I want to be there for you."

The lump forming in his throat was becoming commonplace as his friends stepped up. Clearing his throat, he nodded, "I 'preciate it, Zeke."

With that, they headed out to keep an eye on the crowd. Zeke stopped just before they left the hall to enter the bar and he shot him a questioning gaze.

"Do you find yourself more nervous?" Zeke asked.

"Nervous?"

"Yeah. Here. You know, when you're in the bar. Like looking out more for women to make sure we know who's here and with who."

Nodding his head slowly, he replied, "Yeah. I always just wanted people to drink, pay their tabs, and not cause a ruckus. Now, I search faces, questioning everything I see." Clapping Zeke on the shoulders, he said,

"But that's a good thing. Should've been what I was doing all along."

Stepping into the bar, he made the rounds of the entire room. Checking in with Roscoe at the door and seeing that Zeke had taken his position near the back, he went behind the bar.

"No worries, boss," Joe called out, entertaining a few women sitting at the bar. Charlene had the night off, but the crowd was light, so Joe had no problems keeping up with the orders.

Lynn walked by, placing her hand lightly on his arm. "Doing okay, Zander?"

He smiled as he nodded, stopping as it appeared she had more to say.

"I was telling my husband about what happened. I had no idea my daughter was listening and I don't think she heard much. But, she got the gist that my boss has a friend in the hospital with no friends to visit. She said she'd like to make a card and maybe we should visit and take her flowers."

Smiling again, he stared at his boots for a moment, warmth spreading throughout his body. Lifting his head, he said, "That's really sweet, Lynn, but no way do you want your daughter seeing her injuries."

Wincing at the reminder, she nodded. "Well, tell you what…she can make a card, I'll buy the flowers and we'll get them to you to take."

Giving her shoulder a squeeze, he nodded, "That'd be great."

"You know, what you're doing is making such a difference to that girl's life."

Watching Lynn walk away, her tray tucked to her side as she headed to the bar, he took a deep breath before making his rounds of the bar once more. *I hope that's true.*

Light is trying to pierce the darkness, but a shroud blankets me. Warm. Slivers of light shine at the very edges but the darkness still presses in. I want to reach up to pull the blanket from my face, but I am unable to do so.

It's quiet...where is the voice that speaks softly to me? I'm so tired...tired of waiting...tired of the darkness...

"Hey, Zan."

Zander smiled as he listened to the familiar voice on the other end of the phone. "Rafe. Good to hear from you." Standing in his kitchen, he halted pouring milk into his cereal as he glanced at the clock. "Jesus, man, how early did you get up? It's gotta be about four in the morning where you are." Leaning his jean-clad hip against the counter, he relaxed, ready to listen to his friend's explanation.

Chuckling, Rafe replied, "Don't sweat it. I haven't actually gone to bed yet."

"You okay or working late?"

"It was a late shoot. They wanted to get some shots in a nightclub, so we didn't start until about ten last night and the shoot ended about three a.m. I just got back to the hotel, so I figured I'd give you a call."

Silence fell between them, not as comfortable as normal. Finally, Rafe said, "I hear you're visiting every day."

"Is that what this call's about? Busting my chops?"

"No, no," Rafe hurried. "I just...hell, man. I just wanted to see how you're doing."

Sighing, he said, "Sorry. You're calling to check on me and I'm defensive. Yeah, I'm visiting every day. They still don't know who she is—"

"How the hell can she not be identified in this day and age?"

"Seriously, I wondered the same thing. But, her prints weren't in the system. No one has reported anyone missing to the police. Her purse was at the scene but her wallet, phone, and keys were missing. She must not have driven because no car was left in the lot or the surrounding streets. The police have gone around the neighborhood and to the taxi companies to see if anyone recognized her, but they only have a description they can use."

"Why the fuck don't they take her picture around like in the movies?"

"Because her face was beat to hell."

Zander heard a quick intake of breath. "Oh, fuck. Man, I'm so sorry. I just didn't think. I'm really—"

"Don't gotta be sorry, Rafe. God knows I'm sorry enough for all of us."

"So, what's your plan?"

"For now, I'll keep visiting and reading to her. The

nurses say that it's good for her to have someone to talk to her 'cause she can probably hear voices, even if they don't make a lot of sense. I sure as hell can't talk for hours, so I read."

"The Abridged Classics, right?"

"Uh…"

Laughing, Rafe said, "You used to read from that every night to the rest of us. Miss Ethel barely got to tell us a story at bedtime 'cause you were always reading. Best book ever."

Zander looked down at the large, old book lying on the end of his counter and his hand stretched out to caress the cover. The book had saved the lonely kid who finally learned to read and discovered words had the power to transport him anywhere. The worn edges had their own battle scars, as he had taken it to Afghanistan when in the Army.

"Bet you surprised them," Rafe laughed.

Snorting, he thought of the relief nurse who had come in the other day, visibly stunned that he—large, rough, tatted—was reading a classic. "Yeah, I kind of think some of them figured I might only read comics or porn."

"Bigots," Rafe declared.

"Nah…just the way society is." Silence fell again before he asked, "What about you?"

"Living the high life, Zan—" Rafe started.

"Rafe." With that one, deeply-spoken word, Zander interrupted. "This is me. Cut the bullshit."

Heaving a sigh, Rafe amended, "Okay. Honestly? This is getting old. I get paid a lot of money to walk around, bare-chested or dressed to kill. I know it seems like the life anyone would want, but I swear I'm losing my roots."

"Why don't you come home for a while? Take a break?"

"I'm tied into a contract, but...well, I've been thinking about it as soon as this gig ends. I figure I could crash at Miss Ethel's and help her some."

"When?"

"It wouldn't be for several months, but I've gotta take some time away. This life is pulling me down."

"Sounds good. You know we miss you," Zander said, glad that with Miss Ethel's guidance, none of her boys minded expressing their care for one another.

"Listen, I gotta go get some sleep. Take care, Zan. And, since I know you're on a mission, take care of the girl too."

With the support of his brothers, he felt his heart lighten. "You too," he replied. "Take care of yourself, Rafe."

Disconnecting, he poured the milk into his cereal, ready to face the day.

11

"I wonder who is looking for you," Zander said, holding Rosamond's hand while standing over her bed, staring at her face.

"Good morning," Chloe called out, walking into the room, followed by Dr. Calhoun. Both smiled at him, moving to the other side of the bed. Chloe stood at the computer, typing quickly while clicking through the chart.

Wondering if he should step back, he figured they would kick him out if necessary. Dr. Calhoun carefully probed Rosamond's head wounds before checking her other injured areas, talking in doctor-speak to Chloe.

"Look, I know I'm not family but since there's no one else here, can I ask how she's doing?"

Nodding slowly, Dr. Calhoun said, "What you see on the outside is mostly bruises, which will fade and heal. Of course, it is the internal injuries that we are concerned about. Her ruptured spleen was repaired with surgery and that appears to have been completely successful. Her kidneys did not rupture, but were severely bruised as well, and while blood in her urine was worrisome at first, it has now cleared."

Realizing he was gripping her fingers in a death grip, Zander forced his lungs to expand while loosening his tight hold on her hand. Rubbing her palm, he nodded toward Dr. Calhoun to continue.

"The head injury is our biggest area of concern. On the plus side, her MRI shows little swelling now, no midline shift, nor any mass lesions. Another excellent factor is that she shows normal pupil reaction to light. But, of course, the longer she is unconscious, the more concerned we become. Patients who do not regain consciousness within a month of their injury are less likely to survive."

Zander visibly jerked and Dr. Calhoun quickly added, "But since we are in the early stages of her recovery, we are far away from that concern."

Trying to calm his breathing, though his words belied his nerves, he asked, "What will help?"

The doctor's kind gaze looked down at the still woman lying in the bed and, offering Zander a gentle smile, he said, "What you are doing is perfect. Talk to her. Read to her. Hold her hand. Any stimulation is good and helps the brain to heal...to come back to us."

Dr. Calhoun continued his examination and Zander reluctantly let go of her hand to walk over to the window. Twisting the blinds again, for maximum light on her bed while still keeping her face in the shadow, he looked down over the parking lot. A few minutes later, he heard the doctor's footsteps retreat from the room before Chloe spoke.

"The nurses are all so glad you're here," she said.

He turned around to face her but had no response, so he just stood with his hands in his pockets.

"Really, we are. It's not that we wouldn't care to spend time with her, but there's so little time..." her voice trailed off.

His gaze jumped to hers. "Don't gotta explain," he assured. "You run yourself ragged as it is." Lifting his shoulders in a shrug as he walked back to Rosamond's bedside, he said, "I'm not even sure why I'm here."

Chloe walked over and patted his shoulder, saying, "You know what? Don't think about it too hard. Just be glad you're here." With that, she left the room.

Settling into the chair, he noticed it had been changed. The hard, standard, hospital room chair was no longer beside her bed, a more comfortable, padded chair now in its place. Smiling at the kind gesture, he opened the book, flipping pages until finding the one he wanted.

Taking her hand once more, he said, "How about Mark Twain's Adventures of Huckleberry Finn? I'll bet you read that one in school, also." With a last look at her unmoving face, he began to read.

The sound is familiar. Comforting. Faraway. A deep, melodious cadence. Words, once more as familiar as the voice. Why can I not see where the voice comes from? Dark continues to blanket my world, but still....at the edges light peeks through. Do I want to look for the light? Or stay in the dark? I just want the words to keep coming.

Zander loved the story, first hearing it from Miss Ethel and then from the many times he read it to his brothers. He grinned at the adventures, or rather the misadventures, memories of the antics the boys in Miss Ethel's home could create. How on earth had she been so patient with all that they did? He remembered broken windows from baseballs hit errantly, games of football where some of her prize roses had been trampled.

Shaking his head, he stopped reading for a moment, lost in the thoughts of his childhood once he landed in a safe place. Looking back down at the page, he read,

" **'It was a dreadful thing to see. Human beings can be awful cruel to one another.'** "

Stumbling as he read that line, he quickly lifted his gaze back to Rosamond. The evidence of what cruel things had been done to her was glaringly obvious. Wincing at the pain she must have felt, he hoped unconsciousness came early in her assault.

Leaning back in his chair, he thought about his time in Afghanistan. Infantry, he had seen his share of war. The cruelty inflicted from both sides still caused him to wake in sweat many nights. Scrubbing his hand over his face, he cleared his throat as he worked to clear his mind.

Giving her hand a squeeze, he continued, his voice

animated as he tried to read the dialect intended for the different characters. When Jim was reading Huck's future, he said,

" '**Sometimes you gwyne to git hurt, en sometimes you gwyne to git sick; but every time you's gwyne to git well agin.**'

"You hear that, Rosamond? If I could tell your future, that's what I'd say also. That sometimes you're gonna get hurt, but you'll get well again." Zander rubbed his thumb over the back of her hand, leaned forward, and vowed, "I swear, I'll protect you from now on."

He knew his brothers would call his promise a vow created from guilt. *Maybe that's where it first came from. But now?* He had no idea what was happening, other than he wanted her to awaken and settle her blue eyes on him, beaming her gentle smile his way.

He looked at the clock on the wall and knew his time was nearing an end. "I'll read just a little more and then I've got to get to work. I wish I could just stay here all the time, but know I'll come back tomorrow. I promise."

Reading for another half hour, he came to the place where Huck gives MaryJane one of the biggest compliments he could.

" '**I don't want no better book than what your face is.**' "

Closing the book, Zander placed it in the chair before leaning over and taking both Rosamond's hands in his. He knew how Huck felt. Since Miss Ethel taught him to read, books had been his salvation. Burying himself in the words of a story, he allowed himself to be transported all over the world. Sighing heavily, he stared at the still-swollen and battered face of the beauty lying before him, her hair now limp against the pillow. He reached up and gently soothed it away from her face, his fingertips drifting lightly over her cheek. Bending, he placed his lips against her forehead, feeling the warm skin under his.

Holding the kiss for a moment, he whispered, "If I could just have you look at me, your face would be more precious than a book."

With a final squeeze of her hand, he turned and walked out of her room toward the elevator, missing the blink of her eyes before they closed once more.

Something warm touched me...touched my hand...I want my fingers to hold on to whatever it was but nothing seems to work. There is still darkness but it's not as frightening when I feel the warmth surrounding my hand. More words...deep... melodic. Words I recognize from somewhere familiar. Books...a story.

I feel the brush of a touch on my face. A tingle begins where the touch ends. My face more precious than a book. The warmth spreads. I can feel it...almost enough to bring me out of the darkness.

A flash of light as I struggle to see the cause of the warm touch. This time, when the darkness shrouds me, I am not afraid.

Another bachelorette party. Dropping his head, Zander took a deep breath, remembering when he thought Rosamond was nothing more than part of a group of women having a good time getting drunk and dancing.

Roscoe walked by and Zander caught his arm, saying, "Keep an eye on the women in the back. Make sure they have a ride when they're ready to leave."

"Sure thing, boss."

Making the rounds, he nodded at Lynn and the other servers as he moved toward the back. Zeke had that section covered and, with a word to him, he circled toward the bar. Joe and Charlene were in full form, tossing bottles and keeping the crowd on the bar stools happy as they ordered more drinks and tipped well. Chuckling at their antics, he appreciated anything to keep the customers spending their money at Grimm's.

Hearing deep voices entering, he looked up to see Roscoe greeting Jayden, Jaxon, Asher, and Cael. Grinning, he walked over, hugging and back-slapping each one. "Got a bit of a crowd tonight, but there're some tables by the wall. Come on over."

They settled in chairs, smiling at Lynn as she took their orders. "So, what do I owe the honor, guys?" Seeing the shifting gazes, he prompted, "Seriously?"

"No, no," Cael spoke quickly, lifting his hands up. "No one is here to rag on you. We just wanted to see how you're doing."

He held his eyes for a moment, satisfied Cael was telling the truth. "It's all good. I know you think I'm going in too deep, but you gotta trust me when I say, I just want to be there for her as she is still in the hospital."

"And after?" Cael asked.

"She wakes up and will go her own way. I'm not trying to be a hero...hell, it's too late for that anyway considering how she left here. But, for now, I just feel sorry for her, that's all."

"Just make sure to take care of yourself," Jayden warned. "You won't be any good to her if you wear out."

"Hell, in the Army, you remember what it was like. No sleep, bad food...this is nothing. I got it. Promise."

Lynn delivered the beers and Zander gladly steered the conversation to anything but Rosamond. *How could they ever understand the feelings I have when I hold her hand?*

12

"Goodness gracious, Alexander. Come in and sit down before you fall down."

Miss Ethel ushered him into her home, her thin hands fluttering around. Still in her robe, she led him slowly through the house to the kitchen. "Boy, you got here before I had a chance to get dressed, but don't you mind that. I'll take a visit anytime. Let me get some breakfast going."

He hustled to place his hand gently on her arm and said, "No, ma'am. You sit down and I'll fix breakfast."

She looked askance for a moment, then patted his arm and nodded. "My pride would like to argue, but I don't move quite so fast anymore. My breakfast is usually juice, coffee, and a piece of toast."

As he assisted her to a chair at the large kitchen table, scars still in the wood from the many years she spent fostering boys, he kissed her cheek. "It'd be my honor to fix something for us."

Turning to the old stove, he found her frying pan and soon had eggs scrambled. Placing bacon slices into the microwave, wrapped in paper towels, he set the timer. Taking the twist-tie off the bread, he slid four slices in her oversized toaster. Pouring the coffee into cups, he turned to place one in front of her.

Within a few minutes, he plated eggs, toast with butter and jam, and bacon. Setting the plate in front of her with a small glass of juice, he quickly did the same for himself.

She bowed her head in prayer and he followed suit, knowing it had been many years since he had bowed his head on his own. As her head lifted, she began to eat slowly, her hands shaking slightly.

"Why boys, Miss Ethel?"

She turned her grey-blue eyes toward him and smiled. "I could have just as easily taken in girls," she replied. "But the first child that was brought to me was a boy. It was only for a few weeks, but then social services brought me another. Soon, I had three boys in the house and I just felt like it was best to keep taking boys."

"Keep the temptation down?"

Chuckling, she lifted her cup and took a sip of the hot brew. Nodding her approval at the cream and sugar he had added, she set it down carefully. "Absolutely. I had no idea if I would be keeping the boys for a few days, weeks, or much longer. And, I seemed to have a gift. So, as they brought several more to me, I had twin beds put in the bedroom, so that there could be sharing. In that case, I just preferred to keep to the same gender.

I suppose, if I had been brought girls first, that would have worked too."

"You did have a gift. I don't know that we recognized it or even appreciated it when we were younger. But I do now."

She said nothing, but continued to eat, a small smile dancing around her lips. After a minute she pushed her plate back saying, "That was delicious. Thank you." She leaned back in her chair, her eyes pinning his. "I've got the feeling you have something on your mind, Alexander. I've got nothing but time, so you take yours."

Wiping his mouth with the cloth napkin, he folded it and placed it back on the table. Staring at it, he asked, "Why cloth? You always had cloth napkins when paper would have been simpler with a bunch of boys."

"My, my, you are full of interesting questions today, aren't you?" she grinned, her laugh lines deepening. Fingering her own napkin, she said, "Most of you boys came from rough backgrounds. Besides trying to teach you care, like how to get along, how to look out for each other, how to be a family...I also tried to instill manners. I knew each one of you would go on to be successful and I wanted you to have the basic sense of propriety." Chuckling, she said, "I know that doesn't need cloth napkins, but we always sat down together at dinnertime and it was the one time of the day when you all could talk about whatever you wanted. And we did it sitting at the table like young men."

He nodded silently. Behaving at the table was instilled soon after he came to her home. Before that, he had eaten any way he could, wherever he could.

Pinning him with her sharp eyes, she said, "Why all the questions today?"

Shrugging, he said, "Miss Ethel, I honestly don't know. It just seems as though I have so many thoughts going on all at the same time." She stayed silent, so he continued. "I've spent so much time with Rosamond in the past week. I've described her room hoping she doesn't feel scared if she can hear the machines. I've described what it looks like outside, thinking maybe she would feel some comfort knowing there are trees outside her window." Scrubbing his hand over his face, he shook his head. "I don't know…"

"Sounds to me, son, that in talking to a woman who cannot see anything right now, you've opened your eyes as well."

Her thin fingers reached out to clasp his arm and he looked down at the paper-thin skin covering them, seeing how fragile she now was. His gaze sought hers, the idea that one day she would not be in his life sending a stab straight through his heart.

Opening his mouth several times without saying anything, he finally blurted, "How can I feel something for her? Something so real, based off nothing? Nothing but sitting with her. Talking to her. Reading to her."

"Worrying about her, also?" she asked softly.

Nodding, he swallowed deeply as he whispered, "Yeah."

"God chooses people, Alexander." She held his eyes as she continued to speak. "Sometimes, people are put in our path to walk with us. Maybe for a little while. Maybe for longer. Maybe for a lifetime. You boys think that God put me in your path, but the truth of the matter is, He gave you to me. Becoming your foster mom gave me a purpose…a will to live after my George died. I may not have been a birth mom, but I raised my six siblings, so I knew something about parenting. After George died, I had no reason to get up in the mornings. But you boys…you gave me everything. And honest to God, I loved each of you as soon as you stepped across my threshold."

He said nothing, but the memory of sitting at her feet in the living room as she passed on life lessons to them all came back to him.

"I don't know why, but God put you in the path of that young woman. We can't always see the reasons for what He does, but you were sent to save her. I know the others are afraid you are becoming obsessed because you feel like you were to blame, but that man was going to attack someone, somewhere. He just chose her and your bar at that time. You were placed in her life for a reason. But," she emphasized, leaning toward him, "I firmly believe she was placed in your path as well…for you."

Cocking his head to the side, he stared into her eyes, heavy questions creasing his brow.

"You're a leader, Alexander. I wasn't surprised when you decided to join the Army when you graduated. But you came back different. Not that I was surprised. My George served in Vietnam and I remember the trouble he'd have sleeping when he returned. You threw your-self into the bar. Stayed loyal to your friends and you certainly took care of me, but I felt as though you closed yourself off to life. Maybe, just maybe, this woman was placed in your place to bring you back to life."

They sat in silence for several minutes, the only sound was the tick-tock of the clock in the shape of a cat, hanging on the kitchen wall, it's tail moving back and forth with each second passing. He remembered being fascinated with the clock when he first came to Miss Ethel's, spending minutes just sitting and staring at the black, plastic tail keeping time.

Sighing, he dragged his mind to the present. "You once told me the measure of a man was not in his mistakes, but in how he handled those mistakes."

Smiling, she nodded. "I told that to all my boys. And it's as true today as it was then. And you, Alexander, are a great man."

They stood together as he gathered the plates and rinsed them off. She held on to his arm as she escorted him to the front door. As he bent to hug her, she whispered, "Don't worry about your feelings for this woman. Just know that God has a plan for both of you and it will be revealed in time."

Walking out into the sunshine, he slid his sunglasses onto his face and climbed into his truck. A slight smile curved his lips and his heart felt lighter. Looking at the clock on the dashboard, he knew he had enough time to go to the hospital before getting to the bar.

A flash of light piercing my darkness. The beeps to the side, irritating in their constancy and, yet, I know it is from some-

thing to help me. The deep voice told me that. Another flash of light. Fuzzy. A room. I'm in a room. On a bed. Another flash of light. My head hurts. What's happening. I'll go back to the darkness for a while. To the peace.

Zander's gaze landed on a large bouquet of pink roses in a tall white vase sitting on the shelf near the head of Rosamond's bed, next to a smaller bouquet of flowers, and a bouquet of balloons. His eyes narrowed, stalking over to read the card. Ruefully shaking his head, he felt his lips twitch as he saw they were from Rafe. The smaller bouquet also held a card. The Grimm's employees. His heart lightened, knowing the flowers were sent as much for him as for Rosamond. Seeing another card on the strings holding the balloons, he was unable to keep the smile from his lips as he read the signatures in Cael, Jaxon, Jayden, Asher, and Miss Ethel's familiar scrawl.

Turning back to the bed, he stared down at Rosamond's face. "Hey," he greeted, bending over to kiss her forehead. "You've got lots of admirers sending you gifts."

He settled into the comfortable chair and, as usual, took her hand in his, rubbing the soft skin for a moment. Staring at her face, he noticed her lips had slightly more color. A pale pink. His gaze roved over her face, noting the slight blush on her cheeks.

"Come on, Rosamond. You gotta heal, sweetheart. You gotta come out of the sleep."

She lay motionless and he heaved a sigh. "In the mood for another classic today?" Looking down, he opened the book. Clearing his throat, he said, "I always loved this one. Alex Dumas' The Count of Monte Cristo. It's got everything a young boy could have wanted. Swashbuckling sword fights. Ships on the sea. Bad guys. Good guys who finally get their revenge." Chuckling, he added, "It's got romance but, when I was young, I didn't care so much about that."

Opening the page, he began. After a while, he read,

" **'Often we pass beside happiness without seeing it, without looking at it, or even if we have seen and looked at it, without recognizing it.'** "

Looking up, he said, "I think that was me, Rosamond. I went about each day, but can't say I really saw happiness or, when I did, I didn't even recognize it."

He leaned back in the chair, the vision of Grimm's Bar floating through his mind. Lynn laughing when she talked on the phone with her husband or kids. Joe working hard to capture the eye of one of the female patrons. Charlene with her in-your-face attitude, often hiding a heart of gold. Zeke, excited about learning how to manage, finally feeling like more than a bouncer.

" **'I don't think man was meant to attain happiness so easily. Happiness is like those palaces in fairy tales whose gates are guarded by dragons: we must fight in order to conquer it.'** "

Scrubbing his hand over his face, he thought back to hearing Rosamond's tiny voice as she said, "Excuse me," when she passed by him in the hall and he looked down to first see her beautiful smile. She looked like the sleeping princess in the fairy tale book Miss Ethel read to them and, while he did not recognize it at the time, he wanted to get to know her.

"I should have slain your dragons, Rosamond." Swallowing deeply, he whispered, "Please forgive me."

Blinking against the sting of unshed tears, he sucked in a deep breath through his nose. Managing to quell the desire to cry, he bent back to the words on the page. The story continued through deception, survival, redemption. Friendships betrayed. Love lost and love found.

" 'All human wisdom is contained in these two words—Wait and Hope.' "

Laying the book in the chair as he stood, Zander unlocked the bedrails, sliding them down, and sat on the edge of her bed.

"Wait and hope," he repeated, gliding his hand along her arm. "That's what I've been doing, Rosamond. Waiting and hoping. But maybe not just for the past few days, but for a long time. Waiting and hoping for something...someone. But you gotta open your eyes. You gotta want to get better. I know it must be nice in there...dark and safe. But, I promise you, sweetheart, you come back into the light and I'll make it a safe place for you."

Reaching forward, his hand shaking slightly, he slid his fingertip over her cheek, feeling the petal soft skin. Pushing her tangle of hair back from her forehead, he battled with the desire to get closer.

Her scent, no longer subtle flowers, was hospital antiseptic. And yet, closing his eyes, he could remember the jolt he felt when she first squeezed past him. Her hair, no longer silk and shine, was dull and limp. And yet, he remembered seeing the angelic flow down her back and his hand had longed to reach out and touch her tresses. Knowing he needed to tread carefully, he leaned forward, barely touching his lips to her cheek, the skin cool to the touch. Her body, no longer clothed fashionably in items that hugged her curves was covered in the drab grey of the hospital gown. And yet, he remembered the way his eyes followed her as she walked away from him.

Staring into her sleeping face, he murmured, "Come on, beauty. Come back to me." Closing his eyes, knowing it was wrong, he touched his lips to hers. A barely-there, whisper of a kiss. Keeping his eyes closed, he leaned back, his heart beating furiously in his chest.

Sighing, he opened his eyes. And his breath halted, shock jolting completely through him. Peering back were light blue eyes, staring straight into his.

13

Zander gasped audibly as his body jerked in surprise. He blinked as her eyes held his, his breath leaving his lungs slowly, afraid to move, not wanting to break the spell.

Her fingers twitched and he gently pressed his hand around hers. They twitched against his fingers again. Now blinking, her eyes appeared unfocused, though they stayed locked on his face. He shifted slightly to the left, still holding her hand and her gaze, positioning his body to block out the stream of sunshine coming through the window.

He knew he should ring for the nurse, but the slight movement of her eyebrows gave him pause. The swelling around her eyes made it impossible for her to open them widely, but the light color of her irises captured his attention.

Suddenly aware of his scruffy beard and rough appearance, he rushed to whisper, "Hey."

Her eyes moved slightly, roaming over his face.

"It's okay," he promised, rubbing his thumb over her hand. "You're safe. You've been asleep...uh...for a while. But, you'll be fine now."

Her gaze darted away, jerking quickly to each side before coming back to land on his face. He watched as she swallowed, wincing as though the action caused pain. Seeing the bruises on her throat, he wondered if they made swallowing difficult. Or maybe even speaking.

"You don't have to say anything," he said, afraid she might slip back into sleep. "Just try to stay awake and I'll keep talking."

Snaking his free hand over the top of the covers, he pressed the call button. It only took a moment for Chloe to arrive, immediately calling for the doctor while washing her hands.

She hustled efficiently to Rosamond's side, smiling widely. "Well, hello." She, too, spoke softly, "My name is Chloe. I'm a nurse. You're in the hospital and we're taking care of you."

Zander frowned, observing no recognition in Rosamond's face. "Can she hear us? She doesn't seem to—"

"It's fine," Chloe assured. "I'm so sorry...I should have been preparing you for what happens when she wakes up."

Looking at Chloe's calm face, he forced his panic to recede. Afraid to speak his fears aloud, he simply nodded, watching as she checked the various machines attached to Rosamond. The blood pressure cuff began expanding while Chloe leaned over, saying, "You might feel this on your arm...just a little squeeze...it's fine... we're right here."

He watched as Rosamond's eyes moved between his, seeking reassurance. His heart was beating a staccato in his chest and he was sure the sound was audible to all.

Hearing footsteps coming into the room, he identified Dr. Calhoun by his voice as he spoke to Chloe. He was pleased when the doctor moved around him, bending over Rosamond while still allowing him to maintain his hold on her hand.

Speaking as softly as the others, Dr. Calhoun introduced himself, assuring Rosamond they were all glad to see her awake. He gently examined her, checking her vitals with Chloe. Aware hospital protocol was probably being broken, Zander was glad no one had asked him to leave. He stayed silent, his thumb still moving gently over her hand, observing her gaze continually straying back to him.

As though remembering his audience, Dr. Calhoun twisted his head back and asked, "Zander...can you step outside for a few minutes?"

Inwardly grimacing, he nonetheless nodded, moving back a step. Rosamond's fingers tightened on his as her eyebrows shot down. Her mouth opened, a hoarse grunt coming forth. He stopped, shock firing through him, not letting go of her hand.

Dr. Calhoun leaned over her, a smile on his face while he said, "It's okay. He'll just be outside and then we'll let him right back in—"

Her face, still swollen and bruised, scrunched horribly as a tear slid from her eye. Another animal groan slipped from her lips and her fingers pulled on his. Her pulse rate shot up, the monitor beeping rapidly.

"I'm not leaving," he said, his words firm while still in a whisper. "I'll turn my head...whatever you need me to do, but I'm not leaving her."

Chloe opened her mouth to speak but Dr. Calhoun immediately agreed. "Fine, fine." Leaning back over Rosamond, he said, "It's okay. Shhhh, we'll let him stay. We want you comfortable."

Zander turned his head down to study his boots as more nurses filed into the room and he felt Rosamond's body being moved around gently. Chloe continued a running dialog of soft speech, explaining what they were doing, offering assurances to her.

Finally Dr. Calhoun said, "Everything looks very good. I know this is confusing, but don't worry. Your body needs to complete its healing. We'll run more tests to see how you are doing right now." Moving away, he stood to the side as he ordered new CT scans, Chloe charting his orders.

Stepping closer, filling in the spot where the doctor had been standing, Zander lifted his gaze from the floor, sucking in a breath as he caught her eyes focused on his face.

Bending low, he held his lips close to her ear as he whispered, "I'm Zander." As he raised up, he was mesmerized by the sight of her mouth attempting to curve slightly into a lopsided smile. Even with a battered face, his heart skipped a beat at the beautiful sight.

Zander stood behind the bar, eyeing the customers as he pulled beer for the few on the stools. It was Joe's night off and, though Charlene was always there to step in, he needed her serving tonight.

Zeke walked in from the back, his nod indicating he had finished the stock order. He lifted his chin in return and watched as Zeke took his place near the end of the bar. It was Roscoe's night off as well, so Zeke took a more mid-room position to keep an eye on everyone.

Lynn smiled as she walked up, her tray tucked under her arm. "Peaceful crowd tonight. I know the tips will be down, but I swear I love Tuesday nights."

"You ever think about adding a kitchen?" Charlene asked.

Lifting his eyebrows, he stared at her in surprise. "You kiddin'?"

"No," she replied, an easy grin on her face. "If you added hamburgers, fries, and wings…you'd have the place hopping."

"Why the hell do you think this place needs to be more hoppin' than it is? On weekends, we got more business than we can handle. So, the smaller crowds during the week gives us a chance to breathe."

Charlene winked and Lynn laughed as he shook his head and chuckled. As her mirth ebbed, Lynn cocked her head to the side, still staring at him. "You're different tonight, boss. Is Rosamond doing better?"

His lips twitching, he nodded. "Yeah. Sorry, I should have said something. She woke up today—"

"Oh, my God!" she screamed, jumping up and down. "Charlene, did you hear? She woke up!"

Charlene's head whipped around and, ignoring the customers in front of her, she rushed over to join Lynn in hugging him.

"Good news, man," Zeke said, smiling over the heads of the women.

Unable to keep the grin off his face, he acknowledged with a chin lift. "All right, ladies. Just understand, she's just woken up. She's not talking or moving much yet and has a long road ahead of her."

"Yes, but to wake up must be a good sign," Lynn rushed.

Nodding, he said, "Yeah, it was fucking miraculous to see it."

Charlene moved behind the bar, a bounce in her step as she tossed a few liquor bottles, offering a celebratory drink to the three patrons sitting at the bar.

With another squeeze to his arm, Lynn said, "I'm really happy for you, Zander. I just know your girl will be fine."

Jerking his gaze to hers, he noticed she was not joking. "My girl?"

She playfully gave his shoulder a little push. "Come on, Zander. You know what I mean." Shrugging, she said gently, "From what you say, she's got no one other than you. So, that kind of makes her your girl."

Listening to that explanation, his stance relaxed. "Sorry, Lynn. I know I'm touchy. I'm really just there to give her some company until she goes back to her life."

"So...you're trying to not get emotionally involved?"

He hesitated and she gave his arm a slight squeeze. "Zander, it's not so easy to turn your emotions off just like that. You've become part of her life and she's become part of yours. I don't see why that has to change. Give yourself, and her, a chance." With a gentle smile, she turned and walked back to her customers, leaving him standing alone.

The idea of a future with no more stories shared with his princess hit his gut. "She'll go back to her own life once she remembers everything...one that won't include me," he whispered to no one, a tortured grimace twisting his face.

For the first time since he had been visiting regularly, Zander hesitated outside the hospital door. Anxious to see her again, the desire to feel her eyes resting on him as a wobbly smile crossed her face was overwhelming.

But...what if this is it? What if she's remembered everything? What if she remembers I'm the one who caused her to be outside...alone...with that monster?

His hand shook as he lifted it, holding his palm against the cool surface of the door. Sucking in a deep, fortifying breath, he pushed ahead.

The sight greeting him caused his feet to stumble. She was still in bed, but was now partially raised up to a semi-sitting position. In a clean hospital gown, the pale green color gave a spring-fresh look to her soft skin. Her hair, recently brushed and pulled back in a long braid, was lying over her shoulder. Peach-fuzz, blonde hair surrounded the stitches, much less angry in appearance than a week prior. Her pale hands rested in her lap, her fingers gripping the blanket. Her facial bruises had faded slightly, a lighter purple instead of dark black. Her nose, still covered with a bandage over the bridge, was less swollen, as were her eyes.

Her eyes lifted to his, untold emotions floating in their depths. He righted himself, coming to a halt, wondering what happened next. *Do I leave? Do I say stay? Do I—*

Her mouth, freshly coated in soothing balm, quirked as her lips barely turned up at the corners. Her brows lowered as she lifted one hand, jerking her fingers toward him.

His breath whooshed out from him, his heart pounding in his chest, a smile beaming toward the beautiful woman beckoning him. Stalking toward the bed, he reached out and took her hand in his much larger one. The feel of her fingers moving against his as she gave a tiny squeeze forced him to lock his knees to keep from dropping to the floor. After holding her almost lifeless hand for so long, to feel warmth and movement from her touch made the smile on his face grow larger.

"Hey," he said, his voice raspy. "I'm Zander."

Her eyes brightened as she jerked her head in a short nod. Her eyes cut over to the whiteboard where Rosamond was still written. He followed her gaze before seeing the confusion on her face.

"I know that's not your name," he said. Suddenly unsure how much to tell her and uncertain what the hospital staff had explained, he mumbled, "I…uh…well, didn't know your name, so they let me…uh, just give you one."

Her tongue flicked out, licking her lips, and his gaze dropped to the slight movement. Swallowing audibly, he kept talking to keep his mind on something besides her mouth.

"If you can let me know your name, I'll change it on the board."

Her mouth opened, but no words came forth. Her brows pinched together in evident distress, so he rushed to assure, "It's okay. Honestly. Don't worry about it. All that matters now is that you're awake and can get better."

Chloe entered the room, smiling widely at them. "Hey, how's it going?"

"It's nice to see her awake," he replied, his eyes never leaving Rosamond. "But, I think she wants us to know her real name."

Chloe stood on the other side of the hospital bed, checking her vital signs. Looking down, she said, "Don't worry, honey. Your brain is still healing. You'll be able to talk soon and regain control over your movements." Focusing on Zander, she explained, "We haven't gotten her up yet, because of being a fall risk. As soon as her brain is able to control the muscles in her legs better, we'll have her up and walking."

"And speaking?"

Nodding, she smiled back at Rosamond. "Same with speech. As the swelling of your brain decreases even more, you will be able to control the muscles in your whole body. Dr. Calhoun will be back in this afternoon, but he said this morning that your recovery is going very well."

Looking back to Zander, she asked, "Did you tell her where the name Rosamond came from?"

The heat of blush filled his neck and face. "No…it's…no—"

"Oh, honey," Chloe gushed, placing her hand on Rosamond's shoulder. "After your…uh…accident, we were unable to identify you, so you were listed as a Jane Doe. Zander, here, hated that. Since he had just read Sleeping Beauty to you, he named you after the princess in the story. And you should have seen him fight to keep Jane Doe off the board!" She turned to walk out the room, calling over her shoulder, "You've got a real Prince Charming there."

Knowing his face must be flame red, he grumbled as Rosamond's gaze cut back over to him. "She's got the wrong damn fairy tale. Prince Charming is not in Sleeping Beauty."

Her mouth curved in a smile, her face relaxing once more. Her chest rose and fell with each breath as she settled back against the pillows. She nodded to the chair before moving her focus back to his face.

"Do you want me to sit…stay?"

Receiving another nod, he smiled, sitting in the chair while still holding her hand. Placing the book he was holding on his lap, he questioned, "Do you want me to read?"

Another nod.

Rubbing his chin, freshly shaved for his visit, he

asked, "Do you remember...I mean, could you hear me read before...uh, when you were asleep?"

Her widening smile lit the room, warming his heart. Letting out a long breath, he chuckled. "Well, alright. Let's see what I can find to read today."

14

Zander flipped the pages of his book, his fingers shaking, nerves threatening to overtake him. At the slight pressure on his hand he shifted his gaze from the turning pages to Rosamond's face.

Her brows lowered in question and he instinctively understood she could feel his anxiety. Sighing, he said, "It's been a long time since I read to someone listening. I mean, not that you weren't listening before. But...well, you know...you were sleeping."

Her fingers rubbed along the back of his hand, offering him comfort. Embarrassed that she was concerned about him, he shook his head. "No, no, it's okay. I want to read to you. I just want to choose the best story."

Her gaze dropped to the book still open in his lap and she gave a slight shake of her shoulders.

"Anything's okay?" he asked.

With her nod, he began flipping the pages once

more. Landing on Great Expectations, he hesitated. Another squeeze and he looked up. "Great Expectations by Charles Dickens? Pip and Estelle? And the eccentric Miss Havershim?"

He could have sworn her eyes twinkled and he grinned. "Okay... Great Expectations it is. Thank God it's an abridged version."

She relaxed against the pillows, her gaze on him as he began to read. After an hour, he came to the scene where Pip, now an adult, meets with Miss Havershim and Estelle, his unrequited love.

" **'I loved her against reason, against promise, against peace, against hope, against happiness, against all discouragement that could be.'** "

Stumbling over the words, he jerked his gaze to Rosamond, her eyes closed, and wondered if she had fallen asleep. Her hand lay quiet in his while the words he had just read flowed through his mind.

Barely making a sound, he whispered, "God, I know how Pip felt. I don't dare call this love...I have no idea what it is. But, against all reason, I feel something."

A sound at the door brought him back to the present. Closing the book quickly, he twisted his head, seeing Pete walking into the room. Shooting a glance at Rosamond, he saw her eyes open, moving between him and the new visitor and he wondered if she heard his last whisper.

Before he had time to worry about that thought, Pete greeted them as he approached the bed, his gaze dropping to their clasped hands.

"Zander," he said with a nod. "Hello, Miss. I'm

Detective Peter Chambers. I received a call from the hospital that you were awake and I've been assigned to your case."

Zander noted the flash of dark in her eyes and he rushed to say, "I know Pete. He's a friend of mine." Her hand squeezed his tighter.

"Has she spoken? Told you her name?" Pete asked.

"She understands what you say, Pete. She just hasn't regained her speech yet."

"Oh…" Pete said, his brow crinkling in thought. "Does she remember anything?"

She squeezed his hand again and he turned back to look at her. "What is it, princess?"

If Pete noticed the term of endearment, he did not mention it. "Miss, the reason I'm here is to assist in your case—"

"We need to talk, man," Zander interrupted. Standing, he bent over Rosamond and said, "Now, don't you worry about anything. I'm going to step outside for a moment with my friend and I'll be right back, okay?"

Her arms jerked in response as a grimace crossed her face.

"Shhhh," he soothed. "I'm not finished yet…I'll come back and we can keep reading. You fell asleep before, but we still have some Great Expectations to read."

"Great Expectations?" Pete chuckled. "Never figured you for a classics man…" His words trailed off as Zander glared over his shoulder at him. "Uh…yeah, we'll talk outside." Turning, he left the room.

Turning back to Rosamond he smoothed her hair off her forehead and said, "I'll be right back. I promise. I know you don't know me...not really. But I never break a promise."

At those words, her arm stopped flailing and she loosened her grip on his hand, relaxing back against the pillows. Thrilled that she appeared to believe him, he winked at her before following Pete into the hall.

She wanted to listen to the conversation outside her room, but was unable to hear what was being said. Zander said he would be right back and that he never broke a promise. Smiling, she leaned back, believing him.

Her face felt tight and as she lifted her hand, the fading yellow bruises covering her arms came clearly into view. Barely touching her face, she felt the swelling. Gliding her fingers upward, she encountered rough and puckered skin. Letting her hand drop back to the blanket, she felt the clawing of anxiety as it slid over her body.

An accident. They said I had an accident. *I don't remember an accident.* She wished her mind would work correctly. Thoughts drifted in and out, often before she had a chance to really understand them. *Like flipping the pages in a book without being able to stop to read the words. Book...*

She smiled slightly again, the anxiety easing. *Zander. He read to me. I remember that. I remember his voice. He'll be right back.*

Before Pete had a chance to turn around, Zander was in his face. "Man, I get you need to ask her questions, but you gotta give her a chance to heal."

Eyes narrowing, Pete said, "And just what is your interest here, Zander? She was attacked outside your bar and now you're her champion?"

Scrubbing his hand through his hair, he said, "Yeah...sort of." Heaving a sigh, he admitted, "I felt guilty...responsible. Now, I just want to make sure she's fine. Until we know who she is and who out there is missing her, I want to be here for her."

Pete hung his head for a moment. "Sorry. Really, I'm not trying to be a dick. Her case is so frustrating because we got nothing. Nothing about who she is. Where's she's from. And don't even get me started on who the hell beat the crap outta her. I just really want to get the bastard who did this."

Nodding, he agreed, "I hear you. You better hope you get to him before I do, 'cause I'll fuckin' do to him what he did to her."

Pete stared at him and shook his head. "No...you stay out of it. Let me do my job and you just take care of her." Pausing, he added, "But don't fall for her, Zan. I mean, she might be married or—"

"Got it," he growled. "Jesus, you sound like my brothers."

Pete nodded his head slowly. "Remember when we first met? On the fuckin' plane heading to Bagram

Air Base. Both young and too damn cocky to admit we were scared shitless."

Chuckling, he nodded. "Yeah, I remember."

"We served with some good men over there, but Zander? You are the best man I ever met."

He lifted his head, holding Pete's gaze. "I...I don't know what to say."

"You don't gotta say anything. But, Miss Ethel and all them boys she raised along with you, would tell you the same thing." Pete's eyes cut over to the hospital door and he added, "Tell you what. You spend some time talking to her and when she starts remembering, you give me a call."

Shaking hands, Zander watched as Pete headed to the elevators before he turned and went back inside. His eyes immediately sought Rosamond's, his smile meeting hers.

"You've got no idea how great it is to walk in here and see you looking at me," he admitted, sitting back in his chair and reaching over to take her outstretched hand.

Her gaze jerked to the door and back again in question.

"My friend, Pete, has gone. He's a good guy, I swear. He's a policeman. Well, a detective. He's...uh, well, he's trying to find out how to help you." Her fingers twitched against his hand and he rubbed his thumb in circles over her wrist. Holding her gaze, he continued, "But don't worry about that now. You just concentrate on getting better."

A short nod met his words. Grinning, he asked, "You ready to listen to more Great Expectations?"

She smiled her enthusiasm and watched as he placed the book in his lap, opening to where the bookmark held his place.

An hour later, her eyes closed again as he continued to read.

" 'You are part of my existence, part of myself. You have been in every line I have ever read, since I first came here...' "

Sucking in a quick breath, he lifted his head, seeing her asleep. A strange tightening squeezed in his chest as he stared at her slowly healing face, wishing he could take away all her pain. He knew she needed to remember everything about her past so she could claim her life again, yet he was terrified for her to do so.

Repeating the line again, he whispered, "You are part of my existence, princess. Part of myself. 'You have been in every line I have ever read, since I first came here.' "

Closing the book, he stood, setting it on the chair. Bending over the bedrail, he hesitated before touching his lips to hers. Moving slightly, he kissed her forehead instead. "I'll be back tomorrow, princess. Promise." This time, leaving her caused a greater ache and he fought the desire to stay until she woke again, but he had to get to Grimm's.

As her door closed behind him, a tear slid down her cheek.

15

Walking into Rosamond's room the next morning, Zander was shocked to see her sitting up in the large patient's chair. A fresh gown, blue with white stripes, covered her from neck to feet—which were adorned in fuzzy socks—and a blue blanket was wrapped around her shoulders. Chloe was sitting next to her, assisting as she ate from a breakfast tray on the stand in front of her.

Her blue eyes were bright as she pinned him, smiling in the middle of eating a spoonful of oatmeal.

"Wow," he enthused, "look at you. Sitting up, eating real food." Stalking over, he stopped behind Chloe, peering over her shoulder toward the beauty. Each day the bruises faded a little more. Today, the large bandage over her nose was replaced with a much smaller strip. The swelling around her eyes was diminished, allowing them to open wide.

Chloe stood and said, "Since you're here, do you mind helping? I've got a few other patients to check on."

Doubt hit his gut and he asked, "Is there anything I should know?"

"We want her to work on her motor skills and, to be honest, she's much better today than yesterday. Just be here in case she has difficulties."

Sliding into the seat vacated by Chloe, he looked at the tray dubiously. Upon closer inspection, the breakfast consisted of a meal-replacement shake, a bowl of orange gelatin, and oatmeal.

"Hmmm, well, this probably isn't the breakfast of champions, but for your first food in a while, I'll bet it tastes pretty good."

She nodded as she concentrated on getting the spoon from the gelatin to her lips. Successful, she swallowed. "Goo…" she said, the sound rough.

His eyebrows shot upward as his mouth dropped. "You're speaking."

A light pink color shaded her cheeks and she lifted her shoulders in a little shrug. "Nah mu."

"Not much?" he repeated. "Just hearing your voice at all is amazing."

Her gaze shot over his shoulder and he twisted his neck to see Dr. Calhoun entering the room.

Greeting them both, he reviewed Rosamond's chart before moving to her chair.

"I see you are making a stab at the food. Excellent. You'll need to be on a simple diet for another day or so. We want to see you go to the bathroom on your own.

Your catheter was removed last night, of course, so the nurses will be monitoring your output."

The blush on her cheeks deepened and Zander moved back a few feet to give her privacy, turning his attention to the flowers in the room. He saw another bouquet from Rafe and shook his head in mirth.

"You'll be staying with us until we are certain you are stable. At that time, we can look at rehabilitation placement if needed."

Zander glanced at her face, seeing her brow wrinkle. Recognizing her concern, he said, "Don't worry about that now." Shooting Dr. Calhoun a warning glare, he sat back down in the chair facing her.

After the doctor finished the instructions, entering them into the computer as he talked, he left and Zander noticed she visibly relaxed.

"You know, I hate to call you Rosamond when I know that isn't your name. Or is it? Am I the best guesser in the world?"

She smiled and shook her head as she looked at the whiteboard on the wall, Rosamond still written by Patient Name. "Ra…"

"Your name?" he asked, excitement coursing through him.

Chloe walked back into the room and he called out, "She's trying to tell us her name."

"No way," Chloe exclaimed, her excitement equally showing. Moving closer, she asked, "What is it, honey?"

"Ro…"

Zander's brow creased as he repeated, "Ra…ro?"

"Ro…le."

"Roly?" Chuckling, he said, "Your name's not Roly is it?"

She giggled as her eyes danced. Zander stared, dumbstruck. Her gentle laughter, while hoarse, was music to his ears. Unable to think of anything other than the desire to hear that sound every day for the rest of his life, he was grateful when Chloe continued the guessing game.

"It starts like Ro?" Receiving a nod, she then asked, "Is there something between the Ro and Le?"

Another nod. He watched her eyes move back to the board before shifting to him again. "Ro...a...le."

"Ro-a-lee?" He saw the frustration building as her arms twitched about, her movements still jerky. Jumping up, he stalked over to the board on the wall where Rosamond was printed. Pointing to the 'R' he watched her nod. His finger moved to the 'o' and she nodded again. Sliding along to the 's' and 'a', both receiving nods, he looked to Chloe, her face registering shock as well.

"Rosa. Your name is Rosa?" Chloe asked, now bouncing on her toes.

Zander waited anxiously as she said, "Le. Ro...a...le."

Sucking in a gasp, he said, "Rosalie. Is your name Rosalie?"

A huge smile met his question. Without thinking, he rushed over, enveloping her in his arms. Rocking her back and forth he felt her thin body underneath the blanket, firing his protectiveness even more.

"Do you know your last name?" Chloe asked, her smile wide.

Rosalie's face scrunched slightly as she opened her mouth, but no words came out. Twisting up to look at him, she clutched his shoulders tighter.

"It's okay, princess. A bit at a time," he assured, followed closely by Chloe's assurances.

Chloe congratulated them while she walked over to the whiteboard and wrote Rosalie in place of Rosamond. "You know, Zander…it's crazy that you came so close to her real name. All because of Sleeping Beauty." Grinning, she left the room.

Pulling back until his face was in front of hers, he whispered, "Hey, Rosalie. I'm Zander. Nice to meet you."

Rosalie smiled, a tear falling onto the blanket still wrapped around her. Nodding, she said, "You…too." For the first time since awakening, she felt the stirrings of life once again.

Zander looked over as the door to the bar opened and grinned as he saw Cael, Asher, Jaxon, and Jayden walk in. With a nod toward Charlene, he headed over to greet them.

Sitting at one of the old, round tables, they called out their thanks as Charlene brought over beer.

"Y'all need anything else?" she asked. "Burgers, wings, fries…oh, wait, we don't have that, do we, boss?" Laughing, she patted his shoulder before turning to walk back to the bar.

"What was that all about?" Cael asked, his eyes moving from Charlene to Zander.

Shaking his head, he said, "She's after me about opening a kitchen so we can serve food as well as drinks."

"Grimms' Pub instead of Grimm's Bar. I like it," Jaxon responded.

"Of course, you would," Jayden laughed. "You'd be in here every night just to eat. Aren't you afraid you'd gain weight with all that fried food?"

Leaning back, Jaxon patted his flat stomach. "Hell, the women love my body. And, as much exercise as I get, I could keep the pounds off."

"As fascinating as this conversation is," Zander interrupted, "I've got no plans of expanding. Grimm's is fine just the way it is." Looking over to Cael, he noticed he was staring at him. Crinkling his brow, he asked, "What?"

Cael shook his head slowly, answering, "Don't know, man. You tell us." As the others looked between the two, Cael added, "You look better…more relaxed. Dare I say even happy?"

Now with all four men staring at him, Zander sighed, torn between wanting to share with his friends and wondering what they would say. "Oh, hell, might as well tell you. She woke up—"

The table erupted in a mixed chorus of "Thank God" and "Hell, yeah".

Laughing, he said, "And she was able to tell us her name. It's Rosalie."

"What about her last name?" Jayden asked. "Can the police find out more about her?"

Shaking his head, he said, "Not yet. The doctors say that as her brain heals, she'll regain her strength and remember things."

"Good," Jaxon said, cracking his knuckles. "Then maybe she can identify the prick who did that to her and we can pay him a little visit before the police pick him up."

The others nodded their agreement, but Zander cautioned, "She might not remember. They said that sometimes when memory comes back, the one thing that stays out is memory of the trauma."

"So, she could remember everything about herself except that night?"

His friends watched as his face registered doubt and he rubbed the back of his neck with his hand. Sighing, he nodded.

"Well, that'd be a good thing, right?" Jaxon asked.

"Yeah…" Shifting in his seat, he added, "I can't imagine what the attack must have been like for her. You've seen her…she's small. And the beating she took…" Clearing his throat as anger swarmed over him, he continued, "So, I'd rather she never remember that. Oh, hell, I rather she never remember that it was me who kicked her out, placing her in the way of that asshole."

"But?" Cael prodded.

"Without her testimony, the police will never know who attacked her. He could get away with what he did to her."

"And, if she does remember?" Asher asked, his soft voice cutting through the conflicting emotions.

Swallowing hard, Zander sat up straighter and looked his friends in the eye. "Then I'll have to deal with her memories...and hope the good outweighs the bad."

16

Sitting in the chair, Rosalie looked anxiously toward the door, wondering when Zander would come. If he would come. She did not understand her feelings—only that she knew his was the face she longed to see...the voice she longed to hear.

Maybe, now that I'm awake, he won't come to see me anymore. Closing her eyes, she forced that thought out of her mind. *He promised. He said he never breaks a promise.*

Today's breakfast had graduated to eggs, toast, and bacon. As she pushed the empty tray away from her, she smiled, the taste of food and a full tummy going a long way towards making her feel better. Looking down, she smoothed her hands over her legs, now covered by soft flannel pajama pants. Paired with a matching flannel nightshirt, she felt better. She had questioned Chloe when it was given to her, the answer still causing her to smile. Chloe told her the nurses pitched in together to buy a few things that would make her more comfortable than being in a drab hospital gown.

The night nurse had assisted her with a shower and Rosalie lifted a hand to feel her clean hair, her fingertips barely skimming over the rough scar where the stitches would soon be removed. Glancing at the clock, she wondered what Zander would think when he saw her today. Clean, sort-of dressed, able to feed herself, and walk with help.

And, she remembered more. Looking up at the board, she smiled as she viewed the name Rosalie Noble. It came to her this morning just as her breakfast tray had been delivered. The hospital aide had walked in and called out "Rosalie? Rosalie who?"

"Rosalie Noble," she had replied automatically, almost shouting in joy after the tray was set before her and the aide had left the room. *Rosalie Noble! I remembered!* As soon as Chloe came in, she could not wait to tell her and watched with glee as the kind nurse immediately wrote her name on the board.

Hearing a knock on the door, her gaze shot over, expecting Zander. Instead, an older woman stood there, beautiful flowers in her hands. Snowy white hair, pulled back in a bun. Wire rimmed glasses perched on her nose. A pastel, floral shirt dress, belted at the waist. Stockings and orthopedic shoes completed her outfit, but it was her face that captured Rosalie's attention. A beautiful smile. Light blue eyes that sparkled. Rosy cheeks. And lines emanating from her eyes, giving evidence to years of laughter.

"Hello, my dear. I'm Miss Ethel." She walked to the

window and set the bouquet onto the wide sill. "I see some of my boys have sent flowers as well," she commented as she perused the other bouquets.

"I...didn't know...sent them," Rosalie said haltingly, her eyes never leaving the visitor.

Miss Ethel turned back to her and said, "May I visit for a few minutes?"

Nodding, she lifted her hand, waving it at the chair Zander usually sat in. Miss Ethel settled down into it, setting her purse on the floor before leaning forward and taking her hands in her own.

"My sweet girl, I've been longing to come back, but wanted to wait to give you time to recuperate. I visited last week, when you were still sleeping, but you won't remember."

Her voice tickled the memory banks of Rosalie's mind. *You are strong. So strong. The Psalmist said, 'God is our refuge and strength, an ever-present help in trouble.' I pray that for you, sweet girl.*

"I remember...your voice. God is my strength," she whispered, her eyes wide as she watched Miss Ethel's face break into a beaming smile.

"Oh, my goodness gracious! Yes, child. Yes. I came to visit with you and Zander, and said a prayer for you. How marvelous that you remember."

She met the older woman's smile with one of her own. Cocking her head to the side, she asked, "Zander?"

"Yes, I'm a friend of Zander's. And my other boys, who sent you some of those flowers."

Rosalie twisted around to look at the bouquets in

the room, a quizzical crease settling on her forehead. "I...did not...know...who..."

"Well, it looks like the big pink roses over there are from Rafe. He's one of my boys and a friend of Zander's. Well, more like a brother. Let me see, the carnations and daisies must be from the twins, Jayden and Jaxon." Chuckling, she pointed to the sunflowers, "And those are from Cael and Asher." Looking back at Rosalie, she explained, "My Rafe would send roses because he would assume any woman would want roses. Jayden and Jaxon would have picked out the colorful bouquet...that fits their personalities. And Cael and Asher...well, sunflowers grown in the wild are just what they would love."

Shaking her head, Rosalie said, "I don't underst...know them."

Miss Ethel's face softened as she leaned forward to hold her hands again. "My dear, they are Zander's friends...his brothers. They know how much he wanted you to get well. How full of anguish he was over your...accident." Her tiny shoulder lifted in a shrug, as she said, "The flowers were to brighten your room so that when you awoke, you would have beauty. But they were also a show of support for Zander."

At that, Rosalie smiled, giving Miss Ethel's hand a little squeeze. "Thank you. For visiting...and for your boys."

Laughing, Miss Ethel, said, "Oh, you don't have to thank me. Anyone who has them in their lives is lucky indeed." Standing, she bent over to kiss her forehead and whispered, "You are strong, my dear. And I'll keep praying for your strength to increase."

Rosalie watched as Miss Ethel picked up her handbag and walked out the door, twisting to look at the multitude of flowers only after she was alone. Her thoughts began to swirl. *Zander...friends who are more like brothers...Miss Ethel.*

Blinking rapidly, she realized, just as she could not remember much about what happened in her life before she woke in the hospital, she also did not know who Zander was to her. Before she had a chance to process that, another visitor entered. Recognizing him from the other day, she sucked in her breath. Peter. The detective.

Zander stepped off the elevator, his heart lighter than it had been in a long time. His book tucked under his arm, he nodded as he passed the nurses' station, halting as Chloe called out to him.

"I was going to call, but knew you'd be here soon. Rosalie remembered her last name!"

Eyes wide, he smiled broadly, but halted at her next words.

"We called the police. Detective Chambers is in there with her now."

"Shit," he mumbled under his breath, hurrying down the hall. *I wanted to be here. If he's upset her...*

Pushing her door open, he rushed in, stopping at the sight of her sitting in her chair, dressed in fresh pajamas. Though she was covered from neck to toes, she still looked beautiful. Her cheeks were rosy and her hair was freshly washed and braided. Her eyes sought his, a tentative smile aimed at him.

And there was Pete...*sitting in my chair.* Glowering at his friend, he walked past, bending to kiss Rosalie's forehead. Mumbling against her hair, he said, "You look good today, princess. Did you eat?"

He felt her nod and leaned back to peer into her eyes.

"I ate eggs...toast. And bacon," she whispered in return.

Shooting a glare toward Pete, he said, "Thought I told you I wanted to be here when you talk to her. I don't want her upset."

Pete quirked an eyebrow, "Sorry, Zan. Got a call that she remembered her name."

Looking back into her face, she said hesitantly, "Ros-a-lie No-ble."

He looked at the board on the wall and observed Rosalie Noble printed for patient name. *Noble. How fuckin' perfect. A noble princess.*

Unable to keep the smile from his lips, he kissed the top of her head again. "That's perfect, Rosalie." Leaning his hip on the side of the bed closest to her chair, he looked at Pete, waiting for him to speak.

Clearing his throat, Pete explained, "I've only just gotten here, Zan, so you can keep your fierce looks to yourself."

Rosalie giggled and Zander pretended to glower at her as well.

"So far, she's just been able to tell us that her name is Rosalie Noble. I asked about where she lives or if there is family we can contact, but she was unable to tell me."

Zander caught her lips pinching as her fingers clasped together on her lap. Reaching over, he placed his large hand on her shoulder. "Hey, it's okay. You remember more every day. You shouldn't try to force it." Turning back to Pete, he asked, "What can you do with her name?"

"Ms. Noble, when I get back to the station, I'll run your name through all the databases I can come up with. That'll give us a lot…driver's license, employment, social security, insurance, credit history, address—"

Rosalie sucked in a quick breath, her eyes wide.

"Whoa, don't overwhelm her," he warned.

"Sorry," Pete apologized. "But, I guess what I'm saying is, now that we have your full name, we can find out a lot about you and this is good news. What I find out, I'll come tell you—"

"Only with me here."

"Is that okay with you, Ms. Noble?" Gaining her enthusiastic nod, Pete grinned, looking over at Zander. "Okay, only with you here." Sobering, he turned his attention back to Rosalie. "But, hopefully you'll be able to remember what happened to get you in here."

Rosalie opened her mouth but shut it quickly as Zander stiffened. Looking between the two men, she felt the undercurrent of anger, but did not understand the cause. "What happened? Accident?"

Pete sighed, forging ahead. "Ms. Noble, your accident was not an accident. It was caused by someone who harmed you." He stopped as she reached over to clutch Zander's hand. Staring at them for a moment, he continued, "We want to catch the person who did this to you. But, we've had little clues so far. So, I'm hoping that you'll eventually remember what he looked like and tell us. We want to make sure he goes to jail and can't harm anyone else."

Shaking her head in quick jerks, she said, "I don't know. I don't know."

"Shh," Zander hushed, sliding from the bed to kneel next to her chair. "It'll come back when it's supposed to. Until then, you just concentrate on getting better."

She had no idea why she trusted him so much, but in a world that was mostly blank he was the only voice she knew. Leaning over, she tucked her head on his shoulder and he wrapped his arms around her.

Pete stood, saying, "I'll be in contact with what I find out." With that, he left the room quietly, leaving Zander to comfort her.

17

Zander heard Pete leave but did not take his arms from Rosalie. He tried to convince himself it was because she needed him…his strength. But he knew it was because he needed her. Somehow this beautiful woman had come to mean so much to him.

"Stories," she said, her words soft.

Leaning back, he looked in the direction she was staring. The book of classics was still lying on the bed where he had placed it when he walked in. "You want me to read today?"

When she did not respond, he looked down at her. Moving to the empty chair, he sat, pulling it close so his legs encased her knees, cocooning her. "What is it?"

Her eyes jumped to his as she said, "I remember the stories."

Nodding, he smiled. "Yeah, they said you might be able to hear, even when unconscious. So, I read every day."

Confusion filled her face as she scrunched her nose. "It feels like I knew them. Why can't I remember?"

"Hey, hey," he said, pulling on her hands gently until her face was close to his. "Most of what I read you probably read in high school. Sleeping Beauty you would have heard when you were a little girl."

She nodded slowly, taking his words in. "Okay," she finally agreed. She released his hands, allowing him to take the book into his lap, opening to the pages.

"We didn't get to finish Great Expectations—"

Rosalie spoke suddenly, her voice strong and sure. " 'I have been bent and broken, but—I hope—into a better shape. Be as considerate and good to me as you were, and tell me we are friends.' "

He jerked his head up in surprise, his heart pounding. "What...what did you say?"

"Estelle says that to Pip...near the end of the story. It's one of my favorite lines."

"I didn't get to that the other day," he said, a smile curving his lips.

"I remember...I remember that story. I know that story." Rosalie watched as his smile widened, so handsome it almost hurt to know it was beaming upon her. Her breath caught in her throat at the sight of his penetrating gaze, holding her captive. Forcing herself to relax in the chair, she met his smile as he began to read. At that moment, all was right in her world.

Zander sat in his truck, idling in the hospital parking

lot. He had turned the engine off, but had not moved to get out of the vehicle. Sucking in a deep breath, he pinched the bridge of his nose. Even thinking back to the missions he went on in Afghanistan, when his platoon was heading into unknown danger, he could not remember being more nervous than he was at this moment.

Pete had called him at the bar last night to tell him he was ready to talk to Rosalie. When he asked Pete what he found out, the only response was that he would tell them tomorrow so that Rosalie would hear everything first.

What if she's married? A mom? If so, why aren't they looking for her? What kind of shit job did she have that no one reported her for not showing up to work?

Slamming his hand on the steering wheel in frustration, he knew the answers would not come from the inside of his truck. Looking into the rearview mirror, he scolded himself, "Pull your shit together, man. Whatever comes from this...be there for her." With that vow spoken aloud to no one but himself, he climbed out and walked into the hospital.

As he walked past the nurses' desk, he nodded toward Chloe. She smiled and held up her hand to stop him.

"Hey...listen, I know the detective is coming in—"

"Is he already in there?" he asked, not masking his anxiety.

"No, no, you're first. I just wanted to let you know that Dr. Calhoun wants me in there as well...you know...uh...in case, well, just in case."

Heaving a sigh, he said, "In case the news isn't good."

She reached over and squeezed his arm. "You go on in. I'll come in when the detective gets here."

Nodding his appreciation, he headed to Rosalie's room. Forcing a broad smile on his face, he entered. His gaze landed on the empty chair and empty bed. His heart stuttered until he saw her standing in front of the board, staring at her name. Seeing her dressed in black yoga pants, he tried to keep his eyes off her ass, but the soft white t-shirt was just as distracting.

Not wanting to startle her, he cleared his throat as he entered. She jerked around, quickly wiping her eyes. Rushing over, he swept her into his arms, pulling her close. "What? What's wrong?"

Her only answer was to cling to him tighter, her face buried in his shirt, her tears wetting the material. Allowing her to cry, he rocked her gently, one hand cupping the back of her head and the other rubbing soothing circles on her back.

Finally taking a shuddering breath, she leaned back, an apology on her lips. "I'm sorry—"

"No, princess. You've got nothing to be sorry for. I just want to help. Tell me what's wrong."

Her blue eyes blinked, one more tear sliding down her cheek and his chest tightened with emotion.

Reaching behind her to grab a tissue, Rosalie winced at the twisting movement of her ribs before wiping her nose. A blush rose across her face. "I'm such a mess."

With his hand around her shoulders, Zander led her to a chair. Gently pushing her down, he once more brought his chair directly in front, encasing her legs between his. Taking her hands, he asked, "Now, what's going on?"

Looking down at their hands clasped together, she said, "I couldn't sleep last night. I lay awake and thought of what I know." Lifting her eyes back to his face, she continued, "I know my name. I remember that I know classic stories. I have a memory of a room, with a bed and a suitcase. I have other thoughts that move in and out of my mind, but nothing strong."

"Okay," he said slowly, watching her carefully.

"I understand that no one reported me missing to the police." Her chin quivered, but she fought off the sob, swallowing deeply. "It just makes me sad to wonder what kind of person I was...you know...why no one missed me."

His heart ached for her, overwhelmed with the desire to wipe away all her doubts. Pulling her forward, he settled her on his lap, enveloping her in his embrace. "I don't know, Rosalie. I hope to God you never go away unexpectedly, but I promise, if you ever do, I'll miss you...and never stop looking for you."

She held his gaze for a moment, a tremulous smile curving her lips. "And you never break your promises?"

Smiling in return, he shook his head. "Never."

"Can I come in?"

The voice at the door caused them to look up, seeing Pete standing there with Chloe at his side. Rosalie, blushing, moved off Zander's lap and sat back in her chair. She missed his warmth so she reached over, taking his hand in hers.

He shifted his chair so that he was next to her as

Pete brought in two plastic chairs and set them in front of them. He and Chloe sat facing them and she spoke first.

"Rosalie, I'm here at Dr. Calhoun's request. We don't know what information you will find out today and he wanted a familiar member of the staff to be with you."

Nodding her appreciation, she turned her gaze toward Pete. "Okay, I'm ready...or as ready as I'll ever be."

Pete held Zander's eyes before dropping them to their clasped hands. Turning his gaze fully to her, he said, "Please understand that we are just at the beginning of finding out any information. But I will tell you what I know."

She clung tighter to Zander as Pete took the folder in his hand and opened it. Receiving a reassuring squeeze back, she leaned into his strength.

"Okay, I ran your name through national databases and you are Rosalie Marie Noble. Here is a copy of your driver's license."

He handed her a photocopy of her Maryland license and she stared at the picture of herself. As she devoured the information, he went ahead and told her what it said. "It's a Maryland license. You're twenty-four years old. You have no police record...not even a speeding ticket."

That news sent a breath of air rushing from her body and another squeeze from Zander's hand.

Pete smiled slightly and said, "From that, I ran a check through public records. You owned an older model car and I ran the tags. Assuming you had it when you came here, it obviously has not been reported stolen, nor has it been reported by anyone as being abandoned. My guess, it's still at the place you were living, which we don't know at this time, or your assailant stole it. We expect he has your identification and your keys since they were missing at the scene."

Her mouth opened and closed several times, but no words came. Shaking her head slightly she had nothing to say as she took in the information.

"I did find out you graduated two months ago from a small, public college in Maryland. You received a bachelor's in education and a master's degree in English Literature."

She jerked her head toward Zander, her eyes wide, no longer filled with tears but with surprise. "That's how I recognized your stories," she said.

Zander smiled, loving the sound of her voice full of excitement. Releasing his hand from hers, he wrapped his arm around her shoulders, pulling her in closer.

"Now, about your family..." Pete began, his voice now full of hesitation, immediately drawing their attention. "Rosalie, I'm so very sorry, but the reason no family was looking for you...well, you have no family."

Rosalie's forehead scrunched in confusion and she felt Zander's fingers tighten. Swallowing audibly, she repeated, "No...no family? Not at all?"

"Your birth certificate lists Philip and Elizabeth Noble as your parents. And, I'm so sorry, but I found records of their death. Your father had a heart attack ten years ago and your mother was killed in a car accident your freshman year in college. You were orphaned at the age of eighteen."

Unable to think of what to say, Rosalie sat perfectly still, letting his words flow over and through her. "Orphaned? Orphaned..."

"I found no living relatives. You attended college, living in dorms or apartments for the next six years. Running your social security information, I found that you worked in a restaurant during college to help with tuition. It's possible you had just moved to this area when you were attacked. Your college apartment lease ran out a month ago."

Zander let out a slow breath, taking the information in. The good and the bad. *So, she's not married, but she has no family.* He looked at her face, her fading, light purple bruises stark against her pale skin. She stared straight at Pete, her eyes barely blinking, as though in shock.

"Rosalie? Babe? You with us?"

She blinked rapidly as though coming out of a trance, her head jerking around. Lifting her gaze to his, her breath shuddered slightly, as she nodded. "I...I'm just trying to take it all in."

Chloe spoke up, "Rosalie, Dr. Calhoun has explained to you that memories come back in their own time. Sometimes slowly and other times rapidly. Don't force it. Just take in the information as Detective Chambers gives it to you."

"I understand," she said, turning back to Pete. "So, what now? Do you keep looking to find more about me?"

Pete reddened slightly, squirming in his chair, first

shooting a glance at Zander before answering. "I'm assigned to your assault case and, of course, part of that was needing to identify you. What you have to understand is, I am still assigned to your assault case and I promise to keep working that but, now that we have your name, know that you are not wanted for anything, I won't be digging into your past anymore."

Zander growled, but Pete forged ahead, "Now, that doesn't mean that I won't help you any way I can. But, my priority is to find the man who is responsible for your injuries."

"And what's she supposed to do until you catch him?" he bit out.

"I will give you the name of a reputable private investigator who can ferret out more information about you, but honestly, with your name and social security number, you'll be able to find out a lot yourself."

As Pete stood, Rosalie pushed herself out of Zander's embrace and stood as well. Thrusting out her hand, she said, "Thank you, Detective Chambers. I'm still in shock, but thank you."

Pete took her hand in his, holding it warmly, and said, "This isn't over, Rosalie. Every bit of information that I find, I'll get to you. And, if you would do the same, we might just be able to catch the man who assaulted you."

After Pete left, Chloe walked over, wrapping her arms around her in a gentle hug. "Focus on the good, honey. You're getting better by leaps and bounds. In fact, Dr. Calhoun is almost ready to release you."

As Chloe headed back to the nurses' station, Zander

lifted Rosalie's chin with his finger. "I know you must be overwhelmed, babe."

Her face pale, she whispered, "Orphaned...I have no one."

His heart was pierced at the declaration. Cupping her face with his hands, he vowed, "Not true. You have me."

18

"You sure you know what you're doing?"

Zander glared at Jaxon from across the table at Miss Ethel's house. "You ever know me to not know what I was doing?" he retorted.

"Look, all Jaxon is saying is that you need to think carefully about taking Rosalie into your home," Jayden added. "There's still a lot you don't know about her… hell, a lot she doesn't know about herself."

Sending his glare to the others, he said, "I know she's not married. I know she's not wanted by the police. I know she worked hard to put herself through college and has a master's degree. And I know she's got no one in her life to help her out right now. I think that's enough."

"Are you sure this isn't some kind of hero complex you've got?" Asher asked.

He felt like punching someone and, at this moment, did not care which one of them felt his fist. He knew his face must show his anger because he could feel the red-hot heat pouring off him.

"I think Alexander is a hero," Miss Ethel said, walking into the dining room, a plate of homemade cookies in her hand. Setting them down in the middle of the table, she smiled as they all stood while she took a seat. "I think all of you are heroes."

No one said anything for a moment, allowing her to pass the plate of cookies around. "One thing I can say is, I taught my boys good table manners."

"Miss Ethel," Jaxon said, swallowing a bite before continuing, "you taught us a lot more than just that."

She shrugged her bony shoulders, "Well, I'm glad you think so." Looking around the table, she settled her gaze on Zander. "You've told us the practical reasons why you're taking Rosalie home with you. But what you haven't said is what you feel."

His face heated, this time with embarrassment, as he stared at his plate. "I feel like I want to help her..."

"That's what you might tell your friends, but we're family," she prodded. "Do you just want to be her hero?"

"No," he argued, shifting in his seat, thinking of Rosalie's gentle voice, her smile, her piercing blue eyes. And the way she looked at him, every time he entered her room. Sighing, he said, "She makes me feel...feel things I didn't know about."

He noticed the table had grown quiet and he took a chance, lifting his head, wondering if he would see ridicule on their faces. Instead, what greeted him was calm acceptance. Even Jaxon had no ready quip. He watched Miss Ethel's smile deepen the lines from her eyes.

"You always took charge, Alexander," she said. "Being the oldest, you were the leader, so responsible." Reaching over, she clasped her fingers around another cookie, but paused before taking a bite. "Keep in mind that Rosalie has a long way to go to remember all about her life, and you can't rush a relationship. She's going to your apartment to continue to heal. It's not a large apartment. You have feelings for her, but remember to protect her first."

He understood her unspoken words. Rosalie was under his protection, not for him to take advantage of. "Yes, ma'am," he responded.

Nodding, she said, "All right, then. Who needs more cookies?" She grinned at the unanimous 'yes'.

"Where are all your flowers?" Zander looked around the stark hospital room, seeing Rosalie perched on the edge of the chair. Her hair, neatly plaited in a long braid, was lying across her shoulder. Today, along with the yoga pants, Chloe had provided her with a pair of light blue slippers and a white t-shirt.

She smiled and said, "I had Chloe give them to other patients who didn't have any flowers. I don't want anyone to feel alone."

His heart twinged, but forging ahead, he asked, "So, what do we need to get?"

She lifted her shoulders delicately. "Just me. It's not

like I'm encumbered with a lot of possessions," she joked.

"Come on, you," he said, reaching his hand out to her, gently assisting her from the chair.

Chloe walked in, pushing a wheelchair. "Hospital rules, my dear. I get to wheel you when you bust out of this joint."

Once outside, Rosalie looked up in surprise, as Cael was parked out front in a nice SUV.

Zander explained, "My truck's not so nice, and Cael volunteered to take us to my place in his vehicle. He's got a niece that he hauls around sometimes, so he wanted a safe SUV."

Cael smiled and opened the back door. "Good to see you, Rosalie. I can't promise that the back seat is completely void of graham cracker crumbs, but I'm happy to get you to Zander's place."

"I'm sure it's fine," she grinned, standing. Turning back to Chloe, she threw her arms around her, feeling the sting of tears hit her eyes. "Oh, Chloe, thank you so much for all you did for me."

"Rosalie, I'm proud to have been able to be your nurse. Please take care of yourself and let me know what all you find out."

"I will," she promised.

"Remember, honey," she whispered, "heroes come in all shapes and sizes. And I think Zander is truly one."

Squeezing Chloe's hands, she smiled, "I agree." Cutting her eyes toward Zander, where he stood next to Cael, she said, "I'm lucky he found me. In more ways than one."

With a final goodbye, she allowed Zander to lift her into the back seat. Careful of her ribs, he settled her in next to him as Cael drove away from the hospital.

Zander noticed she twisted her head around to peer at the hospital one last time. "Whatcha thinking?"

She sighed and said, "I just realized that, for right now, the hospital is the only home I remember."

He threw his arm around her protectively, pulling her tight to his side. "Then let's go get settled into your new home."

Zander stood in his kitchen, stirring tomato soup and flipping grilled cheese sandwiches, trying not to think about the woman in his bathtub.

As soon as they had entered his apartment, he showed her to the guest bedroom, explaining that the only person who had recently been there was his friend, Rafe, and he had washed the sheets since then. He had stood in the room, suddenly seeing how spartan it was and wondering what she thought about it. She sat on the edge of the bed and looked around, a smile on her face as though he had brought her to a fancy penthouse.

Next, he showed her where the bathroom was and that was when she squealed that he had a bathtub. Turning to him, she had grabbed his arm and pleaded, "Oh, do you mind if I take a bath now? I so want to soak in a tub of hot water."

Relieved he had scrubbed the bathroom that morning before heading to the hospital, he gladly agreed. And now, she was soaking some of her aches away while he fixed lunch.

Just as he plated the sandwiches, she appeared from the end of the hall. Her pale skin glowed and her cheeks held a rosy tint. Her hair was piled on top of her head, a few damp tendrils curing around her face. She smelled like the bargain soap he always used, but no longer had the scent of hospital clinging to her.

"Hey, there," he said, unable to think of anything else to say.

She smiled as she walked to the short counter between the living room and small kitchen. "Hey, your-self." Looking down, she blushed as she wrapped her arms around her waist. Swimming in his t-shirt, she said, "Thank you for the clean shirt. And for letting me take a bath. I know most people take showers, but I love soaking in a tub full of water." As soon as the words left her mouth, she gasped. "Zander...I remember. I love baths!"

The look of joy on her face shot straight to his heart. Setting the plates down, he rounded the corner as she rushed into his open arms. Nestled under his chin, she felt right. *No, more than right...perfect.*

Leaning back, he said, "How about lunch?"

"It smells good," she said. "Anything but oatmeal, Jello, chicken, and rice!"

Laughing, he served up the plates and bowls on the small table in the corner. "I don't usually eat here, so it's kind of messy," he apologized as he moved some bills and papers.

"Where do you eat?"

"I guess in typical bachelor style...over on the sofa in front of the TV."

She glanced behind her at the living room, complete with a comfortable looking sofa, two chairs, and a large, flat screened TV. "We can eat over there if you'd like. I want to do whatever makes you comfortable."

"Nah," he said, dipping his spoon in the soup. "Miss Ethel would skin me alive if she thought I was serving company in front of the TV."

Giggling, she said, "Well, we certainly don't want that." Chewing her sandwich, she sobered, adding, "But Zander, I don't want to put you out. You're so generous to me..." She laid her sandwich back on the plate with an audible sigh.

"Hey, now, none of that," he admonished, lifting her chin with his knuckle. "I want you here. And I want you to have anything you need."

Looking back down at her apparel, she said, "I suppose the first thing is to get some clothes that fit!" Suddenly, eyes wide, she said, "But money. How will I know if I have any money and, if so, where it is?"

"I've been working on a plan. I just need to go to my workplace this afternoon and settle a few things and then we can start on the *Find Out All About Rosalie Plan*." She tilted her head in question so he explained. "Okay, we know you lived in Baltimore and had an apartment there. Pete talked with your landlord and I got the name from him. We also know the name of the restaurant where you worked. We can drive there tomorrow. Your landlord will have copies of your checks and we can find out what bank you use. Then we can talk to your co-workers and boss at the restaurant to find out more information."

"Are you serious? Oh, my God, Zander. That would be amazing!"

Glad to see the sparkle back in her eyes, he nodded toward her plate and said, "Eat up. Then I want you to rest while I check in with my work."

They ate in companionable silence for a few minutes, each to their own thoughts. He knew his heart was now fully involved. She smiled at him just then, her look saying how lucky she was that he had found her. *No princess, I'm the lucky one.*

19

Rosalie wandered about Zander's apartment after he left to go to work. She shook her head, thinking back to how he made her promise to not leave his place while he was gone. She had looked at him, incredulously, tugging on his large shirt and said, "Where do you think I'm going to go dressed like this?"

Now, he had been gone for three hours and she was bored with channel surfing on the TV. Hating to snoop, she nonetheless decided to explore...*at least that sounds better than snooping!* She started in the kitchen, finding his refrigerator well stocked, and wondered if he bought the food because she was coming or if he kept it that way on his own.

Making her way to his bedroom, she hesitated at the door, feeling like an intruder. The room was not large, the furniture consisting of a large bed, chest of drawers, closet, and nightstand. Seeing their book on his nightstand pulled her into the room, her fingers itching to touch the abridged classics.

Picking it up reverently, she sat on his bed, thumbing through the familiar tales. She loved the feel of pages underneath her fingertips. So much better than an eReader. Jolting, she remembered she had an eReader, but preferred printed books. Excited to have another memory to share with him, she continued to look at the titles.

Closing her eyes for a moment, she listened, hearing his steady voice as he read to her. The comfort in his words...his tone. She smiled, looking back at the pages. Coming across Sleeping Beauty, she hesitated. *I remember...*

" *'And when he saw her looking so lovely in her sleep, he could not turn away his eyes; and presently he stooped and kissed her, and she awaked, and opened her eyes, and looked very kindly on him.'*

"Is that what you'll do with me, Rosamond? Look upon me kindly?"

Sucking in a quick breath, she remembered hearing him ask that question when he read the passage. Hugging the large book to her chest, she squeezed her eyes shut, a smile curving her lips. *Yes, Zander...I look upon you kindly.*

Setting the chairs down from the tabletops, Zander moved through the bar, making sure it was ready for opening. Two days a week they did not open until mid-afternoon and he knew his staff would be in soon. Zeke was already in the back, working on the stock order. He had talked to Zeke about needing to be gone for several days as he took Rosalie to her former residence and Zeke had been more than excited to step into the manager role while he was gone.

"Boss!" Lynn called out as she and Charlene came through the door, both carrying plastic bags.

He watched as they walked over, huge smiles on their faces, plopping the bags onto the nearest table. Digging in, they began to pull out several pairs of yoga pants, numerous shirts, packages of underwear and socks, a pair of tennis shoes, and pajamas. Before he had a chance to process what he was seeing, they dumped a bag of toiletries on the table. The items included hair products, deodorant, razors, lotion, makeup, and tampons.

Eyes wide, his jaw dropped as he looked from the table to the women's beaming faces. Roscoe and Joe walked up behind them, their smiles radiating as well.

"What is all this?"

"We pitched together and bought Rosalie some things...you know...to get her by until she gets on her feet."

"You...you all bought all this?" At their continued grins, he dropped his chin to his chest, breathing deeply for a moment. Lifting his head, he walked over, hugging each one in turn. "This means a lot...she'll be thrilled. But how did you know what sizes to buy?"

"When you told us last night what you know about

her, and how you want her with you as she learns more, we got together and wanted to help," Roscoe explained.

"So we called the hospital and talked to her nurse, Chloe, and she told us what sizes should be good. I also talked to Jayden and he said he and Jaxon were going to fill your refrigerator so she didn't get there and just see bread and beer," Lynn added.

"I don't know what to say, other than, thank you from the bottom of my heart."

Charlene stepped up and said, "Zander, none of what happened to Rosalie is your fault and, at first, I thought you were just acting out of guilt. But, we've all watched how visiting with her has made you happy. Really happy. And we think you deserve that."

As the first customer came through the door, he cleared his throat, adopting his normally taciturn demeanor, and said, "Let's gets ready, everyone. Time to sell some drinks."

Lynn and Charlene repacked the bags and took them into his office, winking at him as they headed onto the floor.

Zander watched his employees hustle about as more customers came in and, for the first time in a long time, his heart felt light as he thought of his Grimm family.

Zander hurried up the steps to his apartment, anxious to see Rosalie. As he put his key in the lock, he hesitated for a second, wondering if she would still be there. *Where else would she go?*

Hustling inside, his eyes immediately found her, asleep on his sofa. Setting the bags down carefully, he walked over, his eyes riveted to her slumbering face. Her blonde hair was waving across her shoulders. The facial bruising was fading and the patch of shaved hair was growing back over her scar. Her pink lips were open slightly, her breathing steady.

Standing there, looking down at her sleeping on his sofa, his heart tightened again. Kneeling, he almost stepped on his classics book, lying on the floor next to her. Glancing down, he realized she had been reading Sleeping Beauty. Bending over, he kissed her forehead gently.

Her eyes fluttered open, unfocused for a few seconds, before she smiled widely. Sitting up with assistance, she scooted to one side so he could sit next to her. "I didn't mean to go to sleep before you got home."

"You should have tucked yourself in bed. Remember, you just got out of the hospital today. You've got to take care of yourself."

"I was terribly lazy, Zander," she admitted. "I finally stole your book and read myself to sleep." Her face brightened, as she said, "And, I remembered hearing your voice read to me."

Smiling in return, he said, "I've got a surprise for you. My employees got together and bought some things for you." As he stood, he turned and offered her his hand. She allowed him to lead her over to the door where he had dropped the bags.

"What's this?"

"Open them and see."

She squatted and began opening the bags, squeals of delight ringing out. "Clothes! Bath oil! Oh, my goodness." Pulling out a pair of soft drawstring pajama bottoms and a matching top, she looked up at Zander's pleased face and said, "I feel like taking a bath all over again."

"You can do whatever you want, babe."

Standing, she said, "That would be silly, but I'll definitely take one tomorrow. For tonight, I'm claiming the pajamas." Rising on her toes, she kissed his cheek before moving into the bathroom. A moment later she emerged, dressed in the soft nightclothes. She approached him, hesitation in her steps as she peered up, eyes shining. "This was kind of your friends. They've been so generous."

"They were glad to do it...truly."

Holding his gaze, she added, "That tells me a lot about you...to have people in your life who care that much for you."

Embarrassed with her assumption, he began, "I don't know about that—"

She stopped him with her hand on his arm. Pale against dark. Blank against tatted. Small against muscular. He looked down at their slight connection and the thought hit him...*opposites and yet, so right.*

"No, Zander. I know. I *know* what kind of man you are. And your friends are right." With a slight squeeze of her fingers, she said, "Thank you...for being everything to me."

He felt the air seize in his lungs as he covered her

hand with his own. "You look beautiful," he admitted, then chuckled. "But then, I liked seeing you in my shirt."

With a soft giggle, her face softened. They piled on the sofa, his arm wrapped around her, loving the way she felt in his arms. No longer bound by the entrapments of the hospital room, having her in his home was just where he wanted her to be.

Rosalie snuggled into his side as Zander turned the ballgame on the TV down low. His body wrapped around her, cocooning her in warmth, and his steady heartbeat's cadence underneath her cheek lulled her to sleep. She had no idea what tomorrow would bring, but for tonight, at this moment, she felt safe...*and happy.*

It did not take long for Zander to feel the heaviness of Rosalie's body as sleep claimed her. Shifting around, he picked her up, careful of her still bruised body. Carrying her into the guest bedroom, he managed to get her in bed and under the covers without her waking up. Bending over, he kissed her forehead. He partially closed her door, not wanting her to awaken in the night and be frightened, and turned out the lights.

Climbing into his bed after a shower, he smiled, thinking of the woman across the hall...and hoped one day soon she would be in his bed where he could be assured she was safe all night long in his arms.

20

Zander glanced sideways, noting the tension radiating from Rosalie with each mile they came closer to Baltimore. Reaching over, he took her hand, linking fingers and pulling them over to his thigh.

She offered a tremulous smile, as she admitted, "I'm nervous."

"Then talk to me," he said. "Tell me what you're thinking. Let's get it out there and then we can deal."

Snorting, she said, "I can't decide if you're practical or bossy."

He barked out a laugh, "Probably both." Giving her fingers light pressure, he prodded, "Come on, out with it."

"I'm excited, but this is scary, Zander. Part of me wants to see and remember who I was. Part of me is terrified of finding out." She sighed heavily, confessing, "You know, right now, I can pretend I was this nice person that people really liked. Successful. Happy. But what if I wasn't? What if we find out that I was a bitch? Or a horrible student? Or maybe didn't really have any friends. Or—"

"Babe, stop right there," he commanded.

"Bossy," she grumbled under her breath.

Ignoring her comment, he plunged ahead, "I don't think we're going to find out any of those things. You might have forgotten a lot of your background which, I remind you, is coming back, but you wouldn't have just woken up a really nice person if you had been the evil queen beforehand."

At that, a smile slipped out and she lifted her free hand to stifle a laugh.

Continuing, he added, his voice now warm, "Having said that, I get that this is hard on you, babe. And, I know it's scary. That's why I'm here. No matter what we find out today, I'm here."

Zander's words soothed her and she felt the tension slip from her body as his fingers flexed against hers once more. She leaned back in the seat, nodding silently. *He's here. Right with me. He's here.*

An hour later, they pulled into the parking lot of an apartment complex. She leaned forward, looking out the window, taking it in. The apartments were located in long, brick buildings, old in style, but the outside was neat and well kept.

"You ready?"

Blowing out a puff of breath, she said, "And if I say 'no'?"

Chuckling, he climbed out and assisted her from his truck. Walking hand in hand, they moved toward the door with the sign **Management Office** hanging next to it. Entering, they stepped into a large room with a long counter dividing the front from the back. Two old, wooden desks were behind the counter, which held metal racks filled with forms. As they moved to the counter, Rosalie could see the forms were for apartment applications and maintenance requests. No one was sitting at the desks, but they could hear voices from the back hall.

"Get over there and fix Ms. Washington's dripping sink and take care of it today!"

Not seeing a counter bell, Zander called out, "Anyone here?"

A full-figured woman appeared from the back, hair in braids arranged in a bun on top of her head, eyes on Zander. Her welcoming smile was white against her ebony skin.

"Sorry, I was sorting out maintenance. How can I help you?" Before he had a chance to speak, she dropped her gaze to Rosalie. "Lordy be!"

She rounded the counter faster than Zander thought a woman her size would have been able to. He was barely moving in to protect Rosalie when the woman grabbed her, pulling her into a warm embrace, rocking her back and forth.

"Rosalie, child, how are you? Are you back? We've just rented your apartment, but I've got another one coming empty next week."

Zander watched nervously as Rosalie's eyes bugged out, her head pressed against the woman's shoulder, mouth open in surprise.

Just as he was about to intervene, Rosalie said, "Martha?"

The woman pushed her back gently, peering into her face, as though just now seeing the bruises and scar. "Well, of course, I'm Martha. Lordy, child, what happened to you?"

Rosalie's hand moved toward her head, fluttering nervously, "I...uh...had a little accident."

"Oh, bless you, girl. But, tell me, did the teaching job not work out? Are you and your man here for an apartment?"

"Teach...teaching job?"

Martha shot a glare toward Zander before looking back at Rosalie. "What's going on? What's happened, Rosalie? And who is this man with you?"

Staring at the woman, now protectively hovering over Rosalie, he almost laughed but managed to hide his grin, figuring the mama bear would take his head off.

"I'm sorry," Rosalie said. "This is Zander...my friend. Well, actually, he's more than that. He's my rescuer."

"What?" Martha asked, her eyes moving between the two of them.

"I was...uh... in an accident and he came to my rescue. I, sort of, forgot a lot of things and he's helping me...uh...put them back together."

Mouth hanging open, Martha said, "Well, I never."

"We thought coming here would help me piece my past together. Did I leave a forwarding address when I left here?"

"No, honey. You said you would stay in a motel until you found a new place and you'd send the address as soon as you got it. I was to hold your mail until you let me know your new address." She turned and went to one of the desks behind the counter, pulling open a bottom drawer. Taking out a small stack of mail, she walked back to Rosalie, handing it to her. "It's not much. You took care of your utilities before you left and you told me to throw away the ads and junk. But, it does include your refund check. Your place was left spotless, so you got the whole deposit back."

Rosalie looked at the check amount and smiled, glad to see that she had money. Feeling Zander's arm wrap around her shoulders, she turned her smile up to him.

"Is there anything you can tell us?" he asked. "Even things in general?"

"Let's sit," Martha invited, pointing to a small table in the corner with four chairs around it. As they sat, she moved to the coffee pot behind the counter and poured three cups of coffee.

Settling into the chair as she joined them, a smile was back on her face. "I could go on all day long about how sweet you are and such a good renter. You always paid on time, kept your place spick and span clean. You even tipped the maintenance men when they had to service your apartment, even though I kept telling you that you didn't need to." Warming to her task, she added, "But you were careful with your money."

"When did I move here?"

"Let's see...you came to us during your third year of college, so that would have been about three years ago. You rented one of our smallest units, a studio. Although, you had a corner unit so you had lots of windows," she added proudly. "And decorated...it was sweet. You managed to find bargain basement deals and it was so... you. Feminine, pretty. Pastel colors throughout."

Rosalie sat still, her mind filling with the image of a bright, corner apartment with distressed white furniture, a coral colored sofa, and floral curtains fluttering in the breeze with the windows open...a tiny kitchen, with white cabinets and colorful jars on the counter.

"Do you know which bank she used when paying her rent?" Zander asked, eyeing Rosalie carefully, glad to see she appeared pleased with what she was hearing.

"Bank of America," Martha said, easily. "I remember because it's the same one I use and they have a branch just down the street. I also remember you saying that it would be nice to not have to change banks when you moved to Virginia."

"About my teaching job? Did I tell you anything in particular?"

Martha's face scrunched in thought, but she shook her head sadly. "No, not really. You were excited. You were going to be teaching English Literature...I do remember that."

"Was it in Richmond?"

"Yes, but you didn't give me any particulars."

Nodding, Rosalie looked at Zander, uncertainty in her eyes. "I don't really know what else to ask," she admitted.

"Ma'am, would it be okay if I give you my contact information, so that if you think of anything else, you can get in contact with her?"

"Lordy, yes, please!"

Zander wrote down his name, email address, and phone number, sliding the piece of paper over to her. As they stood, Martha pulled her back into a hug, this time reciprocated by Rosalie.

"Stay in touch, child," Martha whispered in her ear.

With a nod and a smile, Rosalie linked her fingers with Zander's, allowing him to lead her back to his truck.

Once inside, he looked her over carefully. "You doing okay?"

"Yeah. Especially since I remembered her. I didn't say anything, but I remembered my apartment as well."

Leaning over, he kissed her forehead. "Alright, princess. Now let's find out where you worked."

21

Pulling into the parking lot outside the College Park Bar and Grille, Rosalie sat looking out the window.

"It's weird," she said, softly. Looking over, she noted Zander's quizzical brow. "I can't tell you that I remember this place, but it also doesn't look unfamiliar."

"From the outside, it looks like so many other buildings but maybe the inside will be more striking."

Alighting from the vehicle, again hand in hand, they pushed open the doors to the restaurant. The interior was welcoming and Zander could not help but compare the inviting bar and grille to his more spartan bar. Flat-screened TVs were mounted at every angle and the scent of grilled hamburgers met his nose as a server walked by with a tray. Charlene's pleas to add a kitchen rang in his ears as he watched more servers taking plates of burgers and wings, along with drinks, to customers. Shaking his head to refocus, he nodded toward the back of the restaurant where he knew the management offices would be.

Along the way, a pink-haired server did a double take, a wide grin on her face as she called out, "Rosalie!"

Déjà vu struck as she ran over, pulling Rosalie into a huge hug, similar to Martha's. The server had a name tag on her shirt, alleviating Rosalie from having to remember her name. *Sidney...Sidney...yes! Sidney!*

Sidney smiled up at Zander, her jaw dropping just before she said, "Damn girl. You're gone a month and return with Mr. Handsome." Thrusting her hand out, she introduced herself, "I'm Sidney. Me and Rosalie go way back."

Chuckling, he shook her hand, adding, "Zander."

"Well, hello, Zander," she said, winking at Rosalie. "So, girl, what's happening? I didn't expect to see you back visiting so soon." As her gaze roamed over Rosalie's face, she cocked her head to the side. "What happened?"

"Oh, I had an accident," she replied, the lie now falling easily from her lips. "But, I kind of forgot some things of my past, so we're here to help connect the dots."

"Wow," Sidney said, her eyes wide. "Listen, I've got a break coming up in fifteen minutes. Let me run and tell Jeff you're here and maybe he'll let me take time off early." Without waiting for a reply, she scurried off toward the back hall. After a moment she returned, waving them over. "Come on, he's dying to see you. I filled him in quickly for you."

Walking, hands still linked, they followed the bubbly woman into an office Zander noted was much like his... full of papers and orderly chaos. The manager was an older man, his short salt and pepper hair neatly trimmed. A stomach that hung slightly over his belt indicated he might have tasted his restaurant's food a few times too many. His smile was warm toward Rosalie and she visibly relaxed. Greetings over, they all settled into chairs and she gave a quick rendition of why she was there.

"I'm sorry to hear about your accident," Jeff said, his gaze warm. "You were so looking forward to your teaching job, although I hated to lose you."

"I know I worked here for several years—"

"Eight years to be exact," he interrupted. "You started here when you were just in high school."

Eyes wide, she said, "So you knew me when my mother died?"

Both Jeff and Sidney's faces fell, a solemn pall falling over them. His shoulders slumped as he nodded. "Yes... for a while we became your family. I guess we were until you graduated and moved away last month."

Taking in the information, she sat quietly, sifting through images that floated through her mind—she and Sidney singing Happy Birthday to a customer in the restaurant, Jeff adding a Christmas bonus into her paycheck, Sidney slipping—

"You slipped on a spilled beer and fell on your back, the tray of drinks in your hands flying into the air, landing all over a table of guys!" Rosalie blurted.

Sidney giggled while Jeff rolled his eyes heavenward.

"Oh, my God, that was so funny! I can't believe I didn't break my tailbone!"

Rosalie turned toward Zander, saying, "I don't remember everything, but little snatches of memories are coming."

His smile reached inside her, causing tingles to flow over her body. He reached his arm around her back, his hand caressing her shoulder. "Good for you, princess."

"Princess? Oh, my God, Rosalie. That's so cute," Sidney gushed.

Interrupting, Jeff said, "Are you coming back to Baltimore?"

Afraid to look at Zander, she stumbled, "I...uh...well, not right now. I need to find out about the teaching job—"

"It's too early for her to be thinking about moving," Zander stated, his voice firm.

She relaxed against his side, glad to have someone answering the hard questions. Looking at Sidney, she asked, "Do you know the name of the school I was going to?"

Sidney bit her bottom lip, her brow scrunched. "Let's see...I know it was a high school. You were excited to be teaching English Lit. Um...Kennedy... Lincoln...Washington? It was a president's name, I know that much."

Jeff once more rolled his eyes. "Well that only narrows it down to about 40 something choices."

Laughing, Rosalie said, "That's fine. I should be able to find it with that information."

Looking at Sidney, she asked, "Do you know

anything about my car? I know I have one registered to me, but no one's reported it as abandoned."

"You left it here, Rosalie. It was on its last leg and you weren't sure it would make the trip to Richmond, so you left it here and I was supposed to sell it for you." Blushing, she said, "I've got an advertisement out, but so far, no takers."

"So that's why I didn't have a car there," she exclaimed.

"You took a bus down to Richmond and said you'd buy a car as soon as you could. You said you wanted it to have Virginia tags."

"And my furniture?"

"It's in my mom's garage. You said once you had an apartment, we'd get some of the guys here to help move it to your new place."

They spent the next hour talking, Sidney mostly about their teenage years, reminding Rosalie they had been friends since seventh grade. Memories of her parents began to flow through her mind as well, and gaining her old home address, she determined to add that to her visit.

Zander sat quietly, watching the play of emotions cross Rosalie's face with each story and anecdote shared with her. His fears of her being overwhelmed seemed to have been unfounded, as she appeared to relish each tale.

When they finally stood with promises to stay in touch, and Zander having given them his address and phone number, hugs ensued.

About to leave the office, Sidney said, "Oh, do you

remember Mr. Creepy?" At Rosalie's crinkled brow, Sidney added, "You know, the man who would come in, always ask for your section and leave a big tip?"

"I...I don't remember," she confessed.

"Well, he came in after you left and was not happy that you were no longer here. He asked me where you went and I told him you had moved to Richmond. I figured he finally accepted you weren't interested because he stopped coming in."

Zander's hard voice cut in. "Describe him."

Sidney looked up, surprise in her eyes. "Um...I guess he was in his late twenties or early thirties...brown hair. Built decently. Kind of walked like he owned the place. Always looked at Rosalie like he wanted her to be on the menu."

His gaze shot to Rosalie but she looked towards the ceiling, shaking her head. "I don't remember."

Jeff's intelligent eyes caught and held his. "Is there something I should know?"

He looked at Rosalie, "Princess?" At her slight nod, he said, "Rosalie's *accident* was actually an assault. A man attacked her."

Both Sidney and Jeff reared back simultaneously, mouths open as wide as their eyes.

"What can you tell me about this guy? Do you have surveillance?"

Jeff cursed, "Damn. Not that far back. The tapes are only kept a month and then trashed."

"Name? Credit card receipts?"

"He always paid cash," Sidney said, shaking her head,

reaching over to clasp Rosalie's hand. "Oh, honey, do you think he followed you?"

"I can't imagine anyone would follow me from here to Richmond," she said, her voice strained.

Fury began building in Zander at the idea that she had not only been attacked, but might have been stalked for months. "The description you gave is much like the man that we suspect, but the police have no evidence." Tucking Rosalie into his side, he shook Jeff's hand and with a nod toward Sidney, added, "If you see or think of anything, give me a call."

Outside, after seeing her buckled safely in his truck, he swung up into the driver's seat. Her mood, considerably more somber, hit his heart. "You know you're safe with me, right? I won't let anyone hurt you again."

"Zander, you didn't let anyone hurt me last time. It just happened and you found me."

Her words shot through him and he opened his mouth to confess, but the words stuck in his throat.

"We were going to find my childhood home," she said, her voice soft. "Do you still want to?"

"Princess, you've regained so many memories today and I hate that your smile left with that last news. I'll take you anywhere you want to go."

The corners of her lips curved up as her blue eyes sought his. "Okay, then. Let's not let the last information ruin everything. Let's go."

Meeting her smile, he said, "Sounds good, babe." Plugging the address into his phone's GPS, they pulled out of the parking lot.

Ten minutes later, they entered an older neighbor-hood, sidewalk lined streets filled with neat brick homes. Finding the address, they parked outside her former home and sat for a long time, neither speaking.

Not wanting to interrupt wherever her mind was taking her, he watched her face carefully. For once, her expression gave nothing away.

Finally, sighing, she leaned back against the seat. "I get fleeting images of playing in the yard and riding my bicycle down the street. I think I remember baking cookies with my mom and the kitchen was painted yellow." Rubbing her brow, she sighed again.

Leaning over, he wrapped his arm around her, pulling her in so her head tucked underneath his chin and her cheek rested on his chest. "You've had a big day and you're exhausted. So far, your memories are returning when you see things, interact with them. Maybe when you're rested and Sidney sends the pictures of you two growing up you'll be able to remember more. Don't push it."

Knowing Zander was right, Rosalie nodded against his soft shirt. "You're right. I'm ready to go home, Zander."

"Home?"

"Yeah, back to your place." Twisting her head to look up at him, she said, "Is that okay? I don't want to over-stay my welcome—"

Hearing her calling his apartment *home* warmed his heart. He never thought of it as home as much as just a place to crash. Miss Ethel's house always felt like home.

But with Rosalie going back with him, home was just where he wanted to be.

Smiling, he whispered with his lips touching her hair, "It's more than okay, princess. Let's go home."

2 2

Zander fumed while staring at Pete, sitting in the police station. "I'm telling you, I got a bad feeling about this—"

Lifting his hand in protest, Pete argued, "I get it, Zan. I do. But we've got nothing to go on. What you're telling me is good information and I promise to contact the manager of the restaurant to see if there is an employee who can give us more details about the man. However, right now, we don't even have a photo of him to circulate. His description is too vague, even by you, to come up with more than a drawing of what he looks like."

"So, we've got nothin'," Zander bit out.

"We have the DNA from underneath Rosalie's fingernails from the attack, but it doesn't tell us who the assailant was. If we get someone, we can nail him with that, but it doesn't lead us to anyone now."

"What if he's still after her? What if he's out there watching her right now?"

"If he is, then he's not making a show of it. The hospital reported that no one asked about her and they were on alert, since they knew she was a Jane Doe. When that happens, the hospital personnel are trained to be on alert if anyone calls in with a description that matches their Jane Doe. That's often how they identify an accident patient who comes in with no identification —a relative or friend calls and starts describing the person with enough detail for there to be a tentative match, which is then verified."

Leaning back with a huff, Zander shook his head. "I thought it was just a guy with anger issues who had too much to drink, got rebuffed so he went ape-shit and attacked her. I never thought about it being someone who might have been after her." Scrubbing his hand over his neck, he added, "I just feel like she's a sitting duck."

"She with you most of the time?"

"I've got her at my apartment..." Seeing Pete's lifted brow, he added, "She's in the guest room."

Throwing his hands up, Pete defended, "Hey, I know you're a good man. But, I also know she looks at you like you're the only man on earth."

"Well, I wouldn't mind something happening, but only when the time is right. So, for now, I'm giving her a safe place to continue to heal."

Walking into his apartment that evening after visiting

the police station, he smiled at Rosalie before his eyes slid to Jaxon, offering his friend a chin lift.

"Jaxon came by and I told him I didn't think you'd be too much longer," she said, standing at the oven, pulling out a large pan of lasagna. "Look what Miss Ethel sent over." Setting the pan on a folded dishrag on the counter, she invited, "Jaxon, will you stay and eat with us tonight?"

"No thanks," he replied affably, standing to leave.

Rosalie cocked her head to the side, considering him carefully. "But I thought you needed to talk to Zander?"

Blinking rapidly, he nodded. "Yeah…uh…yeah. It's about his truck." Shooting a glance at Zander, he said, "Can I take a look at it now?"

"Sure," he agreed, then turned to her. "Be right back."

Zander walked with Jaxon down the stairs, pausing at the bottom. "Thanks for coming, man."

"No problem, Zander. What did Pete say?"

"Still a big, fat nothin'. We've got no picture, not from the night of the attack nor from the restaurant where she used to work. The description sounds like the same man, but who the hell knows."

Jaxon glanced up toward the apartment. "What are you going to do? I mean, me and the guys have no problem dropping by and checking on her when you're out and you know Miss Ethel would love to have her around, but you can't keep her locked in an ivory tower forever."

Blowing out his breath, he nodded his agreement.

"And when you're at work half the night?"

"I don't know. Hell, I'm flying by the seat of my

pants, here. I've got no fuckin' idea what I'm doing, other than I want her in my life and will die trying to protect her."

Slapping him on the shoulder, Jaxon said, "Well, let's not have it come down to that. Go on and get your supper. Miss Ethel wanted to send something, so you know it's good. She'd like a visit soon, you know."

"Rosalie got her security deposit back from her last rental, so I'm taking her to the bank tomorrow so she can get back into her account. We'll stop by afterward."

Waving Jaxon off, he headed back up the stairs, taking them two at a time.

Zander looked across the small table, seeing a small dab of sauce on the corner of Rosalie's mouth. As her tongue darted out to lick it off, he shifted uncomfortably in his chair at the familiar hard-on he was constantly trying to hide.

Rosalie looked over, noting Zander's eyes were on her lips. Lifting her napkin, she wiped her mouth. "Do I have more sauce on my mouth?"

Blinking, his gaze jumped from her lips to her eyes, widely staring back at him. Clearing his throat, he said, "No, no. Sorry...must have had my mind somewhere else."

"Oh," she said, chastising herself for wishing his mind was on her.

Standing, they reached for the platter at the same time, their hands touching, sending a tingle zipping up her arm. From his quick intake of breath, she wondered if he felt it too.

Insisting she sit down while he cleaned, she sat on the sofa, watching as he finished washing the plates and putting the lasagna leftovers in the refrigerator. His body moved with a natural grace she admired. His black t-shirt strained over the muscles in his chest and the sleeves were tight against his arms. The ink on his left arm only accentuated his tone and her eyes followed his every move. His hair, shorter on the sides, looked like he casually ran his hands through the top, leaving it messy and oh, so sexy. Suddenly, he tossed the dishrag on the counter and turned around to face her. His light-colored eyes landed on hers, causing her breath to catch in her throat.

"You keep staring at me like that and…" he drifted off, his voice like gravel.

"And what?" She stood, taking a step toward him, wondering what she was doing.

Stalking around the corner, Zander headed toward her, stopping a few feet from her. Not letting go of her gaze, he battled the desire to take her in his arms. "Rosalie, I'm trying to do the right thing here. I don't want to take advantage of you."

"Take advantage? You've cared for me since we first met."

"You've been injured," he added, his hand twitching at his hips, longing to reach out and touch her.

"My injuries are healing. I feel fine."

Sucking in a deep breath before letting it out slowly, he said, "You don't have all of your memories back."

"We know I'm not involved with anyone." She took a small step forward, stopping with her bare toes right in front of his socked feet, her head tilted back to peer into his face. Placing her hands on his warm chest, she said, "I want you. I want this."

Her hands seared his skin as he let go of his last inhibitions. Lifting her up by her waist, her legs wrapped around his hips, her body pressing tightly against his. The feel of her in his arms was the last puzzle piece falling into place. It was right...and right where he wanted her to be. Her hair, like silk, flowed over his arms and he lifted one hand to thread his fingers through the tresses.

His mouth slanted onto hers, molding their lips together, sucking, nipping, tasting. The evidence of his need was pressed against her core and she moaned into his mouth. The sound reverberated through him, making all thoughts of slowing things down almost impossible.

Carrying her down the hall, he entered his bedroom, maneuvering their bodies so they were both lying on the bed, she on top of him. Lips still attached, he slid his hands to her ass, molding the flesh with his fingers.

Sliding up on her knees, Rosalie straddled his hips, her hands on his hard chest, her breathing ragged. Staring down at his face, his eyes pierced into hers and he opened his mouth to speak. Knowing he was about to say they should stop, she pressed her fingers against his lips, stilling them. His eyes widened as she reached to the bottom of her t-shirt and pulled it up slowly over her head.

Zander watched as the pale skin of her stomach was exposed and the material snagged for a second at the bottom of her breasts. With a deft move, she sent the material over her head and down onto the floor. Wearing a simple, white cotton bra, his gaze focused momentarily on her full breasts before sliding upward, latching once more on her face.

Rosalie reached back, unfastening her bra, letting it slide down her arms. Dropping it to the side, she suddenly became unsure, crossing her arms over her breasts.

Reaching up, he gently pulled her arms away, saying, "You're so beautiful. Please don't feel embarrassed. If anyone should be embarrassed, it's me. You're way too beautiful to be with me."

A giggle slipped out as she rolled her eyes. "That's ridiculous. You? Mr. Gorgeous, muscles, tattoos, and kind heart and—"

"Now who's being ridiculous?" he grinned.

Sucking in her lips as the pleasure of his hands gliding over her breasts threatened to take away all thought, she whispered, "Maybe we're just perfect for each other."

With a deft maneuver, Zander rolled them over, looming above her, his penetrating gaze roaming over her face. "Can't think of anything better anyone's ever said to me. To be someone's *perfect*." Leaning down, he kissed her lips, slow and sweet, savoring every taste.

Finally, dragging himself off the bed, he stood, sliding her pants down her legs, taking her white panties with them. Peering down at her, stunned that she was in his bed, giving herself to him, he wondered if it were a dream.

"Perfect," he agreed. "You're my perfect."

He grabbed the back of his t-shirt and pulled it over his head. His hands went to his jeans, unbuttoning them as quickly as he could.

As he shucked his jeans, Rosalie's eyes traveled down from his wide shoulders to his naked chest. A tattoo was inked from his left shoulder, extending down his arm, the flowers and patterns creating a mesmerizing piece of art. She could not wait to trace the intricate design with her fingers, memorizing it as she went. He was powerfully built with thick chest muscles, chiseled abs, and a tight stomach that ended in a perfect V that traveled downwards. By the time her eyes had moved to the end of the V, his jeans and boxers were off and her eyes feasted on his cock. Blowing out her breath, nerves threatened to overwhelm her.

I don't know if I've had sex...or with whom...or how many—

"Whoa, come back to me," he said gently, seeing the panic in her eyes. "We don't have to do anything but just lay here and hold each other. And we can do that dressed, if it would make you more comfortable." He bent over to snag his jeans off the floor, but she leaned up on her elbows and stopped him.

"No, no," she protested. "I don't want to stop. I just got scared." He moved to sit next to her on the bed, rubbing his large hand over her leg. Soothed by the motion, she continued, "I don't know when the last time I had sex was. Or if I've had sex. Or who—"

"Shhh, it's all right," Zander nodded, her expression searing him. She looked so lost. "I hadn't thought about how this would seem to you. Are you sure you want to go ahead?" Gaining her enthusiastic smile, he said, "Okay, here's what we'll do. We'll go slow...we'll go easy. If at any time you feel uncomfortable, you just tell me. Part of our being perfect together means that even stopping will be perfect."

He saw the second of hesitation and made the decision for her. Maneuvering her gently, he pulled the covers down before tucking them both into bed.

Curling his body around hers, he whispered, "Sleep, babe. That's all we need to do tonight...just sleep in each other's arms."

He heard a long sigh, but she did not protest. With her pressed against him, he felt her body become heavy as sleep claimed her. The light from the hall created a halo of blonde, silken hair, sifting through his fingers as Rosalie lay with her head on his chest. His heart full, Zander tucked her closer as his hand drifted near the scar running at the edge of her hairline. A flash of memory came to him, reminding him of what she looked like when he first found her...battered, lying in the dirt. Closing his eyes, he willed the remembrance away, focusing instead on the soft breath caressing his chest and her small hand resting on his stomach.

Not sorry they stopped, he strengthened his resolve to take care of her, in all ways. Tucking the covers up higher around her shoulders, he drifted to sleep, a smile on his lips.

23

A porch swing. A front porch swing...Mom and I would sit, swing, and sing songs as we waited for Dad to come home. Cookies on the counter when I got home from school. My dad teaching me to ride my bike when I was six years old. My parents reading fairy tales to me when it was time for bed, in a bedroom decorated in pastels like a fairy castle. Holding Mom's hand while standing in the cemetery, wondering who would slay my dragons now. Mom and I sitting on the porch swing, no longer singing, but just talking...holding on to memories. Professor Mullins telling me I had a gift for under-standing and loving literature. Pure imagination. A phone call...this time leading to standing alone in a cemetery. It's up to me to slay my dragons.

Now the way is dark, lost and I'm running but my feet feel like lead. I turn to look behind me and can see the fiery breath as it blasts all around. The sound, like thunder, crashes and I can feel the ground shake. It's coming...coming for me.

Suddenly, the dragon is almost upon me. I open my mouth to scream, but nothing comes out. Ahhhhh—

"Rosalie. Rosalie. Wake up."

Blinking, she sat up quickly, bumping her head on something, her arms and legs flailing out as she tried to escape. "No, no!" she screamed, fighting the invisible danger.

"Rosalie, babe. Wake up," Zander called, shifting quickly to throw off the sheet, untangling her legs. Grabbing her shoulders, he lowered his face directly in front of hers, chanting, "It's okay, I'm here. You're okay, I'm here."

Her wild eyes slowly focused on his, her chest heaving as she sucked in great gulps of air. Her hand grasped his shoulders in return, her fingers digging into the muscles. Understanding flowed over her and tears filled her eyes.

"Zander," she cried, falling forward, planting her face into his chest.

"Babe, shhh, babe, I've got you," he soothed, feeling her body shivering. Uncertain if it was from fright or cold, he reached back, snagging a hoodie sweatshirt he had tossed on the floor. Managing to slide it over her head, he maneuvered her arms through with difficulty as she clung to him. Once she was partially covered, he leaned back against the pillows, pulling her with him, before grabbing the covers.

Rosalie felt the iciness slowly subside as he cocooned her in his embrace. She felt the warmth from his hand as it moved up and down her back, the motion bringing a modicum of peace. Leaning back, she turned her gaze to his, seeing no condemnation in his eyes.

"Nightmare?" he asked, still rubbing her back.

Nodding, she worked to steady her breathing. "Yeah…I remembered my parents. Not everything but, a lot."

"Tell me," he encouraged.

She rested her weight on him, her cheek against his heartbeat, drawing strength from him. Allowing her mind to drift back, she said, "My mom used to have homemade cookies for me when I got home from school. She taught kindergarten in a private school and it was only half-day, so she was always there for me. We had a front porch swing…God, I loved that swing. My dad used to read me bedtime stories…fairy tales when I was little. He taught English Literature at the local college, but I never knew much about that since he died when I was young."

Sighing, she remained quiet for a moment, her fingers splaying on his chest. He was about to prompt her for more memories, but she began to speak again.

"I remember my dad's funeral. Not too much about it…just standing there with Mom. I remember hearing her cry at night in her bedroom when I was supposed to be asleep. When I got older, I understood they shared one of those amazing loves…the kind that lasts through all time. I remember living at home my first year of college, just so Mom wouldn't be alone. But when she died, I couldn't bear to be in the house any longer. I sold it and put the money in my bank account, using some to pay for college and some just to save for the future."

Looking up, she pierced him with her big, blue eyes, holding him captive.

"You know what? I remember that when I was little, I thought my dad could slay all my dragons. But then, when he died, I knew I would have to slay them myself."

"Babe, listening to your former friends yesterday confirmed what I already knew. You're smart, driven, hard-working, dedicated, independent—"

"I haven't been very independent since meeting you."

Sitting up, with her still in his arms, he said, "Rosalie, just because you were hurt, doesn't mean you're not independent. It just means you needed some help. You had a life full of friends, people who cared about you because of the beautiful person you are...inside. I witnessed that caring yesterday, but like I said, it only confirmed what I already knew."

Holding her gaze, he continued, desperate for her to accept how strong she was. "You don't remember, and I'm glad...but you fought that night. You were fighting a dragon. Babe, I promise that, from now on, I want to be the one to slay them. If you'll have me."

Rosalie lifted her head the inch needed to touch her lips to his. Cupping his face in her hand, she slid her fingers over his beard-stubbled jaw. She felt his hesitation, allowing her to lead the kiss.

Mumbling against his lips, she said, "I know who I am now. I know what I want. And what I want...is you."

Taking over the kiss, Zander molded his lips against hers, the slow-building fire flaming higher with each taste. His hands skimmed over her skin, exploring every delicious curve.

Rosalie felt the shock from her nipples to her womb and down to her sex as he cupped her breasts. Deciding to explore on her own, her fingers drifted from his shoulders over his chest, and glided over every muscle defined in his abs. She heard the sharp intake of his breath when her fingers moved lower and grinned against his lips at the power she held over his body.

"I want this to be good for you," Zander groaned, moving her hand away from his aching cock. "It'll be over too fast if you keep going like this."

Sliding his hand over her stomach, his fingers skimmed the scar from her surgery marring her delicate skin. Anger flamed, but she shook her head gently, bringing his eyes to hers.

"There's no past here, Zander. No one but us."

Moving his finger through her slick folds, he found her wet and ready. Her body taut with need, it only took a few minutes of sliding his finger in and out of her sex before tweaking her clit and he watched her fall apart in his arms.

The orgasm rushed through her, the currents tingling throughout her body as she held on to his shoulders, her fingernails digging in as though afraid she would drown without his body to anchor hers. She leaned up, pulling the sweatshirt over her head and throwing it off the bed.

Not knowing how long it had been since she had been with someone, if ever, he lifted himself over her body after rolling on a condom. Holding his weight up with his forearms, he kissed her softly. The blush of sex painted her breasts and he bent to suckle each one, savoring the taste and feel of her. Entering her slowly, he filled a little bit at a time, allowing her to adjust to his size. She moaned at the feeling of fullness and the pressure that immediately began to build. With a final push, he was in all the way and began to pump slowly. Her legs circled his waist and she dug her heels into his ass, moving in time to his thrusts.

"More, I need more," she said in a whisper, and that was all it took for him to move faster.

The delicious feeling of friction had Rosalie hanging on, the sensations threatening to drown her as she was flung over the edge again. As the shock waves pulsated from her inner core outwards, she felt their bodies moving perfectly as one.

Zander felt her inner walls grab his cock, her natural juices making the thrusting easier. He captured her lips once more, imitating the motion of his thrusts with his tongue. He could feel his balls tighten and knew that he was close to his own orgasm. Peering down, he watched as her gaze held his, and the pleasured smile that covered her face was all it took. Throwing his head back, he powered through his orgasm, pulsating deep inside as her channel tightened around him again.

Rolling to the side, he lay panting as he pulled her body in close to his. Sweaty, still shaking with the intensity of the moment, they clung to each other. Neither of them spoke for several minutes, the emotions of the act too overwhelming. Too important.

Finally, able to speak, Zander only said one word, but it meant the world to Rosalie. "Perfect."

2 4

Walking out of the bank, Zander led Rosalie to the truck, his arm over her shoulder as he admired her relaxed smile. "Feel good?"

"Oh, my God, you have no idea!"

They made a trip to the DMV that morning to get a new driver's license based on the copy of her Maryland license Pete had provided, along with her birth certificate and a copy of her social security card. Then, they went to the bank where, with her identification and bank account number, she was able to receive a new debit card and put a stop on her former one.

He had asked the teller if anyone had used her card in the past weeks and Rosalie breathed a sigh of relief that the answer was no. Then he inquired if her card had been used for a motel in the area in the past month. From that, the teller gave them a printout of the last activity for her account. Scanning it quickly, they were easily able to see the last charges were at a small, local hotel, only about six blocks from Grimm's Bar.

Now, climbing up into his truck, Rosalie placed her new cards and bank checks in the small purse Lynn had provided. Turning to her, he grinned as she clutched her purse in her lap as though afraid to let it go.

She returned his smile, saying, "This is like getting more pieces of my life back together. I'm finally starting to feel like Rosalie Noble again."

Meeting in the middle, over the console, he kissed her, hard and fast. Moving back, he said, "Next stop, let's go to the motel and see if we can get some of your things back."

As Zander pulled into the modest hotel's parking lot, Rosalie leaned forward, her gaze pinned on the building.

"It looks vaguely familiar." Huffing, she flopped back against the seat. "Why is it that I can remember my childhood, my teen and young adult years now, but I can't remember the time right around the attack?"

Shifting in his seat, he said, "Dr. Calhoun said that most of your memories would probably come back, but for some people they never remember the trauma that caused the brain injury. I guess since you were here for a short while before that night, this is part of what is still hidden."

Nodding, she agreed, "Makes sense."

Once inside the small lobby, they approached an older man sitting behind the counter. His grey hair was neatly trimmed, while his suit was slightly wrinkled. He looked up, staring at them over the rim of his glasses, which were perched on the end of his nose.

"Can I help you folks?"

Zander approached and said, "Ms. Noble was a customer weeks ago when she had an accident. She's just now out of the hospital and was hoping you still had her belongings."

The man's penetrating gaze turned toward Rosalie and his eyes narrowed for a moment, before widening. "Oh, my goodness! Yes! I remember you."

She noted his gaze lifted slightly, focusing on her forehead where the jagged scar and barely-there hair was growing back over it.

"I went out one evening," she said, "and…uh…well, was unable to come back."

He nodded, "Yes, yes, I know. You had paid for a week and when the week ran out, the housekeeper told the manager she had not seen you in days. I was gone to visit my daughter and when I got back, I overheard them say someone's belonging were in the storage if they came back." His face scrunched as he shook his head. "I'm real sorry…now I realize I should have tried to figure out whose belongings they were but I never took notice."

"It's fine," she said, seeing his distress, offering him a small smile. "But, can you let me have my things now? I'll be more than happy to pay for the time they were here."

Clucking, he said, "Lordy, no. I reckon the manager just put them in the storage room back here and, God knows, that room's so messy, no one even goes in anymore."

He disappeared for few minutes and returned with a sheepish expression. "I got the smaller suitcase, but" looking up at Zander, "do you mind helping with the other things? It seems Ms. Noble had quite a few items."

Zander disappeared around the counter as Rosalie immediately opened the suitcase and breathed a sigh of relief, recognizing her clothes. Looking up, she grinned as Zander returned, carrying much larger suitcases in each hand while the clerk carried another suitcase and laptop cases.

"Oh, my, thank you," she gushed, hurrying to take the case from the clerk as Zander moved out the door.

"No, problem, my dear. I'm just glad you're reunited with your belongings."

Throwing her arms around his neck, she gave him a quick hug and, as she pulled away, she watched him blush, grinning back at her. Zander walked in again, this time picking up the next two suitcases and with *thanks* thrown out, escorted her back to the truck. She stood, watching as he placed her cases in the bed of the truck.

Zander walked over to her, his heart light as her smile lit his world.

"That smile warms my heart," he said, pulling her into his arms, kissing the top of her head.

"I can't thank you enough, for all you're doing for me," she breathed into his shirt, her arms around his waist.

Her body fit perfectly underneath his chin and he fought the desire to take her home and spend the rest of the day in bed. Fighting the urge, he said, "Come on, princess. I've got somewhere I'd like to take you. Somewhere nice and easy. And somewhere we can get some homecooked food."

Rosalie leaned back in her chair, her tummy full of good food and her face hurting from all the smiling she had been doing for the past hour. Looking at her hostess, she said, "Miss Ethel, how do you fry chicken so crispy? I swear, I've never had better."

Miss Ethel preened, lifting her hand to smooth a few loose wisps of her hair back into its bun. "Oh, my, how sweet you are. But I've been frying chicken for as long as I can remember. My grannie used to sit me on a stool, near the stove...not too close, mind you, 'cause of the splattering oil, but close enough I could watch her cook. And, I reckon, she sat at her grannie's stove as well."

"Maybe you could teach me, sometime," she asked, suddenly feeling shy, wondering if it was presumptuous.

Zander reached under the table, linking his fingers with hers, recognizing the slight tremble in her voice.

"Rosalie," Miss Ethel declared, "there would be nothing I'd like more than to have you spend some time with me. And if some chicken gets fried at the same time, then we're both winners!"

"You wouldn't be the only winners," Zander said. "I'd expect to share that chicken."

Beaming, Rosalie teased, "I suppose I might share with you."

He barked out a laugh, loving the relaxed banter coming from her.

"All I know is, if you two are cooking, then I want to be invited," Jayden said, reaching over to grab another piece of chicken.

"Boys, save room for pie," Miss Ethel reminded, immediately drawing the interest of the rest of the group. She looked at Rosalie, "When I decided to start taking in my boys, I had no idea how much they would eat."

"That was so brave of you," Rosalie said, awe in her voice.

"Oh, fiddle. It was the boys who were brave."

She glanced around the table and could easily see from their expressions they disagreed with Miss Ethel.

"I had this big ol' house and my George had died. We never had children and, when a friend from church called me to say that she knew social services needed a foster mom for a young boy, I accepted. Best decision I ever made." Her grey eyes landed on Zander, a smile playing about her lips. "He was my first to stay for any length of time and was such a good boy. It made it easy to decide to take in more."

Rosalie peered up at him, noting the blush staining his cheeks.

"Good thing she didn't get us first," Jaxon quipped. "She woudda stopped right there."

The others laughed, but Miss Ethel just shook her head. "You might have been a bit of a scoundrel at times, but just like all the others, you were a good boy."

"We were the lucky ones," Zander said, immediately gaining agreement.

"I'll get the pies—"

"Miss Ethel, sit back down. Asher and I can get them for you." Cael and Asher pushed back their chairs and headed into the kitchen.

"Don't cut the pies in there," Jaxon called out. "Bring 'em in here so we can make sure the pieces are even."

Laughter rang out as a scowling Cael walked in carrying two pies, followed by Asher with dessert plates and clean forks. "Man, you gotta forget what I did when I was about six," he complained.

"You were twelve and I remember it clearly," Jaxon retorted. He turned to Rosalie and explained, "He used to always help Miss Ethel serve the dessert and we soon figured out he cut the largest piece for himself."

"I was scrawnier than you all. I had to do something to bulk up."

Rosalie laughed as Cael tried to defend himself. She felt Zander's fingertips caress her shoulder and twisted her head up to look at him. Moving closer, she whispered, "Thank you." Bending, he touched his lips to hers, quick but sweet.

As the apple pies were being devoured, Jayden asked, "So, what now, Rosalie?"

She halted in her chewing, licking the juicy apple from her lips, carefully considering her response. "Well, the last part of my life that I need to find out about is where I was going to be working. My friend in Baltimore said I had a teaching job at a high school. But she only remembered the name was a president's name. I haven't looked yet, being too busy trying to get my identification back in order." Shrugging slightly, she added, "So I hope to tackle that tomorrow."

Asher said, "There's a Jefferson High School in the county…about ten miles from here."

Jayden pulled out his phone, flashing an apologetic look toward Miss Ethel.

She laughed and said, "It's okay. I'll allow it this time, since it's for a good cause."

Zander leaned over to her and said, "Miss Ethel's rules…no cell phones at the table."

"I think that's a good rule," she agreed. Biting her lip, her eyes gained a faraway look in them.

Zander stayed quiet, his gaze shifting from her to the others across the table in a silent message to let her have her moment.

Eyes clearing as though coming out of a trance, she grinned, looking up at him and said, "My parents always had the same rule! Although, my mother included books at the table too." Seeing his surprise, she explained, "My father and I could get lost in a book and if we were reading during a meal, no one talked. Mom always said that mealtime was for sharing."

"Absolutely," declared Miss Ethel, her grey eyes shining.

"What's it like…remembering things?" Asher asked. Catching Zander's glare, he hastened to add, "I'm sorry—"

"No," she rushed, placing her hand on Zander's arm.

"It's fine to talk about. Really." Turning back to the others, she thought for a minute before explaining, "You know how sometimes when you wake up, you know you were dreaming but you can't remember the dream?" The others nodded and she continued. "Then maybe later, something happens or someone mentions something and you suddenly remember the dream you had." Shrugging, she said, "That's the best description I can give."

Zander shifted their chairs so that there was no space between them, tucking her in closer. "Proud of you, babe." Seeing her open her mouth, he added, "Nope. Not listening to you deny it. You're braver than you realize."

"Absolutely," Miss Ethel agreed and the others joined in as well.

Blushing, she tucked a long lock behind her ear, aware her scar showed but refusing to hide behind her hair.

Jayden piped up, "There are two high schools in the area with names of Presidents. Jefferson and Madison."

Gifting him with a smile, she said, "That's a big help, thank you Jayden. Miss Ethel, allow me to help with the cleanup."

She quickly realized Miss Ethel had, indeed, taught the boys table manners, as they all stood and carried plates and platters into the kitchen. With everyone helping, the dining room and kitchen were soon neat.

As she and Zander moved to the door, she found herself engulfed in goodbye hugs. Each of the men made her promise to call them if she needed anything, especially while Zander was working. "I don't have a cell phone yet—" she began.

"We're taking care of that tomorrow," Zander stated. "First thing, before we go talk to the schools."

Grinning, she looked at the others and said, "I'll get your numbers from him and plug them in as soon as I have a phone."

Zander moved to say his goodbyes to his brothers while Miss Ethel stepped forward to hug Rosalie.

"My child, you are making this old woman very happy. I know the circumstances of the two of you meeting was not good, but God has a way of bringing light into darkness. And you, sweet Rosalie, are light."

"Null and void."

Once they had gotten home from Miss Ethel's the previous evening, and Zander had carted Rosalie's suitcases to his apartment, she was thrilled to pour through each one, discovering her clothes, toiletries, books, files, and her laptop. As though reunited with long lost friends, she sat on the bed in the guest room, going through her belongings. Firing up the laptop, she remembered her password and was soon checking her emails.

Walking into her room, Zander had looked at her crestfallen face. Before he had a chance to ask, she spoke.

"It was Jefferson High School that had hired me and I've been getting emails wondering where I was." Sighing, she said, "The last one states that due to my being a no-show, my contract is null and void."

"Oh, babe, I'm so sorry," he said, moving to sit next to her, pulling her into a hug. "What can I do?"

"Nothing...it's just that now I'm unemployed. I guess I'll call them tomorrow to see if there is something that I can salvage from this mess." She shifted on the bed to face him, her mouth pinched into a line. "I feel like I lost so many things and that...that...monster who took them from me is still out there."

Rosalie voiced his same concerns and Zander slid his hands down her arms to clench her fingers.

"He won't get near you again. And we'll figure out something."

The next day, Zander stood in the kitchen, the refrigerator door open, listening to Rosalie's phone conversation. They had gone that morning to get a new cell phone for her and he delighted in her joy over her new purchase. She immediately put in his number, Miss Ethel's and his brothers', as well as Sidney's and Jeff's.

He went to the grocery store after that to give her some privacy and check on Grimm's. Now, as he listened to her voice, it appeared things with the school were not going well.

"Yes, yes...I understand. All right. Well, can you tell me what the next step is?"

He watched her roll her eyes before her lips turned down.

"Okay, thank you very much. I'll be sure to go online and do that this afternoon." She disconnected and looked over at him. "I guess you can tell that I don't have the job. I told them I could provide them with the police and hospital records so they would know I was telling the truth. They were sympathetic, but they had to have a teacher, so they hired someone else. Given my circumstances and excellent application, they did say that I could do substitute teaching this year and reapply for full-time teaching next year."

"Babe, I'm so sorry, and I'm pissed because it feels like I keep having to say that—"

"Zander, none of this is your fault," she said, jumping up from the sofa, rushing over to him. "You've done nothing but rescue me, take care of me...my God, you've been my hero."

She wrapped her arms around his waist, slipping her head underneath his chin. He enveloped her, his heart aching.

If she only knew it was my fault she was attacked in the first place.

The words were on the tip of his tongue, begging him to confess all to her. But, tucked into his embrace, she felt like his other half, as though all the missing pieces of him, since his mother had abandoned him as a child, had fallen into place. Swallowing the confession, he kissed the top of her head.

———

"I want to go to the bar with you."

Zander halted the sandwich on the way to his mouth, as he looked over at Rosalie, still munching on her chips.

"Uh..."

"I don't want to keep you from work, but I don't

want to spend another evening by myself. We now know I don't have a job right now, so I'd like to go see where you work."

"Babe, I don't know if that's such a good idea—"

"I know you're worried about me, but I laid awake last night thinking about what all that man took from me and I'm sick and tired of being afraid. I know you said I was attacked there and you found me behind the building, but I don't think avoiding it is the right thing to do."

"You want those memories?" he asked, incredulity in his voice.

"No," she huffed. "Not necessarily." Tucking her hair behind her ear, she rubbed her forehead, her fingers barely grazing the puckered scar, the ever-present reminder of her attack. "I don't want to be afraid anymore," she confessed, her eyes pleading. "I want to be with you. And a big part of you is your bar."

Leaning back heavily, he tried to think of another reason for her not to go, but the hopeful expression on her face undid him. He knew he would grant her any wish, even if it meant she would remember the first time she had been in his bar—and was kicked out by him.

Nodding slowly, he suggested, "How about this? We go early and you can meet some of the staff, but mostly sit in my office or the break room?"

She smiled but her eyes held questions.

"It's just that you haven't been in crowds since the attack and I don't want you overwhelmed. And," he added, his voice stern, "you stay with me. I don't want you out of my sight."

Readily agreeing, she tossed her last chip back to the plate and launched herself toward him, planting her lips on his.

―――――

Pulling into the parking lot, Zander's sweaty palms almost slid on the steering wheel and he bit back a curse. Feeling Rosalie's eyes on him, he forced a thin-lipped smile out.

"Does it make you upset that I'm here?"

He heard the concern in her voice and inwardly cursed more. Parking, he continued to grip the steering wheel, afraid if he let go, she would see his hand shake. Swallowing, he turned and pinned her with his gaze. "This is my business, but this is the place that caused you untold harm. I have a hard time reconciling the two."

Her gaze left him and moved to peer out the front windshield. The brick building was set back with the parking lot in the front and what appeared to be additional parking at the side. The neighborhood was in an older part of town, but not run down...just slightly worn out. Rosalie recognized the hotel she had been staying at when they passed it and noted it was only about six blocks from the bar.

Shaking her head, she said, "Nothing. Nothing looks familiar." Tilting her head to better see the sign above the door, she laughed. "Grimm? You named your bar Grimm?"

A chuckle finally broke through Zander's nervousness and he replied, "I had no fuckin' clue what to call the place. I think it was Rafe who said I should name it after one of the books I was always reading. Then Jaxon said it should be Grumpy from Snow White. Somehow the two ideas took shape and it's named after the Brothers Grimm."

Her head whipped around, blonde hair flying as she grinned, leaning in for a kiss. "I love it…it's perfect."

Entering the bar a minute later, he called his employees, who were setting up the bar, to come over. Rosalie smiled as the eclectic group met her with smiles of their own. She met the servers, bartenders, and security, and thanked Lynn and Charlene for the clothes and toiletries.

Roscoe took her hand in his much larger one, the smile on his face not matching the agony in his eyes. "Miss Rosalie, I'm so—"

Zander interrupted, clearing his throat loudly.

Roscoe shot him a glance before amending, "I'm glad to make your acquaintance."

She smiled up at him, wondering why the specter of agony was in his eyes, but chalked it up to someone getting hurt on their property. "Thank you," she said, before her hand was pulled back into Zander's.

"And this is one of my brothers," he said, introducing a handsome man, his dark blond hair long and shaggy.

"I'm Zeke," he said, shaking her hand. "I came to

Miss Ethel's later than Zan did. He was a teen and I was just a scrawny, punk kid."

Laughing, she looked up at the large, muscular man and said, "I wonder what Miss Ethel fed you all. All of her boys are big."

"All right, everyone get back to work. I'm gonna spend time in the office and will have Rosalie with me." With that, they headed down the hall, her body tucked up underneath Zander's shoulder as they entered the office.

Zander looked down, heaving a sigh of relief when she showed no signs of remembering Grimm's at all. He was thankful, for her sake—and selfishly, for his own.

Walking back from the stock room hours later, Zander stepped into the office, ready to call it a night. A quick glance told him Rosalie was not sitting on the old sofa where he last left her. His brows lowered, he turned and hustled down the hall, stopping at the edge of the counter, disbelieving what he saw. Rosalie, a waitress apron tied about her waist, was walking around the uncrowded bar room with Lynn, laughing as she took drink orders.

Stalking over as she made her way to the bar, he growled, "Princess, what the hell are you doing?"

She looked up, a complete lack of guile in her eyes, and placed her palm on his chest. "Don't be mad. I'm bored just sitting in your office and Lynn told me that you are down a server."

He had forgotten that one of the college girls recently went back to school. His gaze cut over to Lynn as she walked up.

"Sorry, boss. She wanted to work and said she had waitressing experience."

"Zander," Rosalie's soft voice called his attention back down to her. "This place doesn't scare me. I've walked around...nothing. I don't remember anything here. Other than substitute teaching, I have no job."

He propped his hands on his hips and stared at her, his eyes roaming over her face. Dropping his chin to his chest, he steadied his breathing. Finally, he wrapped his arms around her, pulling her into his embrace.

"You can only be here when I'm here—"

"Agreed," she rushed.

Scowling, he dropped a kiss on the top of her head, his gaze moving over the sparse crowd. "And I don't want you here when it's busy. I want to be able to see you at all times."

Leaning her head back, she bit her lip as she stared up. "Are you worried that he'll come back?"

Sucking in a gasp, he said, "Fuckin' hell, babe. If I ever see his face again, he'll suck meals through a straw the rest of his life when I get finished with him."

Zander's voice, more of a growl really, reverberated through Rosalie's body as she clung to him, both awed by his strength and concerned over his anxiety. "I know you're worried, Zander, and honestly, I don't want to put myself in harm's way. But here, with you and the others around, I'll be safe. I need to do something.

Something normal. I don't want to confuse healing with hiding."

Her words hit him and Zander knew she was right. *I've been so busy trying to protect her, I've forgotten to let her live.* "Okay, princess. You can work, but I'm still going to keep an eye on you."

Laughing, she winked as she moved out of his arms. "I'd be disappointed if you didn't!"

Trailing his fingers over the petal soft skin of Rosalie's shoulders, Zander sighed, his body relaxed after their lovemaking. It surprised him how much he had enjoyed having her at the bar. For the past two weeks, he watched her smile while serving drinks, laughing with Lynn, watching in awe as Joe and Charlene tossed bottles around behind the bar, and joked with Zeke and Roscoe. He made sure she did not get tired and immediately swooped in when she yawned. His employees commented that they saw more of him on the floor in one night with her around than they usually did in a whole week. He just rolled his eyes, but knew they were right.

Now, lying in bed, legs tangled, arms wrapped tightly around each other, her head on his shoulder, he thought about how his life was changing with her in it.

"Can you tell me about Miss Ethel?"

His fingers halted on their path over her skin, her question halting his musings. "Miss Ethel?"

"I just wondered how you ended up with her," she said, her soft, warm breath against his chest. Leaning back slightly, she lifted her eyes to his. "It's just that you know so much about me and I...well, I want to know about you as well."

Shifting in the bed, so he was on his back and she was half lying on him, he sighed, "It's not much of a pretty picture before I got to Miss Ethel's."

"You met me when I wasn't much of a pretty picture either."

He looked down at her, shaking his head. "You were always beautiful to me, princess."

"And you've always been my hero." Kissing the underside of his jaw, she waited patiently for him to tell his story.

"Never knew my dad...not sure my mom did either. She was mostly high, or drunk, or both. I can't say I was abused, just neglected. I don't have memories before about the age of four...I guess that's pretty normal, but I assume she, or someone, must have fed me enough to keep me alive. My first memories are of sitting on the floor of our two-room apartment, waiting to see if she would come home and bring food. I started going to the apartment next door to ask for some. They were nice enough and would make me a peanut butter sandwich. Then they'd yell at my mom when she came staggering in about not feeding me. That'd piss her off."

Rosalie gasped, her fingers flexing on his arm as she held him tight. "Oh, Zander...oh, my God."

He continued to stroke her back while shaking his head. "It was all I knew, babe. By the time I was six, I'd learned to steal food from the local grocer. Mom would be gone for days, so I'd wander the neighborhood and manage to take enough that I had plenty to eat."

"But what about school? Didn't you get some food there?"

"Didn't go to school, babe."

Bolting upward, she leaned her hands on his chest, pushing an "umph" from his lips as she shifted to see his face.

He chuckled. "Damn, honey. You're strong when you're upset."

"Of course, I'm upset! How could she do that to you?"

Her indignation sparked warmth deep inside him, staring into her wide, blue eyes. A flash of what kind of mother she would be flew through his mind, knowing she would be the best, and he admitted to himself he wanted to be the one to witness that as she became the mother of his children.

"Zander, what are you grinning about?"

"Sorry, I'm just awed at your mama-bear coming out, that's all. It's nice to have someone care."

"I do care," she said, her voice soothing as she leaned forward to plant a light kiss on his lips. Settling back, she asked, "When did you get to Miss Ethel?"

"I got caught one day by a policeman who had seen me sneaking around the grocery. He was kind...probably took one look at me, skinny kid, clothes a mess, hair a mess, and had my situation figured out. He took me home and it was one of the few times my mom was there. The place was a wreck...she was drunk...no food in the kitchen...he saw my bed was a blanket on the floor. He told her he was taking emergency custody. I was scared, thinking I was going to jail."

"What did he do?" Rosalie could not imagine how frightened a six-year-old Zander must have been to be taken off by a policeman, no matter how kind he was.

"A nice lady showed up and took me to a house. I had no idea at the time, but she was a city social worker and I was placed in a temporary foster home. The couple was nice, but it was only temporary. I had a bath, good food, a bed to sleep in, and clean clothes. They enrolled me in school, but I hated it. I remember going in front of a judge and my mom actually showed up to court. Drunk and disorderly."

"Oh, my God," she breathed, her heart hurting for the little boy Zander.

"Judge took away Mom's rights and I went to live in another foster home. They were also nice, but," he shrugged, "I kept sneaking out of school to run the streets. Hated school. Hated feeling stupid because I didn't know how to read. When I was eight, they placed me with Miss Ethel. I'd never met anyone like her in my life."

"Tell me," she demanded, her eyes now sparkling.

"You've met her...she was pure love...pure discipline...pure patience. She taught me to read. She told the teachers to just care for me and let me learn at my own pace. Then at night, she would read to me. I must have soaked it all in."

"And the others?"

"She took in boys...there were about six or seven of us at a time. Rafe, Cael, Asher, Jayden, and Jaxon and I pretty much grew up together. When I was graduating from high school, she had room to take in others. You met one of them...Zeke."

"I'm so glad you ended up with her."

"She saved all of us, that's for sure." He was quiet for a moment before adding, "That's why I got this tattoo."

Her eyes dropped to his upper arm, where the inked, swirl of flowers ran down his arm.

"Miss Ethel always had flowers in the yard from spring to fall, but her favorites were her roses. She always smelled of roses as well. Me and Rafe sat in the tattoo parlor when we were eighteen and the guy asked what I wanted." Chuckling, he said, "I didn't have a fucking idea, but he showed us a book of some of his work. I saw the flowers and it just hit me. If I was going to have something permanently on my arm, I wanted it to be a reminder of Miss Ethel."

"Can I ask what happened to your mom?"

"When I was fifteen years old, Miss Ethel informed me that my mom had died. I never asked, but I'm fairly sure it was from a drug overdose. You might think I'm hard-hearted, but I didn't shed a tear. It was as though I was told of the death of someone I didn't know."

She leaned forward, her lips pressed against his chest, right over his heart. "What about after Miss Ethel's?"

"Joined the Army right after graduation. Did tours in Afghanistan. Saw shit...did shit. Hated it, but met some good men there. Rafe and Cael joined the year after I did. Hell, Jaxon and Jayden were in the year after that. We weren't trying to be heroes, but none of us wanted to go to college and the military just seemed like a good way to get a steady paycheck. Our paths crossed occasionally while we were in. By the time we all got out, we found our way back here, keeping track of Miss Ethel, making sure she was still in our lives."

"That's so sweet," she gushed. "I love that you still take care of her."

"Babe, we could never repay our debt to her. But, each one of us would die trying."

"What about Grimm's?"

Chuckling, he shook his head. "I don't know...I guess I just always wanted something that was mine. All mine. My mom sure as hell never had money coming in on a regular basis and in the military, I got a paycheck but was always at someone else's beck and call. I wanted my own business...be my own boss. I didn't know a lot about other businesses, but I knew about bars. Spent time in them when I was younger and in the military." Shrugging, he said, "It just seemed like a good idea and when I found the old, run-down bar for sale, it called to me."

"And the name Grimm's?"

The silence stretched and she patiently waited, watching the emotions roll through his eyes.

"Like I said before, I had no fuckin' idea what to name it, but Fairy Tales always made me feel like anything was possible. I know the original Grimm Brother's tales were not like the kid versions today, but that didn't matter. They just make me think of happy endings."

Shifting, he rolled so that they were side by side, faces close with their bodies tangled together. "Now you know all about me." His hand slid up to her breast, kneading the pliant flesh, tweaking her nipple. "And, I'd like to get to know you again…intimately."

Her eyes twinkled as she reached down to stroke his engorged cock. "My pleasure."

"Oh, it will be," he promised, rolling her on top.

She threw her leg over him, straddling his hips, her core settling at his throbbing cock. With his hands, still on her breasts, he felt their weight as he rolled her nipples. One hand moved over her stomach to her mound and, as she lifted, he pressed his thumb against her clit. Throwing her head back, she rubbed her slick folds over him, desperate for the friction her body craved.

"Take me, babe. Ride me."

His voice, rough and commanding, washed over her, creating a want she needed to satisfy. Centering over his cock, she slowly slid down his shaft, the fullness filling her.

Zander allowed her to choose the speed, but was barely holding on to his patience. When she was fully seated, he groaned as she began to ride him, rocking up and down on her knees with her hands planted on his shoulders. Her long, blonde hair hung like a curtain around them and he slid his hands from her breasts to her hips, his fingers digging into her ass.

As her movements slowed, he lifted her slightly, then

began pumping his hips, taking over the thrusts. Her inner walls squeezed his cock as her orgasm rushed over her and she cried out his name.

He flipped them, causing her to squeal as he landed on top, his weight supported on his forearms. Lifting her knees, he pushed her legs wider as he continued to power through his thrusts. "Give it all to me, babe," he growled.

"You've got me, Zander," she panted, watching his face as his muscles corded in his neck. "All of me."

At her words, his orgasm hit and he poured himself into her. Thrusting until the last drop was milked, he managed to roll to her side so as to not crush her when his much larger body collapsed.

Their breaths, ragged, finally slowed, their racing hearts beginning to beat as one. As reason returned, his eyes widened. "Shit, babe, I forgot to use a condom." Her eyes jerked open and he rushed, "I'm clean...I swear, I'm clean."

"I am too," she assured. Trying to think of when she last had a period, she confessed, "But, I haven't had a... uh, period since I've gotten out of the hospital. I know antibiotics and trauma can mess up a woman's cycle. But, I'm sure...well, I uh..."

Cupping her face with his hand, he peered into her eyes, now full of worry instead of passion, and hated he put that emotion there. "Listen, Rosalie. I take responsibility...full responsibility. But, honest to God, if you get pregnant, I won't be upset. I've fallen in love with you, princess, and the idea of making a baby with you would be the best happily-ever-after I can think of."

Rosalie looked up, a tremulous smile meeting his self-assured one, and her heart leaped at his words. "I love you too, Zander. I think I fell in love with you while I was still sleeping."

"I wish I could go to work with you tonight," Rosalie said wistfully, sitting cross-legged on the bed, watching Zander getting dressed. "I don't feel bad."

He plopped down on the bed next to her, his fingers halting as they tied his boots. Twisting his head, his deep voice rumbled, "Babe."

Shaking her head, she said, "Babe? You know that one word has so many different meanings, depending on your inflection."

"Yeah, and what did that one mean?"

"It meant that you think I'm silly in wanting to go with you."

"No," he argued. "It meant that I don't believe you when you say you don't feel bad. I was there, remember? I saw them move your arm around, trying to ascertain if it had healed properly. Another CT scan and another x-ray on your ribs."

Huffing, she leaned her elbows on her bent knees, placing her head in her palms. "I'll be bored tonight."

"But, I won't have to worry," he added, kissing the end of her nose. "Anyway, you said you were going to get called this week for substitute teaching, so you don't need to be staying up till the wee hours of the morning and then getting a call a few hours later."

Nodding, she knew he was right, but it still rankled.

He stood, placing his hands on her shoulders, his face just inches from hers. "I hate like hell to leave you, but my truck was making noises when we were out today and I need to take a few minutes to make sure it's good before I go."

Unfurling her legs, she stood, his hands still warm on her shoulders. Smiling as she lifted to her toes, she wrapped her hands around his neck, her lips moving to his. Soft and steel. Firm and pliant. He groaned into her mouth, taking the kiss deeper.

His phone buzzed on the dresser and he pulled back reluctantly. Holding her gaze, he said, "We keep this up, I'll never get to work." His phone buzzed again.

With her palms resting on his chest, she gave a little push. "Go on," she grinned. "I'll be fine and here when you get home."

Kissing the tip of her nose, he swiped his phone off the dresser and glanced at the screen. Hitting a few buttons, he said, "It's Rafe. I'll call him back later."

Moving together to the front door, she kissed him once more before shutting and latching the door behind him. Standing with her back flat against the door, her eyes roamed around the small room, wondering how she would occupy her time. Landing on the sliding glass door, she remembered Zander's truck was parked below. Grinning, she hurried over to the door and out to the balcony, waiting for him to come into view.

It only took a moment before he was below, stalking toward his truck, his tall, muscular frame capturing her attention. Leaning only slightly over the rails, she admired the hug of his black, long-sleeved shirt over his chest. His jeans, worn and comfortable looking, show-cased his thighs and ass. Nothing fancy but, all man.

Opening her mouth to call down to him as he lifted the hood of his truck, she caught the phone at his ear. Not wanting to interrupt, she remained quiet, deciding to wait until he hung up before calling down.

"Rafe? What's up?" Zander asked. He propped the hood of his truck up and leaned over the engine. Laying his phone down, he pushed the speaker button.

"Hey, Zan. Just wanted to see how things were going."

"Good, all good. How about you?"

"Hell, I can't complain," Rafe joked, his voice belying his words. "But, I didn't call about me. I talked to Cael and he mentioned you've got your Sleeping Beauty still at your apartment. What's up with that?"

"Her name's Rosalie, dickhead, and what do you mean?"

"Come on, Zan, don't you think your guilt's gone far enough. I mean, I'm sure she's a nice girl and all, but you takin' her in, just because you think it's your fault she got assaulted, is going overboard."

Still jiggling a few wires underneath the hood, he felt

his temperature rise. "Rafe, what's your problem? You've always had my back before—"

"I've still got your back, Zan. Probably me more than anyone else there, 'cause I don't have to see her dependence on you. But, I gotta tell you, the other guys are concerned as well." Before he had a chance to retort, Rafe continued, "One of these days, she's going to remember that it was you who kicked her out of the bar. And, even though it wasn't your fault, she's going to remember being in the parking lot that night, a target for that asshole who grabbed her."

"You think I don't worry about that? You think I'm not afraid that she'll blame me?"

"Yeah...I know you. I know you're torn up with guilt. Man, that was not on you. But, you've become her everything. She's in your apartment...working at Grimm's...with you almost twenty-four-seven."

Still fiddling with his truck, he wiped the sweat forming on his brow, Rafe's words hitting low. "So, what the hell is wrong with that?"

"Fuck man, let me list the reasons. Number one, the relationship isn't built on full disclosure. Number two, she's so dependent on you, she's got no life outside of you. One day, you might look around and realize, if it's not right, she's too ingrained in your life to be able to get out. Number three—"

"Fine, fine, I get it," he growled. "But you're forgetting one major thing and that's how much I care about her."

"I haven't forgotten that, Zan. But if she's only with you because she sees you as her saviour, is that really what you want? She can't get on without you right now and you're locked in with a woman who doesn't even remember the first time she ever lay eyes on you."

He picked up his phone, slamming the hood of his truck. "Fuck, man, I care about her. I love her. And I'm a selfish enough bastard to want to keep what we have. I'll tell her sometime…when I think she's ready to hear the whole story."

"And in the meantime, you've got her dependent on you. Is that real, Zan? Are you in love with Rosalie or with the fairy tale princess you've built up in your mind? Is she falling in love with you, or just idea of her prince? Do you even know the difference?"

"I hear you, Rafe," he bit out, frustration pouring from every pore. "I think you're wrong, but I hear you. Listen, I'm headin' to work. Talk to you later." Disconnecting, he shoved his phone back into his pocket, walking to the driver's door. Climbing inside, he backed out of the parking space, his eyes lifting to the balcony of his and Rosalie's apartment, smiling as he thought of her safely tucked inside. *Rafe's wrong…I do love her. The real Rosalie.*

His gaze missed how the sliding glass door had just shut, the woman inside retreating, a tear sliding down her cheek.

The last suitcase was packed. Her books were in a box. The bathroom was now devoid of her toiletries. Her laptop was in its case, her purse sitting by the door.

And, the handwritten letter was lying on the kitchen counter.

The taxi pulled up outside and she picked up the first few items before making her way to the bottom of the apartment stairs.

"I've got a few more things to take," she explained, grateful when the taxi driver got out and offered to help. It only took the two of them another trip to have her belongings inside and he twisted around, lifting an eyebrow. Rattling off the address, she leaned back in the seat. Wanting to keep her eyes forward, they slid to the side, as if pulled by a magnet, to watch as Zander's apartment building faded into the distance.

Closing her eyes tight to stem the fear of more tears falling, she focused on Rafe's words. *Dependent. Fairytale. Not real. Guilt.* She understood all of his words except the guilt. *What guilt was he talking about? Why would Zander feel guilty? What happened that night?*

Watching the city streets slide by her window, she wondered if she should be heading to a hotel. *It would be good to disappear.* But her destination also made sense. *As long as I don't swap one dependency for another.* As the taxi stopped outside the house, she climbed out, her nerves now at an all-time high. *Oh, God, was this a mistake?*

Slipping the driver his fee, he nodded in acknowledgment before helping to lug her cases to the front porch. Her stomach somersaulted as the door swung open and Miss Ethel hurried out, her arms open wide. Rushing into the older woman's embrace, she felt the heaviness in her heart burst forth, new tears streaming down her face.

"Oh, child, come in, come in."

With Miss Ethel's arm around her shoulders, she was ushered into the living room. Sitting on the sofa, she held tightly to the older woman's hand, the lifeline necessary at the moment. As her eyes dried, she observed the tea service sitting on the coffee table in front of her, homemade cookies on a small platter. Smiling weakly, she wiped her eyes.

Patting her leg before rising, Miss Ethel poured the cups of tea and placed a few cookies on a saucer. "Drink, my dear, and have a little snack. I always think tea and cookies help us feel better about whatever distress is going on in our lives."

Obediently following her lead, Rosalie sipped the sweet, peppermint tea, the scent and taste cutting through the confusion of her mind. Munching on a cookie, she allowed a small smile to slip out. "I remember my mom used to make homemade cookies all the time."

Miss Ethel's face crinkled as she smiled and said, "I'm so pleased you're regaining memories of your family. I think that it's important to remember those we've loved."

At the word *love*, her heart plummeted, but she fought through the darkness. Heaving a sigh, she said, "I'm sure you're wondering why I called you earlier, so upset you felt like you needed to invite me to stay—"

"Rosalie, nothing made me feel like I needed to invite you. Yes, I did hear the distress in your voice and, yes, I do realize you are running from something and that must involve Alexander. But, I want you here and not wandering somewhere or even holed up in a hotel somewhere. My home is always open to you."

Clearing her throat, she leaned back into the deep cushions of the sofa after placing her cup back on the coffee table. "I'm sure you're curious...and I know," she rushed to say, "that you said you don't need to know what happened, but I want to tell you. I want to talk about it."

Miss Ethel nodded and copied her movements as she settled back in her chair, her hands folded in her lap. "Okay, sweet child. I'm all ears."

She gathered her tumultuous thoughts for a moment, trying to decide how best to proceed. Finally, with a frustrated shake of her head, she blurted, "I overheard Rafe."

Miss Ethel blinked, confused, and she realized how stupid that sounded. "Rafe called Zander today and he had him on speaker phone, so I heard their conversation. I know it was wrong, to eavesdrop but...well, if I had tried to move, Zander would have heard me. So, I just stayed still, and...uh..."

"Naturally, you listened. You could hardly have just shut your ears."

Snorting inelegantly, her lips curved slightly. "I suppose God should have given us ear flaps like eyelids, so we could just close them when we needed to."

Miss Ethel cackled, clapping her hands. "Oh, my dear, how funny." Sobering, her gaze never leaving Rosalie's, she said, "So, tell me what Rafe said that had you running."

With a great sigh, Rosalie began telling her what she

heard. Finally, she summarized, "So, all of Zander's friends are wondering why I'm still at his place. They think I'm too dependent on him. They think he's acting out of guilt or a misplaced fairy tale in his mind. And, it was hinted that Zander's the reason I was attacked."

The silence of the room was broken by the tick-tock of the old cuckoo clock on the wall, its metronome comforting as she waited to see what Miss Ethel would say.

"Do you remember the night of the attack?"

"No," she replied, shaking her head. "I don't remember anything about that night. I have memories of the hotel I was staying in, but nothing after that until I awoke in the hospital."

"Well, it is Alexander's story to tell you, of when he first met you," Miss Ethel said, "but it's no secret that he blames himself for not keeping you from danger."

"Then he's blaming himself for the actions of someone else," she argued, pleased to see the other woman nod her head in agreement.

"Yes, but we can't always control our thoughts. Especially for someone like Zander. He always took his responsibilities of being the oldest of the boys in my house very seriously."

"So, he is with me out of guilt?" Rosalie asked, pain lacing her words.

"Tell me, what do you remember of being asleep? In the hospital?"

That was not the question she was expecting and her head jerked slightly as she pondered. "Uh…I remember darkness. But sometimes it seemed like there was a light at the edges. Sometimes I wanted the light, but other times, I welcomed the darkness."

She looked up, wondering if Miss Ethel would have a comment, but she just continued to look at her with an expectant expression. "So, uh…I remember hearing a voice. I suppose I heard more than one, but it was the deep, constant voice of someone in particular that I remember. At some point, I heard words, phrases, I recognized." A small smile slipped out as she continued, "It was as though the words and that voice wrapped around me, keeping me safe. Keeping me anchored."

"Alexander," Miss Ethel said, her voice soft.

"Yeah," she agreed, smiling at the memory, "Zander. He told me his name when I was sleeping and when I awoke and heard his voice, I knew it was him."

"My dear, he may have visited you the first time out of a sense of worry, but I have no doubt he continued out of a sense of caring."

They sat quietly again, each lost in their own thoughts. Closing her eyes, Rosalie went back in her mind, to those days of just hanging on, hearing his voice.

The sun began to slide further into the horizon, shadows now creeping into the living room of Miss Ethel's house. Rosalie watched as she reached up to flip the light switch on the old, Tiffany lamp over her chair, sending a soft glow about the room.

"My boys have always been unusually close," Miss Ethel said, startling Rosalie, who stayed respectfully quiet as the older woman continued to reminisce.

"They all came from such diverse backgrounds, and

yet were all so vulnerable, so similar in that way. Alexander was the first and remained the oldest. I often relied on him to help with the younger ones, feeling that the responsibility was good for him. I would never have asked him to give more than he was able to give, but due to his mother's neglect, I gave him love and a safe harbor and he wanted to give that to others in return."

"He told me you taught him to read," she said, her voice soft with gratitude toward the unselfish foster mother who did so much more than just take in lost boys.

"Yes, yes. He and I used to pour over books. He had a thirst for learning and especially a desire to read stories. I think he loved the places they could take him to. Growing up, his imagination was all he had. And, of course, he would read to the others at night before they went to bed."

Folding her hands in her lap, she continued, "They not only became my family, but they also became family to each other. Fiercely protective. I suppose that's what prompted Rafe's call. The others might have been concerned about Alexander, but they've met you. They understand that what he is feeling is real. Rafe is...well, Rafe isn't here. He's less trusting, more suspicious of people's behavior. But, someone will come along to knock him for a loop. Until then, he's more likely to believe in what he can see and touch."

"He was right, though," Rosalie said. "I didn't want to admit it at the time, but as I sat in Zander's apartment and thought about everything, I realized he was right. I *am* dependent on Zander and I shouldn't be. I woke up from a long dream, finding my body battered, not remembering why. All of my memories were fuzzy, and that was so scary. And there he was, larger than life, the one thread I remembered from my deep sleep in the hospital." Closing her eyes, she battled the sting, as she swallowed deeply. "He was so handsome. Big and rough, as though he could battle anything and, yet, so gentle with me. And it was so easy to just give it all over to him. My worries, concerns, fears, doubts. He took them all and made me feel safe."

"I don't think that's a bad thing, my dear. Through that care, you have remembered more of your past, he helped you discover who you were and used to be."

Leaning forward, her eyes wide, she said, "Oh, Miss Ethel, please don't think I'm ungrateful for everything he did for me. I know my feelings for him are real. But Rafe kept mentioning guilt and said that our relationship wasn't built on full disclosure. He accused Zander of being in love with the idea of a fairy tale."

"Pffft," Miss Ethel huffed. "Rafe has grown cynical and spreads that around to others. Believe me, if Alexander feels something, it's real. That boy's head was never in the clouds." Reaching over to clasp her hand, she added, "But, if you need some space, that's a good thing too. And you're welcome here as long as you want to stay."

Standing, Miss Ethel peered down at her and said, "Now, before I show you to your room, tell me if you let him know where you are."

Blushing, she responded, "I left a long note on the counter."

"You do know he will be here as soon as he reads it."

"I asked him to give me some space…that I needed some time alone."

Miss Ethel just smiled, saying, "Come with me, dear. You must be exhausted."

Following obediently, she picked up her suitcases and trailed up the stairs after her, wishing her heart felt lighter. At the top of the stairs, she observed a long hallway, with two doors on each side. A quick glance revealed a large bathroom through one of the doors.

Miss Ethel directed, "My bedroom is downstairs next to the kitchen. These three bedrooms were for my boys. They generally shared the bathroom, but one room up here has its own connecting bathroom." She smiled over her shoulder toward her and explained, "I wanted one room to have privacy in case I was given a child that had difficulty integrating. If not, then usually the oldest had the privilege of a private bathroom. In fact, Alexander lived here the last two years he was with me."

Stopping at one of the doors, she followed the older woman inside, seeing a clean, functional bedroom, obviously with the connecting bath. The wooden, twin-sized bed, covered in a light blue, chenille bedspread was against the far wall with a nightstand and lamp next to it. A matching wooden dresser was against the other wall, the clean surface containing a few nicks in the wood, bespeaking of years of use.

"It's not much for a young lady," Miss Ethel began, "but I'll be pleased to have you stay here as long as you wish."

Smiling her gratitude, she set her case down and grasped Miss Ethel's hands. "It's perfect." A giggle slipped out and she shook her head. "In fact, I just realized that even though I've only been in Virginia for about two months, this is now my fourth room. First, the hotel. Then, the hospital, followed by Zander's and now here."

Patting her hand, Miss Ethel nodded silently, her face full of understanding. Walking out of the room, she stopped at the door, looking back over her shoulder. "Come on down when you get settled and we'll have some more tea."

Once alone, she lifted her suitcase onto the bed. Placing her belongings in the closet and drawers, she felt a sense of connection at the thought of Zander's teenage belongings in the same space. Heaving a sigh, she peered into the mirror in the bathroom. Staring at her reflection, she squared her shoulders, lifting herself to her full height. "You've got this, girl. Stand on your own...then you'll be someone with something to offer."

Full of determination, she flipped off the light on her way downstairs.

28

Zander gripped the steering wheel with white knuckles, forcing his lead foot to not speed down the neighborhood streets. His stomach gripped with anxiety and his heart ached...a real, physical ache. Ever since he had gotten home to an empty, Rosalie-devoid apartment and read her note his heart had seized in pain.

Recrimination slammed into him as he realized she must have overheard his conversation with Rafe. He should have never put his phone on speaker. Pulling into Miss Ethel's driveway, he observed the front porch light on and bolted from his truck. Not wanting to wake her, he used his key, entering the foyer quietly.

"I'm in here, Alexander," came the familiar voice, soft in the night. Rounding the corner, he saw Miss Ethel, her white hair in a long braid lying over her shoulder, dressed in a pink robe. She blinked as she turned the lamp on, chasing away the shadows.

He rushed into the room, squatting in front of her.

Before he could speak, she said, "She's fine. She's in one of the bedrooms upstairs."

Dropping his chin to his chest, his voice full of anguish, he asked, "I've lost her, haven't I?"

The feel of her hand on his head lent a spirit of calm to his storm and he inhaled a shuddering breath.

"Alexander, be at peace. You haven't lost her. She's still figuring out who she is, and Rafe's words made her realize that she needs to do that on her own."

"I can't believe she heard the crap he was spouting—"

"Was it?" she interrupted, holding his gaze as he lifted his face to hers. "She *is* dependent on you. She doesn't know the whole story of what happened the night she was attacked. She awoke to a lover's kiss and has been in a fairy tale ever since...or, at least, she wonders if she has."

"What do I do?" his pain poured out in each word.

"Talk to her. Tell her everything. Stop trying to be a prince...just be a man she can trust."

He caught her eyes moving over his shoulder and at that moment he felt Rosalie's presence. Twisting his head, his breath hitched as she stepped into the faint glow of the lamp. Feeling Miss Ethel rising from the chair, he stood, assisting her to her feet.

"Well, children, it's late and this old lady needs to sleep."

Bending to touch his lips to her soft cheek, he accepted her warm pat as she moved toward the hall. Taking Rosalie's hand in hers, she said, "Talk, my dear.

And listen. But, remember, you have a home here as long as you need it."

After Miss Ethel left the room and soft footsteps could be down the hall, Rosalie lifted her gaze to Zander, still standing in the middle of the room.

His ragged voice matched his face. "All the way over here, I kept thinking what if you had decided to not come here...had gone somewhere else. I just kept thinking that I had to find you even if I had to search every corner of the earth."

"You once told me if I ever went away, you'd never stop looking for me."

Stepping closer, he kept his eyes on hers. "I wasn't lying." Swallowing audibly, he added, "I wasn't lying when I said I loved you. I've never lied to you, Rosalie. But, I'm so sorry you heard the phone call between me and Rafe."

"He's your friend...he cares about you."

"I know, but he also hasn't been here to see what's happening. How you make me feel. Getting to know you. He's far away, so it's easy for him to make snap judgments."

"But the others are here and they're worried."

Reaching his hand out, he gave a tiny tug on her arm. "Can we sit?" At her nod, he led her to the sofa, sitting next to her. Close, but making sure to give her some space.

"We need to talk about the guilt, Zander. I don't know what that means."

Blowing out a deep breath, he said, "I never lied to you, but I also never told you about the night you were attacked. At first, I didn't want you to relive the horror. But, I also didn't want you to remember me as anyone other than your champion. Selfish, I know...I guess I just wanted to stay your hero."

"Miss Ethel said it best—just be someone I can trust. Without all the facts, I can't trust you."

He stared at her wide eyes and became lost in them. Her blonde hair fell in sleep-tousled waves over her shoulders. Her flannel pajamas peeked from from beneath a pink robe tied haphazardly at her waist. Forcing his gaze from her rosy mouth, he knew she deserved the truth.

With a slow nod, he swallowed deeply, knowing his relationship with her could change forever. "You came into Grimm's on a crowded, busy, noisy night. I noticed you when you moved past me from the ladies' room back into the bar. Your beauty knocked me for a loop and your soft voice captured my attention. But, you seemed too innocent for a bar like mine." Shrugging, he admitted, "What can I say? Before you, I was a grumpy ass most of the time." Rubbing his hand against his forehead in an ineffective attempt to ease the tension he felt, he continued. "So, I was behind the bar, thinking you were too young to be there. A man came up and you seemed surprised. Then you seemed annoyed. Then he put his hands on you and I kicked him out. I had Roscoe take him out and get him a cab. He was pissed, said some nasty things, which just made me angrier."

"Okay," Rosalie said slowly, understanding why he was irritated at the man. "So, what happened then?"

Heaving a sigh, Zander plunged ahead, knowing

that, if she were going to hate him, he might as well get it out into the open. "I turned on you. I was pissed at him and turned it around on you. I said you shouldn't be at a bar like Grimm's and I cut off your alcohol. I called a cab and escorted you to the door. Roscoe took you from there to make sure you got in the cab."

Her brow lowered, confusion evident. "You kicked me out?"

"No...yes...I mean...fuck, Rosalie. I thought you were too good to be hanging out alone in a rough bar. I was attracted to you, but acted poorly. I hated that I might see you hook up with someone. So, I took away your choice and made you leave."

Her face gave nothing away, so he plunged head. "The taxi pulled into the parking lot, but a fight broke out near the back of the bar at the same time. Roscoe told you to take the cab home and he came back in because he heard the ruckus. After we got the fight settled, I went back out to make sure you were okay and saw the cab driving down the road."

Her mouth opened slightly, but no words came out. Sucking in a shaky breath, she said, "So, I didn't make it to the cab. He was out there. Biding his time until I came out."

"I...I don't know. I guess he must have been."

"And he didn't have to wait long. There I was."

"Yeah...I was the last to leave. I heard a noise on my way out and followed it. That's when I found you." A choking sound left his chest and his eyes squeezed shut, as though to get rid of the memory. In order not to see her condemnation, he kept his eyes closed as he confessed, "I might not have attacked you, but it's my fault he got to you."

Just as before, Rosalie heard nothing but the tick-tock of Miss Ethel's clock on the wall. His words swirled around in her head, her heart aching at his honesty. Reaching out, she placed her pale hand on his forearm.

Zander's eyes shot open, head down, staring at their connection and her fingers stroking his arm. Afraid to look away from her hand, he finally forced his head to lift. Her intense gaze hit him, his breath leaving his lungs in a rush.

Clearing her throat, her voice tentative at first, she began, "I don't know why I was there that night. Maybe, being new in town, I was just hoping to meet some people. Or maybe I was tired of sitting in the hotel. Who knows?" Letting out a shaky breath, she continued, "But I do know this. Zander, you may have been a grumpy ass, but you're a good man. You cut off my drinking when you thought I needed to leave. Even though, according to you, I hadn't had too much to drink, you thought it wasn't safe. Your intent was to get a cab for me."

Lifting her shoulders in a slight shrug, she continued, "Who knows why things happen? When a plane crashes, is the person who missed the flight just luckier than the ones who were on it? I don't know. But I do know that you didn't assault me. You were trying to take care of me before the assault and you certainly did afterward."

"I felt horrible, Rosalie. The idea that I put you in his

path just killed me." His words, laced with anger, felt like they were torn from his lips.

Squeezing his arm, she said, "If he was lying in wait for me, Zander, he would have been out there an hour later or whenever I left. He could have followed me back to the hotel. I know it feels like it couldn't have been worse, but it could have. He could have left me where no one would find me. He could have finished the job and killed me."

Jerking at the idea her not living, he grasped her hand in his, his thumb finding her pulse on the inside of her wrist. Feeling the thrum of her blood pulsing in her veins, he calmed. "I haven't been able to forgive myself."

The confession struck Rosalie and she said, "That's the guilt Rafe was talking about. He thinks you're with me out of guilt. So, I'll ask you point blank, Zander...are you?"

Twisting his body so he faced her fully, Zander stared into Rosalie's eyes, the blue shining in the glow of the lamp. Taking both hands in his, he held her gaze. "When I visited you the first time in the hospital, it was out of concern. Guilt...and concern." A grimace of pain crossed his face. "When I saw you lying on the bed, so bruised and battered, my heart sunk at the damage done to your beautiful body. And the guilt ate at me. I felt as though I just handed you over to the monster."

Listening to his description, Rosalie witnessed the evidence of his guilt written on his ravaged features. He gave a slight tug on her hands, bringing her attention back to his words.

"When I first began to read to you, I felt...I don't

know…like we were connected. It's hard to explain, but as you lay there, unmoving, I hoped you could hear the stories. I looked forward to visiting. It was no longer just guilt, but caring. I wanted to be the first one you looked at when you finally opened your eyes. I wanted to be the one you turned to." Zander's chest hurt as he held her gaze, his words choking him. "Please forgive me."

"So, what started as guilt…" she prompted.

Rubbing her hands in his, he nodded as he finished, "Ended up being love. Rosalie, I didn't want you to move in with me out of guilt. I wanted you with me because I was in love. Am in love." Hoping she was not just hearing his words but hearing his heart, he held his breath watching the play of emotions cross her face.

Blinking slowly, she whispered, "I've realized that I put you on a pedestal. You were my hero…my dragon slayer…my prince."

Fear gripped his chest, his heart beating so loudly he was sure she could hear.

"But, the reality is, you're just a man. A man who makes mistakes. Sometimes falters. Sometimes disappoints." Her lips curved slightly as she continued, "But I forgive you, Zander. Because, even though you're just a man, you're still my hero."

Her words took a few seconds to sink in, but the pull on his hands, bringing his face closer to her, caused his eyes to widen as he sucked in a fast breath. Her lips landed softly on his, a gentle movement. His heart soared but he held the kiss steady, afraid of breaking the fragile spell. Focusing on just the kiss, he angled his mouth, barely licking her lips.

Rosalie's hands slid around his neck, pulling him closer, drinking him in. Their tongues explored slowly, savoring the taste of their love. Shifting back, she blinked several times, running her tongue over her kiss-swollen lips.

"Oh, babe, I know it's late, but let's go home," Zander said, his smile firmly in place, relief flooding his chest.

"Uh...no, Zander. I'm not going," she said, her voice soft but strong.

"Okay, we can spend the night here and go back in the morning," he agreed.

Biting her bottom lip, she shook her head. "No, honey. I'm not going back with you. Not tonight. Not tomorrow. I'm staying with Miss Ethel for a while."

His brows lowered with confusion. "I don't understand. I thought—"

"Rafe was right about something," she said, tucking her hair behind her ear. "I am dependent on you and I need to stand on my own two feet for a little bit."

"Wha...no. I mean, Rafe's got no idea what he's talking about—"

Her fingers landed on his lips, her touch burning, and he had to fight the desire to kiss their tips.

"Please, listen to me."

He eyed her pleading gaze and nodded, settling back, making sure their legs were still touching, taking her hand back into his. "Okay...anything you need, sweetheart."

Releasing a deep breath, Rosalie looked down at

their connected fingers, linked together, and her heart warmed at the sight. Lifting her gaze, she said, "I do love you, Zander. And this is not me breaking things off with you. It's just that when I was in the hospital, I was scared. I had no one. No belongings. No place to stay. I didn't even have clothes to put on. But you were there... larger than life. You took care of everything. With you, I felt safe, secure, and didn't have to worry about anything."

"Was that so bad?" he asked, reaching to smooth her hair back from her face, his hand warm on her cheek.

Her lips curving, she shook her head. "No...it's been wonderful. A place to stay. A job until I can teach again. My belongings. Sharing an apartment with a man I adore. What's not to love?"

"Okay, princess, you're going to have to break this down for me. If it's so good, why do you not want to keep it going?"

"Zander, we never even dated. We didn't go on a single date. There was nothing normal about our meeting...about our coming together...about my moving in with you. It just happened."

"Okay..." he said, confusion still written in his crinkled brow.

"I want to take a step back. I want Rosalie Noble, recent teacher-to-be, transplant from Baltimore, to meet Zander King, local businessman. I want to come to you, standing on my own. Not out of need, but out of want."

Her words swirled around Zander's head and, after his initial protestations, he knew she was right. The crazy situation they found themselves in had them hurdling forward at light speed. And, while their love was true, they had not taken the time to slow down and savor the new beginnings of their relationship.

Rubbing his thumb over her soft cheek, he nodded slowly. "You're right. It kills me to think of you not sharing my home right now, but as long as you're not saying goodbye to us, I'll do anything to make sure you know we're perfect together."

29

"You ready?"

Zander stood on the bottom of Miss Ethel's porch step, his eyes to the top where Rosalie was bent over, stretching her calves. Limber, she was able to bend her leg in a position that he was sure was impossible. But it afforded him a view of her perfect ass, lovingly caressed by a pair of tight, running pants. *Oh, I'm ready, but maybe not for running.*

She jogged down the steps to him, a wide smile on her face. Her long hair was pulled up into a ponytail and he was taken back to the dream he had of seeing her running after seeing her toned legs in the hospital. Staring at her upturned face, blue eyes twinkling, he had to admit, the reality was better than any dream he could have conjured in his mind.

Her fingers plucked at the sleeve of his t-shirt, a concerned wrinkle creasing her brow. "How can you be wearing just a t-shirt and shorts on this chilly morning?"

Bending to place a chaste kiss on her lips, he grinned. " 'Cause when I'm around you, I'm always overheated, princess."

She threw her head back, laughter ringing out, the sound melting his early morning grumps.

"Come on," she said, rolling her eyes.

The run today was just one of the many ideas she had come up with for their dates over the past few weeks. They began to jog down the street toward the park where they had enjoyed a picnic last week, complete with a red-checkered tablecloth on the ground and a basket loaded with fried chicken that Miss Ethel had taught her to make. Last weekend, she managed to get him into a movie theater after wrangling an admission from him that he had not been in one since he was a teenager.

A few delivery trucks and early commuters passed them by, but for the most part, the world had not woken yet. The sun painted the sky in yellows and oranges as it peeked over the horizon. Puffs of air left their lungs as they began to run in unison. He shortened his stride to match hers, finding the run to be invigorating, though effortless.

They jogged companionably as they made their way around the small lake in the center of the park and he confessed, "The first time I saw your legs, you were still in a coma, but I remember thinking at the time that you must have been a runner."

Smiling up at him, she said, "I discovered my

running shoes packed in one of my suitcases and the memories flooded back. I ran in high school, both cross country and track. I didn't have time to run competitively in college, but continued to run for the exercise. It's freeing, don't you think?"

"Freeing?" he barked. Shaking his head, he thought of the Army's boot camp runs. *Hardly freeing...more like forced runs until everyone dropped.* Looking down at her upturned face, blue eyes full of life as they stared into his, he grinned. "Yeah, as long as I'm running with you it's...freeing."

Punching his shoulder, she argued, "You just agree to be nice. You can disagree, you know."

He pondered her statement, knowing they were supposed to be getting to know each other better. "Well, I have to admit that when I was in the Army, forced runs at all hours of the day...running till we puked our guts up...having to run more if one of us dropped back...well, I guess *freeing* isn't the word I would have used."

"Oh, Zander," she rushed, her brows drawn down. "I never thought about being forced to run. For me, it was always something I did out of pleasure."

"That's exactly what I want running to be for you... pleasure." He watched her lips curve slightly and grinned in response. The dawn's light caught her hair, spinning the blonde into gold. "I gotta tell you, if I had your image to focus on when I was in the Army, I would have been the fastest fucker on the trail."

Another giggle slipped out and they continued along the path. This was the time of day he was usually ensconced in bed, but an early night at Grimm's last night afforded him the opportunity to take her up on her offer of a run. "You seem to know this trail," he commented, seeing her feet sure and steady on the mulched running trail.

"I've come here a couple of times," she confessed, "but just walking. This is the farthest I've been able to run. I think it helps to have a partner."

"I think a partner in all things is good," he said, winking at her, unable to keep the smile from his face as she laughed.

Rounding a curve in the trail, he noticed her pace slowing. Ever conscious of her former injuries, he asked, "You okay? Why don't we stop and walk for a bit?"

"Oh, I hate this," she moaned, her hand pressing into her side.

"Runner's cramp?"

She nodded, but a grimace crossed her face. "I'm sorry," she said, "I thought I was ready for this."

Concern was etched on his face as he leaned over, his hands on her shoulders, halting her steps. "You don't have anything to prove to me, babe. Walking with you is just a good as jogging." He noted her curt nod, but his heart stumbled at the way she kept her head down as they continued along the path, the smile gone from her face.

Snagging her hand, he led them to a bench before gently pushing on her shoulders to have her sit. Kneeling, he massaged her tight legs while she drank from their shared bottle of water.

"You don't gotta prove anything to me, Rosalie. You've come so far in your recovery...it's fucking amazing." She sucked in her lips, a sigh heaving from her body. He lifted her chin with his knuckle, peering deeply into her eyes. "Come on, princess. What's going on here? This is the time when we're supposed to be getting to know each other, right?" He knew it was uncool to use her words against her, but was desperate to know the reason behind her hesitation.

"I found my running shoes, like I told you, and remembered how I felt when running. I just thought that you'd see me as strong...you know, if we were out doing something physical. Not some patient trying to heal, but as a strong woman." Lifting her shoulders, she sighed again. "I'm tired of being weak. I want to come to you whole, so I guess I've pushed it a little too much."

"Oh, babe," he said, pulling her forward until her head was tucked under his chin, his arms wrapped around her back. For a moment, he said nothing, simply allowing their hearts to beat as one. Feeling the tension sliding from her body, he said, "Rosalie Noble...you are the strongest person I know." He felt her shake her head and loosened his embrace just enough to allow her to lean back so she could see his face.

At the confusion in her eyes, he continued, "Don't you see? You were beaten, but not broken. With every step that you've taken in your recovery, you've shown your strength."

"Zander, I couldn't have done this without you. We don't even know if I would have woken up in the hospital if you hadn't been there talking and reading to me every day."

Cupping her cheek in his large, rough palm, he stared into her eyes, so full of doubt. "You didn't need me to slay your dragon...your strength comes from within. We did it together, princess."

A slow smile curved her lips until her whole face beamed with the pleasure of his words. "Together," she whispered.

A breath apart, they moved toward each other until the touch of lips flamed into a kiss. His thumb caressed her cool cheek as her arms snaked around his waist. Pulling back slightly, his breath ragged, he said, "I need to get you fed before I forget we're in the middle of a public park. Come on, I saw a food truck over there."

A few minutes later, continuing their walk, breakfast burritos in their hands, they laughed and talked, the worry disappearing. Ending at Miss Ethel's front porch, he bent to take her lips once more. As he reluctantly ended the kiss, she waved, her heart soaring at the thought of going home with Zander. For now though, her home was with Miss Ethel. *But soon...*

30

"So, let me get this straight," Cael began, sitting on Zander's sofa, his eyes pinned to the man in front of him wearing dark jeans and a navy, button-up shirt. "You're dating the woman you were living with?"

"Isn't that backward?" Jaxon queried, stuffing Doritos in his mouth, *umphing* as Jayden elbowed him in the arm.

"I get it," Asher said, bringing a fresh beer into the room before settling down in one of the chairs. "You gotta know if she wants you or was just with you 'cause of the fucked-up situation."

"Her stayin' with Miss Ethel is a good thing," Jayden stated. "Miss Ethel could use some company—"

"Agreed, but we've been dating for weeks now and if I have anything to do with it, she won't be there for much longer," Zander quipped.

Jaxon stopped eating long enough to ask, "She still like the car?"

He had an old car at his shop and had it running perfectly. Zander had wanted her to buy a sturdy SUV and she had insisted on a small hybrid. In the meantime, Jaxon had suggested she drive his extra car until they could decide.

"It's perfect, man," he replied. While not an SUV, the older, heavier automobile was safe, in his opinion. "She's appreciated having a set of wheels to run around in. And with her substitute teaching, it gives her something reliable." Running his hands through his hair, he stood. "I'm heading out...y'all can hang and watch the game from here if you want."

As the door closed behind him, he heard a call of, "Don't be late, son." Laughing, he knew they could not see the middle finger salute he flipped, but it made him feel better to offer it anyway.

Last week he took Rosalie to a ball game and was pleasantly surprised when, dressed in the team sweatshirt, she had cheered as loudly as the rest of the spectators. He also remembered glaring at a few men whose attention had been snagged by the beautiful woman next to him.

They had continued with a few, early morning runs, her strength gaining with each. Dinner dates ending with him kissing her on the front porch of Miss Ethel's house had him wondering if he had taken a trip back in time to his teenage years. Although, with Rosalie's body pressed against his, he knew she was no fumbling teen, but a fully grown woman. His cock twitched at the memory.

Parking outside Miss Ethel's house, nerves hit

while he sat, staring at the large, old house he always considered home. Sucking in a deep breath, he left the safety of his truck and walked up the front walk approaching the porch. The door swung open, Rosalie appearing.

He stared, as though seeing her for the first time. Gorgeous in a floral dress and with heels encasing her feet, she had more height, but still much shorter than he. Noting she had a sweater hanging about her shoulders, he was glad it would keep away the chill, observing it also made her blue eyes shine. He felt light-headed and realized he had forgotten to breathe.

"You shouldn't be here," he blurted.

Rosalie stared down at him, her brow furrowing at his words. Tilting her head, she stared at him in question.

"I mean," he corrected, "you should be waiting inside for me to ring the bell."

A smile spread across her lips, brightening the evening sky. "Should I let you come in and tell Miss Ethel how honorable your intentions are?" she teased.

Hoping the evidence of his intentions were not showing, he shifted his stance and rethought saying hello to Miss Ethel. Before he could make that decision, she appeared behind Rosalie, her smile beaming at him as well.

Startled out of his appreciative perusal of Rosalie, who had moved to the side when Miss Ethel came out, he jogged up the steps to place a kiss on the older woman's soft cheek. She reached up and squeezed his arm, her affection warm.

269

"Have fun, you two," she called out, giving them a little wave.

After goodbyes, he stuck out his elbow for Rosalie to slip her hand through. With a huge smile still on her face, she allowed him to escort her to his truck. When they reached it, she blinked.

"You washed your truck?"

"Hey, don't be so astonished," he laughed. "Wait till you see the inside."

As he assisted her into the seat, Rosalie observed the cleaned seats, dashboard, and floor mats. "Oh my!" she exclaimed, laughing. As he climbed into the driver's seat, she turned to him, asking, "So, are you trying to impress some girl?"

Leaning forward, he placed a soft kiss on her lips, his smile matching hers. "Not just some girl...but one, very special girl."

The drive to the restaurant was short and once inside, Zander walked with his hand on Rosalie's lower back as they followed the hostess to the corner table in the back, next to a window overlooking a nearby park. He fiddled with his napkin after the server took their orders. She watched him for a moment before sliding her hand across the top of the table, placing it on his.

"Hey," she said, "Don't be nervous. It's just me."

His eyes jumped to hers and he offered a slight nod as he flipped his hand palm up, linking fingers with hers. "I know...but I don't want to fuck this up. It's been a while since I've been in a really nice restaurant."

"Oh, Zander, you're not going to mess anything up.

Anyway, that's part of being a couple. Good times mixed with some not so good."

"We've already had our not so good," he quipped.

Nodding, she agreed. "Don't worry. I'm just taking time to get my feet under me."

"So, how's the substituting going?"

Her smile brightened, as she said, "You know, up till now, I've been all over the school, often just being a glorified study-hall teacher. Yesterday, I actually substituted in an English class."

"Really? How was it?" His eyes twinkled as he watched her face become more animated.

Laughing, she said, "I was so nervous. It was at one of the high schools in the area, in the English department. They were seniors, which I was really grateful for. I know ninth graders can be more difficult. But anyway, most of the day went really well. One class wanted a substitute to do nothing, so I had to really work to get them to do the assignment, but the other classes had no problem following directions."

Her excitement was evident and he finally understood why she wanted some independence. *Isn't that what I wanted when I joined the military? And then again, when I was discharged, and bought Grimm's?* "So, do you know when you go back?"

"Usually I just get a call early in the morning when they need me, if it's for a teacher who has called in sick. But, they've got an English teacher who will be out for a whole week for a conference and at the end of yesterday, the principal asked if I would be available. I jumped at the chance. He also hinted that another English teacher will be having a baby in a couple of months and, if I wanted, they would offer the full-time sub position to me."

"Would that be better?"

"Absolutely!" she enthused, a confident smile firmly in place while her fingers absently rubbed his hand. "I'd get to know the kids instead of just being in a different class every day. I could work with the teacher and actually do lesson plans. And, the pay is significantly higher if you have a long-term sub contract."

He watched her blue eyes twinkle in the candlelight, the feel of her fingers on his hand zinging straight to his cock, while the warmth spread to his heart.

"In fact, I might be busier than ever. One of the teachers suggested I put my name on the school's website as an English tutor. That way, I could have some students to tutor in the afternoons or evenings when you're at work." After a moment, she confessed, "I like this," her voice barely above a whisper. Recognizing his unstated question, she added, "This. Feeling like I'm an equal partner and not just some poor waif needing to be rescued."

"I never wanted to make you feel less," he said, his hand clutching hers.

Her smile warm, she shook her head. "You never did, Zander. You always made me feel like the center of your world. But, it was me. And, don't blame Rafe. He just said what I knew in my head but didn't want to admit in my heart. I now feel like I'm more of a true partner in our relationship."

Before Zander had a chance to respond, their food

arrived, the scent tantalizing. As they ate, the conversations turned lighter, enjoying each other's company. Her teaching plans and his thoughts about finally expanding the bar filled their evening, right through dessert.

Standing on Miss Ethel's front porch at the end of the date, he wrapped his arms around her, pulling her close. Lowering his head, his lips teased hers. What began as a slow smolder soon flamed into intense passion. Angling his head, he delved deep into her mouth, his tongue devouring her flavors. Tasting the spices, wine, and chocolate from dinner, mixed with the essence of her, intoxicated him more than any alcohol. With one hand anchoring against her back, the other slid upward, tangling in her long hair, the silken tresses teasing his fingers as he gripped them gently.

Lost in the sensations that narrowed her world down to Zander and his sensual assault, Rosalie's knees weakened and she wondered, fleetingly, if she could stand on her own if his arms were not holding her up. The sounds of the street faded away as all thoughts centered on the feel of his firm lips moving against hers. She faintly heard a moan, but had no idea if it came from her or him. Eyes tightly closed, she felt him lift away from her and she mewled in discontent. Opening her eyes, she stared into his intense gaze.

With his cock painfully straining against his pants, Zander lifted away, his eyes memorizing every facet of her face for the hundredth time. Her lips, now plump and slick. Her cheeks, rosy with arousal. Her eyes peering back, their brightness now intensified with a hungry need.

Sucking in a shuddering breath, he groaned, "I want you, princess. More than you can know. But, I'm going to see you inside now, before I give in to the urge to toss you over my shoulder and carry you back to my lair."

A delightful laugh escaped her kiss-swollen lips. "Lair?"

Grinning, he pressed her tightly to his chest. "What else would I call a place where I dwell, lost in my thoughts of possessing you?"

Whispering against his shirt, she nodded, "I guess lair is the perfect word."

Kissing the top of her head, he nodded toward the front door. "Go on, sweetheart. I've no doubt Miss Ethel is waiting up for you."

Watching her step inside the house, he waited until he heard the lock click in place before walking back to his truck. Driving toward his apartment, he smiled at the memory of her excitement over the permanent substitute teaching position. As much as it hurt not having her in his arms all night, he knew Rafe had been right. She needed this time. But, as soon as she was ready...he wanted her back in his place, ready to make it *their* place.

31

"Are you not going out tonight?"

Rosalie, sitting on the sofa, an English Literature book in her lap, smiled at Miss Ethel. "Not tonight. Zander needs to be at Grimm's for a delivery that got delayed and since it's Saturday, he needs all his staff on the floor." Shrugging, she said, "I haven't been working there since the substitute jobs have been rolling in and, I have to admit, I miss it. But, it's all good. I wanted to get some lesson plans completed tonight since I'm seeing him tomorrow."

Shaking her head, Miss Ethel murmured, "Grimm's. I swear, when I heard what he was going to name his bar, I laughed out loud."

"I think it's cute."

Miss Ethel chuckled, "Oh, Lordy. Have you told Alexander that you thought the name of his bar was cute?"

Joining her mirth, she answered, "No, ma'am. I think my words were something along the lines of the name just fit."

They settled into a comfortable silence, Miss Ethel with her knitting and Rosalie fiddling with her pen.

"Something on your mind, dear?"

She jerked her head up, surprised at the question. "You really are good at this, you know."

"Good?"

"Yeah...reading people. I think that's why you were such an amazing mom to all your boys." She smiled as Miss Ethel blushed, waving off her praise. "But, I do have something on my mind. I just don't know how to tell you."

Miss Ethel set her knitting needles back on the bag at her feet and turned her attention fully to Rosalie. "I think, perhaps, you have decided that you'd like to be with Alexander more and you're afraid of leaving me alone."

Mouth open, she shook her head. "How do you do that?" Sighing, she set her book to the side, holding Miss Ethel's gaze. "You're right. During the past weeks, my feelings toward him haven't diminished at all. In fact, they've grown. And, while I'm not working full time yet, I do substitute about three days a week, so my self-reliance has grown as well."

"Let's not forget the car that Jaxon was able to get for you, so you can get out and about more."

"Oh, my gosh, yes! Now that I can drive, I feel so much more independent. I've got money in the bank, a car I can use, and some income coming in."

"So, what's stopping you?"

Dropping her gaze to her lap, she sighed heavily. "Being here is...safe...comfortable. I remember living with both of my parents, before my dad died. And then, it was just Mom and me for a while and, while I remember her lovingly and we certainly had some good times, her sadness was always just under the surface." Lifting her eyes, she swept the room, saying, "But this house is so full of love. You can feel it from every room."

A benevolent smile graced Miss Ethel's lips, her eyes crinkling at the corners. "That was such a lovely sentiment, Rosalie. Thank you. As much as I loved every boy who graced my home, I always knew they were not mine to keep forever. When the time was right, they needed to move on into the world. For some, it was while they were still young and went back to their parents who had managed to overcome their difficulties so the children were safe again. For others, it was when they graduated and became adults. I never kicked them out of my house just because high school was over. Many stayed until they had jobs and enough money to make it on their own. Some, like Alexander, joined the military, but they all managed to come back to visit."

"And that's a testament to their love for you," she avowed.

Chuckling, Miss Ethel nodded. "Yes, I would have to agree, this house was full of love." Her mirth slowing, she leaned forward and pinned her with her gaze. "However, they did leave when the time was right. And so must you. I am fine here...and hardly lonely with all the boys checking on me so often." Shifting back against the well-worn cushions, she picked up her knitting needles once more, adding, "And I hope you will return often as well." Glancing at the cuck-coo clock on the wall, she asked, "Are you anxious to tell Alexander your decision?"

With a wide grin, she bounded off of the sofa. "Yes! Absolutely. I won't be long since I know he's busy, so I'll be back soon." Bending to kiss Miss Ethel's cheek, she grabbed her phone and purse before heading out the door with her keys.

———

Zander viewed the crowd with a practiced eye. Loud. Noisy. But, so far, under control. Making his way through the crowd from the back, Zeke stopped him near the bar.

"Boss, you've got a visitor. I escorted them into your office to wait until you had a free moment."

Staring at his employee and friend, he narrowed his eyes. "Visitor? Who the hell did you let into the office?"

"Just go on back and see," Zeke quipped, walking away. Looking over his shoulder, he grinned. "But take your time…no rush…we've got this out here."

Glaring at his back, Zander stalked down the hall, throwing open the office door before immediately coming to a halt. His eyes widened at the sight of Rosalie perched on his desk, her legs encased in tight jeans and with a revealing pink top showcasing her assets which, he couldn't miss, were pushed out as she reclined with her hands behind her, flat on the desk. A quick glance to the side revealed a jacket. *Thank God, she was covered when she came in.*

His dick responded immediately to the buffet presented, but he held himself in check, lifting an eyebrow in silent question.

"Um…I missed you," she divulged, licking her lips nervously.

Grinning at her obvious uncertainty, he nonetheless loved the way she had boldly come to him. Flipping the lock behind him, he stalked her way until his body was planted between her legs. With his erection pressed against her core, he felt the heat of her need through their layers of clothing. Leaning forward, he pressed his chest against hers, feeling her heartbeat pounding in time to his.

"Yeah?"

"Yeah," she breathed.

Nuzzling his nose across her face, his lips tantalizing close to hers, he asked, "So, what are we going to do about that?"

Swallowing deeply, she confessed, "I was hoping you'd tell me. Trying to seduce someone in their office is new for me."

He inhaled her scent, floral mixed with arousal, and admitted, "Me too, princess. Never had anyone in here like this before." Pressing his pelvis closer in, his swollen cock made his jeans uncomfortably tight.

She reached out, palming its length, eliciting a gasp from him. "Seems like you miss me too."

"Minx," he growled, the feel of her hand on his crotch almost unmanning him. Grasping her hand to still its movement, he added, "You plannin' on ending our dry spell?"

"Actually..." she began, drawing his immediate attention, eyes widening. Staring into his piercing gaze, she continued, "I came to tell you that I talked with Miss Ethel tonight about moving back in with you. That is if you—"

He halted her words, slamming his mouth onto hers, his tongue plunging into her warmth as their noses bumped awkwardly. The kiss quickly flamed as their tongues tangled, both giving and taking at the same time.

His hands found the bottom of her shirt and with a deft lift, only parting long enough for the material to pass between them, he tossed it to the chair behind his desk. She attempted the same maneuver with his shirt, but was unable to achieve the same effect.

Chuckling at her noise of protest, he leaned back and whipped his Grimm's t-shirt over his head. Her fingers managed to unbuckle his belt and were in the process of unzipping his jeans when he unsnapped her bra, his lips immediately dropping to latch onto a nipple.

Gasping with the intensity of his teeth raking across the swollen bud, Rosalie's lost her purchase on Zander's zipper as she moved to prop herself up on the desk more firmly. Leaning back, she landed on a pile of papers and he unceremoniously swept them onto the floor. With a hand placed between her breasts, he gently pushed her backward until she lay on the top of the desk, her ass at the edge. Unzipping her pants with more success than she had with his, he jerked them off, snagging her panties on the way. Sliding his fingers through her folds, he discovered her wet and ready. He stopped for a second, staring at the hooded gaze she landed on him, her oversensitive skin blushing.

Snapping out of it, he dropped his jeans and boxers to his ankles, palming his erection after grabbing a condom from his wallet. Rolling it on before placing the tip at her entrance, he halted, holding her gaze.

His voice rough with need, "What do you want, princess? You gotta tell me...I gotta hear it."

Reaching up, her fingers grazing his chiseled abs before sliding up to squeeze his shoulders, she said, "I want it all. You...us...now."

With a grin, Zander plunged into her warm channel. Like sweet nirvana, the sensation of her grabbing him almost had him coming immediately. Forcing his thoughts to her pleasure, he palmed her breasts, his thumbs flicking over her nipples.

His thrusts were hard, but Rosalie met each one with a thrust of her own. She crossed her ankles around his hips, her heels digging into his muscular ass, urging him on.

Watching her breasts bounce with each movement, her beauty laid out before him, Zander dropped his gaze to their coupling, watching as his cock, slick with her juices, moved in and out. He was struck with the intimacy of the act—the complete joining of two bodies. Feeling his balls spasm, he knew he would not last long but wanted her pleasure to come with his.

Reaching between them, he rubbed her swollen nub, eliciting a groan pulled from the depths of her lungs. Feeling her inner walls clamping onto his cock, he thrust again, climaxing into her warmth, his neck straining with the orgasm. As the last drop left his body, he fell forward, his chest landing on her, catching himself from crushing her at the last minute with his hands planted on the desk.

Gasping for air, he slowly became aware of the smile of contentment on her face. Dropping a kiss on her lips, he nuzzled her nose as he breathed in her essence.

"Mmmm," she moaned, satisfaction moving through her body.

Reluctantly pulling from her, he took care of the condom before grabbing some tissues to wipe moisture from her folds. Assisting her to a seated position, still perched on his desk, she looked around at her scattered clothing.

"Wow. I'll never look at this office the same."

Barking out a laugh, he quipped, "You? Hell, I don't know how I'll ever sit at this desk and work without getting a hard-on just from this memory."

Grinning, Rosalie blushed as she sat up, considering which article of clothing to go for first. Zander snagged her bra and dangled it from his fingertips. Shooting him a pretend glare, she took it, quickly fastening it on.

Pouting, he leaned over to kiss the tops of her breasts, saying, "Hate to say goodbye to these beauties."

"Well, you won't be missing them for too long," she teased.

After they both straightened the rest of their clothing, he reached out, taking both hands in his. "Were you serious? About moving back in?"

She heard the wistful hope in his voice and nodded. "Yes, but not tonight." Seeing his smile drop, she rushed to explain. "I've got to get my lessons in order this weekend while you're working, because I'm subbing on Monday and Tuesday. And, I know Miss Ethel said she doesn't mind me leaving, but I'd kind of like to have a few more days with her." Reaching up to cup his stubbled jaw, she admitted, "She's kind of become a mother to me too. Or maybe like a fairy Godmother."

Nodding, he agreed, his gaze warm on her. "Sounds familiar."

"How about if I move back in on Wednesday? If you take that day off, we can have the whole day together."

Leaning down, Zander planted a sweet kiss on her lips, his heart full. "You got it, princess."

Walking her to her car, he waved goodbye as she drove down the street before moving back into Grimm's. The bar was packed with the Saturday night crowd, but it appeared his staff had things in hand, despite his absence from the floor. He stood for a moment at the hall entrance, his hands on his hips.

Zeke passed by with a grin splitting his face. "All's well, Zander?"

"All's right with the world," came the easy reply. Making his way around the room, he relaxed slightly seeing the patrons having a good time, his servers hauling drinks and making tips, the bartenders keeping the crowd at the bar happy, and Roscoe and Zeke in place. Roscoe had moved to the back, giving Zeke his turn at the door. It was much noisier in the back, but they said they preferred it to the door, which was more boring. *Whatever...as long as we're covered.*

No bachelor or bachelorette parties—thank God. While Grimm's was full, it was a calm chaos. Groups sat at tables or the bar, couples danced in the back.

Lynn walked toward the back, her arms laden with two trays full of drinks. A man was shoved by another and knocked into her. With a scream, she fell forward, trays and glass crashing onto a table full of patrons. Pandemonium ensued as Lynn landed on several seated customers whose chairs tipped over, screaming in surprise.

"Fucking hell," he cursed. "There goes the peace."

By the time he pushed his way to the back, Roscoe was bent, assisting Lynn from the floor.

Zeke was coming from the front, while Zander grabbed the two men. "Time to go, assholes," he seethed, shoving them toward the door.

Walking back inside, he quickly scanned the room. Lifting eyes to the heavens for a second, he sucked in a huge breath. Moving into action, he assisted customers up, apologizing while promising free drinks. Several had wet clothes and he offered to pay their cleaning bills as well.

Lynn stood to the side, her eyes filled with tears. Charlene threw her arm around her, leading her toward the staff room. Thankfully he had just hired some new servers for the busier nights, so they jumped in, sweeping up the glass and mopping the floor. Roscoe moved the chairs back into place, his affable personality soon having the customers laughing at the commotion. Within ten minutes, the bar was set right and everyone was settled in with their drinks, listening to the music.

Jerking his head toward Zeke and Roscoe, he motioned for them to follow him to the back hall. "Seems the two drunks were fighting over a woman who had no desire to be around either of them. As a precaution, walk every female customer to their car—every single one."

With chin lifts from the two, he headed to the staff break room. Stalking over to Lynn, he pulled her into a hug. "So sorry, honey. I want you to call your husband and see if he can pick you up early."

"I'm fine, boss, really. I was just embarrassed and my wrist hurt a bit when I fell. But it's not broken, or even sprained. I just landed funny."

Looking at his watch, he said, "We close in half an hour. Lynn, you stay in the breakroom until your husband comes to pick you up."

An hour later, the bar was closed and everyone was ready to go home. Zeke and Roscoe had escorted all the female customers to their cars as they left, just as requested. Seeing everyone leave, Zander and Zeke locked up the bar after counting the till and locking the deposits into the safe.

"You okay, man?" Zeke asked.

"Yeah," he replied, clapping his friend on the back as

they approached their trucks. "Just a helluva way to end a night that started out so well."

With a laugh, Zeke waved goodbye and Zander climbed into his truck, wishing it was Wednesday already.

32

"Rosalie?"

Not recognizing the man's voice, she hesitated, Zander's cautions ringing in her ears. "Uh...who's calling, please?" she asked.

"I'm sorry. I didn't mean to catch you off guard. This is Rafe. I'm a brother...well, friend of Zanders—"

"Yes, of course," she replied, her nerves jumping as she remembered the conversation she overheard. "This is Rosalie."

"Listen, I owe you a huge apology," he confessed. "I know you heard the things I said to Zan and I never should have doubted you or his feelings for you."

"No, it's fine. Really, it is. After I thought about it, I realized you were right. I was dependent on him. And if we were to ever have a normal relationship, I needed to be autonomous and he needed to not have any guilt. Your opinion just forced us to both realize we needed to take a step back and give us some time."

"Wow," he said, the relief evident in his voice. "I felt terrible when Zan told me that you had left. He said you were staying with Miss Ethel?"

"Yes, and it's been wonderful. My parents have both passed, so she's been good for me to connect with."

"I'm glad and I'm sure she's loved having another woman around, as well."

Uncertain what to say, she picked at a piece of fluff on her sweater, her nerves taut.

"I'm glad I got to apologize before meeting you," he said. "I care for Zander and I'm starting to understand what you two have. I wish both of you all the best."

"Thank you," she gushed. "You mentioned meeting me…are you coming home?"

"Yeah, it looks like my contract here will end sooner than I thought and I'm heading back to Richmond to spend some time getting in touch with my roots and to decide what the hell I want to be when I grow up."

A laugh erupted from her, recognizing the humor Zander always claimed Rafe exuded. "Well, I'm sure Miss Ethel will keep you straight."

"You got that right," he agreed. "I'm hoping to get out there this week, so I'm looking forward to meeting you."

Disconnecting with a smile, she looked up as Miss Ethel walked into the room.

"What's put that smile on your face?"

Standing, she took the tea tray from the older woman's hands and set it on the coffee table. "Believe it or not, that was Rafe. He called to apologize and say that he's coming home soon."

"That boy always finds his way back, no matter how

much success pulls him far away." Sitting, she asked, "Did he say when he was coming?"

"Not for certain, just that he's hoping this week. I guess it's a good thing that I'm moving out."

"I certainly don't mind all the company, but I have a feeling Alexander is anxious to have you back with him."

Rosalie zipped up her suitcase and placed it on the floor of the room. With a smile, she twirled in a circle, her arms wrapped around her waist. *Today...I move back in today.* Zander was coming to Miss Ethel's at lunchtime so they could eat with her before she moved out. Rafe was expected imminently, although which day, he was unable to say until he could make the flight arrangements.

Walking down the stairs she passed Miss Ethel putting on her coat. "Are you cold?"

"I was just going to get the mail from the mailbox," she explained.

"I'll get it," Rosalie offered, kissing her on the cheek. "You sit down. We should have time for tea before Zander gets here for lunch."

Patting her cheek, Miss Ethel turned to head into the kitchen as she walked out onto the front porch. The sun beamed down, but the late fall day gave evidence that winter was just around the corner. Wrapping her light sweater about her tighter, she walked toward the mailbox at the end of the front walk. Seeing a man alighting from his vehicle, staring at her, caused her to slow her steps. She returned his smile, tentatively, as she took the envelopes from the mailbox.

"Rosalie?" he called out as he neared.

She blew out a breathe in relief. "Rafe?" He tilted his head to the side as though inspecting her carefully. Suddenly uncertain, she asked, "Um…are you Rafe?"

A wide grin crossed his face. "Yes, yes, I am."

Taking a step towards him, she attempted to hide her surprise that he did not match her expectations. "It's so nice to meet you finally. I know Zander will be so pleased you are here in time for lunch."

His smile lessened slightly, as his eyes shifted to the house behind her. Not wanting to seem uncharitable, she had a hard time reconciling the man in front of her with the knowledge that he was a model.

"Um, do you want to come inside? Miss Ethel was just fixing tea."

"No, no," he replied in haste. Looking back at his car, he said, "Um…I have some things in my car. Perhaps you would come help me with them."

With a backward glance at the porch, she noticed Miss Ethel had stepped out. Reassured, she nodded, "Sure." Waving toward the house, seeing Miss Ethel walking down the steps, she called out, "I'm going to help Rafe get some things out of his car and then we'll come in."

"That's not Rafe," Miss Ethel's voice rang out, her steps taking her closer to Rosalie. "That's not Rafe!"

Blinking in confusion, she looked back at the man and his face twisted in anger, but before she had a chance to move away, he grabbed her arm, dragging her toward him. A cloying scent of cologne filled her nostrils and she stumbled. The memory of him crowding her, touching her back, leaning over her, annoying her slammed into her. Other scenes of him coming into the restaurant in Baltimore began to flip rapidly through her mind. She cried out as her memory now included feeling him hit her over and over in the dark parking lot at Grimm's.

"Get back, old woman!" he yelled, wrenching her arm as she tried to jerk out of his hold. "Stop fighting," he growled, "if you want the old woman to stay safe."

She immediately stopped struggling, her chest heaving. "Why are you doing this?" she cried, fear clawing at her gut, her gaze shooting between his face and Miss Ethel, who continued to approach.

"You let her go," Miss Ethel ordered, her face set in anger.

"She and I've got unfinished business," he spit out, opening the trunk of his car. Looking down, he said, "Get in, or the next thing you'll hear is the old woman's screams."

Gasping, she looked up just as his fist made contact with her jaw. She fell backward into the trunk and the lid slammed down, then blackness descended.

Zander's tires squealed as he came to a halt outside Miss Ethel's place and jumped out of his truck, barely allowing the vehicle to come to a stop. Racing up the porch, followed by Zeke, he was met by Asher, Cael, and Rafe. His eyes raked over Miss Ethel, assuring she was safe, as she stood shaking in Cael's embrace. Another squeal of tires sounded and within a few seconds, Jayden and Jaxon arrived.

Pete, standing with two police officers, had just taken her statement and was issuing a BOLO for the man's license tag. Looking at Zander, he said, "Miss Ethel got his make, model, and more importantly, his tag number."

Cael assisted her to a seat, but she pushed their concern away. "I'm fine, I'm fine. Just so angry I could spit nails!" Looking at the others, she said, "Rosalie didn't remember him. When he approached, she thought it was Rafe."

"Fuck," Rafe cursed, then immediately apologized.

"Son," she said, "right now, I could cuss as well." She lifted her eyes to Zander, saying, "Please bring our girl back to us."

Dropping to her feet, he grabbed her hands. "I promised I would keep her safe," he said, his voice breaking. The others moved in, hands on his back in a show of solidarity.

"Martin Burgess," Pete said, looking at Zander. "The man's name is Martin Burgess. Address is listed for Baltimore. I've got someone sending his driver's license picture to Rosalie's former employer to see if he's the man from the restaurant that used to ask about her." Pulling his phone out, he turned it toward him. "Is this the man you saw next to Rosalie the night of the attack?"

He looked at the image, his heart seizing in his chest. "Yes," he growled. "That's the asshole."

"He used to work for the post office, but was let go last year due to allegations of harassing women on his postal route," Pete said, staring at the information coming through his phone. Looking up, he continued, "He's in a small, grey Honda sedan. Miss Ethel said the back, driver's side had a dent like someone had hit him with their bumper at some time."

Zander stood, then leaned over and kissed her cheek. Shooting a look to his friends, he said, "Cael, watch her." Gaining a nod, he turned and headed out the door, quickly followed by the others.

"Zander!" Pete yelled. "Don't get involved. Let me do my job!"

Whirling around, he stalked over. "My job was to protect her," he ground out. "I didn't and now my job is to get her back."

Lifting his hands, Pete said, "I get it, man. I do. But you running around, half-cocked, looking for his car, won't help her. And if you did happen to find him, you killing him won't help her either."

"Only way you can stop me is to arrest me, Pete." They stared at each other for a few seconds.

Dropping his hands, Pete responded, "Fuck." Looking over at Rafe, he added, "Keep him safe."

Rafe's own glower hit the policeman. "She's in this fucking mess because she thought the asshole was me. She was just trying to be nice. You don't gotta worry about Zander, 'cause if I get to him first, ain't gonna be much left for you to arrest."

With that, Zander headed to his truck. Calling out to the others, he said, "Drive around. The asshole hasn't been far and if he's kept an eye on her, then I'll bet he's still in the area." Climbing into his truck, he ignored the shaking of his hands. Pulling into the street, he willed his thoughts to slow. *Gotta focus...this is one dragon that won't get away again.*

33

Déjà vu crept over Rosalie as she blinked her eyes open. She was uncertain where she was, but she knew the pain in her jaw was from being hit. A trickle of fear slid down her spine, but instinct took over and she stayed motionless, closing her eyes to slits. *On a bed. Very little light...perhaps from a lamp. The sound of cars driving in the distance. The sound of a toilet flushing in the room next to me.* Moving her ankle and hands slightly, her heart leaped. *I'm not restrained!* Hoping her jaw was not broken, she felt anger slide into her being, replacing the fear from earlier.

Zander filled her mind, knowing he would be frantic and wondering how he would find her. The reality hit her...*I've got to take care of this on my own.*

Jolting upward, she shot her gaze around, seeing she was in a cheap hotel room. Recognizing the bedspread and standard picture on the wall, she realized it was the same hotel she had stayed at when she first came to

Richmond. *That means I'm not far from Grimm's! If I can get away...*

Hearing the water in the sink turn off, she scanned the room for a weapon, but found none. As the door opened, she watched as the man stepped into the room, his eyes narrowing when they landed on her.

"I thought you were dead," he said.

Stunned at the anguish in his voice, it still did not match the venom in his eyes. Feigning ignorance, she lifted her shoulder in a barely-there shrug. "I...don't remember you. I don't remember a lot of things."

His pupils dilated as he stared, hard and unyielding. Tilting his head to the side, he repeated, "You don't remember me? You don't remember anything?"

"No...should I know you?" Fingering her jaw, she adopted a confused tone, asking, "How did this happen?"

He jerked around, his eyes narrowing further. "You truly don't remember?"

"No," she lied, then looked around the room. "How did I get here?" Seeing the tension on his face ease, she hoped he continued to believe her subterfuge.

His shoulders relaxing, he smiled, stepping forward. Lifting his hand slowly, he barely touching her bruised jaw. "We're old friends, you and me. I saw you were hurt and brought you here to take care of you."

Her stomach lurched as his finger ran over her face. "Oh...uh...thank you," she murmured, scooting back. "Can I use the bathroom...please?" Attempting a shy façade, she hoped he would fall for her deception.

He stared for a moment, indecision in his eyes, before replying, "Yeah…sure."

She stood, holding herself steady while walking past him into the small, windowless room. *Nothing to use as a weapon here either.* Waiting a moment, she flushed the toilet so he would not be suspicious before washing her hands.

Opening the door, she spied him standing at the window, holding the curtain back slightly to peer out. "Will you be taking me home now?"

Turning to her, his eyes flashed dark. "Your place is with me. It's always been with me…I just had to prove to you that no one else can have you but me. I'm the only one who can take care of you."

Unease slithered over her, recognizing his loose hold on sanity. Continuing to pretend ignorance, she nodded slowly. Desperate for a reason to leave the room, she placed her hand on her stomach, rubbing in circles. "I'm really hungry. Can we go get something to eat?"

His eyes darted wildly about the room. "No," he bit out. "We need to stay here. But…but, I can order something. There's a pizza place nearby. I can call them."

Forcing the panic to recede, she agreed, "Sure, that'd be great." Maintaining her distance, she perched on the side of the bed, farthest away from him, keeping her eyes pinned on him. He picked up the phone in the room, dialing the number from a flyer laying on the small table. *I've got to get him when the pizza is delivered. That'll be my chance.* Determined to keep him calm in the interim, she waited until he hung up.

"Um, so we've known each other for a while?" she

asked, her voice soft, belying the pounding of her heartbeat.

He smiled, easing into the single chair in the messy room. "Yeah…we met in Baltimore. I'm Martin. Martin Burgess. You worked at a restaurant and that's where we met. We got to talking, started to see each other, you and me. Had some good times."

Knowing he was lying, she nodded encouragingly, clutching her hands in her lap to hide the trembling.

His smile was replaced with a scowl, as he continued, "But then you left. Didn't tell me where you were going. You just up and left."

"Oh, well, I'm glad it all worked out." Spying the lamp on the nightstand nearest her, she considered using it as a weapon. *When the pizza delivery comes, I can hit him from behind.* Swallowing deeply, she hoped that would be true.

"But it didn't work out at first," he ranted, standing as he raked his hand through his hair. "You pushed me away, so I had to punish you." His eyes darted to her face, his Adam's Apple bobbing, as he continued, "You understand that, don't you? If you're not with me, you can't be with anyone."

He took a step toward her, so she rushed, "Yes, yes. I see that now. I need to be with you."

Her words appeared to soothe him. Nodding, he heaved a sigh, "Good. It'll all work out now that I have you."

Attempting a smile, she prayed Zander would find her in time, but knew she had to be ready at any moment to take him on herself.

Eyes peeled for a light grey sedan with a large dent in the side, Zander raced through the streets. With his cell phone on, he and the others stayed in contact, expanding the grid they had determined would be the best plan.

"Zander? Jaxon and I've just circled the neighborhoods spreading out from Miss Ethel's. We've checked all the parking lots and alleys."

His heart heavy, he replied, "Keep going north. Rafe and Asher've got the west side, near the mall and the shopping centers there. Also, they're checking the—hang on, Pete's calling." Hitting the button, he bit out, "Pete? Talk to me."

"Your hunch was right. Seems he just used his credit card at Tino's Pizza Place, not too far from us. I've got units on their way to get the delivery address."

"I want him."

"Man, let us do our job. I'm calling you just to let you know that he's still in the area, like you thought. Not for you to do a damn thing."

"Let me know the address—"

"No. You and your brothers stand down. I'll let you know as soon as we have him."

Slamming his hand on the steering wheel, he opened his mouth to argue when a little red car with a Tino's Pizza sign on the top drove by, turning into a parking lot. "Fine, Pete," he agreed, "call me when you know."

Disconnecting, he dialed Rafe as he made a U-turn at the next intersection. Quickly explaining, he said,

"I'm on his tail. Might not be the right delivery, but I'm taking a chance. I'm on James Street and he's...shit! He's heading into the Westside Hotel. Let the others know and get here ASAP."

Watching the young man alight from the car, jogging up the stairs, Zander recognized this place. Rosalie had stayed here when she first got to town. Feeling a punch to the gut, it hit him Martin must have been here all along, just waiting for his chance with her.

Spying a grey sedan in the lot, he hoped he wasn't too late.

Martin turned from the window, his assessing gaze landing on Rosalie before moving toward the door.

He noticed as she stood and turned toward her, but before he could speak, she smiled while asking, "Is the pizza here? I'm starving."

He snapped his mouth closed and nodded. "Yeah... I've already paid, so I just have to tip the guy." He peeked out the security hole while reaching into his back pocket for his wallet. He opened the door, counting out a couple of dollar bills.

Not hesitating, she grabbed the lamp, giving a herculean tug to make sure the plug pulled from the wall, and hefted it over her head as she charged forward. Barely noting the delivery boy's wide-eyed expression, she brought it down just as Martin turned, throwing his hands up to protect his head.

Zander ran up the stairs at the end of the hotel, rounding the corner on the third floor, seeing the pizza delivery boy standing in a doorway. The pounding of his heart matched the pounding of his booted feet as he raced along the outside corridor. Barely aware of the squealing of tires in the parking lot below, he neared the door.

The delivery boy visibly flinched as an ear-piercing scream and crash from inside the room rang out, driving all thoughts from Zanders's mind except one. *That was Rosalie's voice.* With his hands in front to push the boy out of the way, he was halted as the boy stumbled backward into him almost bringing both of them down.

Moving the boy out of the way, he made it to the door in time to see Rosalie standing over Martin, the remnants of a broken lamp in her hand, just before she tried to jump over him to get to the door. Martin, his head and arm bloody, reached up to snag her foot just as she jumped and caused her to stumble. Looking up, she saw Zander standing with the light shining behind his body, looking every bit the avenging angel.

Zander rushed forward and kicked Martin's arm, releasing Rosalie and causing Martin to scream out in pain. She fell into his arms, crying, "You came, you came."

Red with rage, he gently moved her outside before turning back to the man dragging himself to his feet. With a punch to the abdomen, Martin doubled over in agony, his hands clutched around his middle. Grabbing his shirt, he pulled Martin up straight before landing a full-fisted hit to the jaw, dropping him back onto the bed, unconscious. Bending down to go at him again, he felt his arms pulled back and he whipped his head around.

"No, no, baby, please no more," Rosalie begged, hugging his arm to her chest. "It's over, please no more. I don't want you to get in trouble."

His chest squeezing with emotion, he turned, cupping her face with his rough hands, his gaze now landing on her bruised and swollen jaw. Rage returning, he bit out, "He put his hands on you—"

"Zander, I'm right here. I'm okay, I promise," she assured, clutching his hands with her own, desperate to leave. "Please, baby, take me home. Take me home."

At the word *home*, he felt his fury abate as her blue eyes held his, love shining through to his soul. Pulling her in tightly, pressing her face against his chest, he willed his heartbeat to slow. "Jesus, princess…all I could think of was what if I was too late—" His words halted as her fingers landed on his lips.

Raising her eyes to his, Rosalie said, "You're my hero, Zander. You've always been my hero."

A few minutes later, after the police arrived and sorted things, she watched Pete escort a bloody Martin to the cruiser, and grinned. "This time, we both slew the dragon."

3 4

The large group sat around Miss Ethel's table, extra chairs having been found and pushed into every available space. The older woman had rushed down the front steps to envelop Rosalie in her embrace as soon as Zander parked his truck and helped her out.

She assured Miss Ethel that she was fine, just banged up—again. Her joke fell flat as Miss Ethel spied her crooked smile due to the bruise. Ushering her in, she immediately began to pour coffee and serve sandwiches. The men helped and, soon, the gathering was more relaxed. Rosalie smiled, recognizing Miss Ethel had the gift of making everyone feel as though the crazy world was right again.

Zander kept tucking her into his embrace, so she finally gave up her seat, preferring to sit in his lap. She saw the furtive glances the men sent her way, their eyes dropping to her bruise before their grimaces made their own jaws tense with anger.

"Guys, I'm fine," she said. "You can stop with the glares. Pete's got him in jail and," she turned to him, adding, "he won't be getting out anytime soon, right?"

Agreeing, he explained, "I told the others that Martin Burgess used to work for the post office, but was let go last year due to allegations of harassing women on his postal route. He also has two counts of domestic battery, filed by two previous girlfriends. He'll try to lawyer-up, but with his past brushes with the law, this time he'll go to prison. Charges will be assault, kidnapping, stalking." Looking at her intently, he added, "And attempted murder. You name it, I'm asking the District Attorney to go for it."

Blowing out what felt like a long-held breath, she shook her head slowly. "It's hard to believe it's over. Finally, over."

Rafe grinned at Rosalie sitting on Zander's lap and said, "Gotta say, seeing the whoopin' you put on him before we got there...you did all right."

Laughing, Rosalie added, "And I have to say that meeting you in person is certainly more what I expected than when I thought he was you!"

"Yeah, Rafe's a real pretty boy," Zander quipped. As the mirth died down, he looked over at the others, saying, "I know you're gonna say that I don't need to do this, but thanks...to all of you for immediately jumping in to find her—"

"You're right, man," Jaxon interrupted, his gaze warm on the couple sitting across from him, "you don't gotta say it."

Pete stood to leave, saying goodbye to Miss Ethel

before turning to wave toward the others. After he left, Miss Ethel sat down next to the twins and smiled at Rosalie.

"My sweet girl, I predict only good things for you from now on."

Agreeing, she twisted her head to stare into Zander's eyes. "I think we both have our happily-ever-after."

His heart full, he leaned over, taking her lips in a sweet kiss. "You got that right, princess."

One Year Later

"Order up!"

Lynn grinned as she passed by Zander on her way to the counter, now in the back of Grimm's, picking up the platter of wings to deliver to customers. He rolled his eyes, but his lips turned up at the corners. Scanning the room, the large, flat-screened TVs gracing the four corners had the rapt attention of most of the patrons.

Walking by the bar, he gained nods from Joe and Charlene, indicating everything was under control.

Zeke clapped him on the back, saying, "I'll be out back. Got a delivery coming in."

"Everything okay?"

Barking out a laugh, Zeke said, "Hell, partner, with me running the kitchen, everything's great!"

He watched his new business partner stroll out back

and, with another glance around the crowded, and newly named Grimm's Pub, he knew it had been the right decision. The old regulars still came in for drinks —some to watch the games on TV, some to just chat with Joe and Charlene, others to sit quietly in a corner knowing one of the servers would keep an eye on them —but now, a newer clientele also came in, for the drinks and food.

His musings were interrupted as Roscoe, at the front, yelled, "Beauty on the floor!"

Eyes darting toward the door, his feet automatically headed that way. The smile that greeted him was almost as wide as his own as he wrapped Rosalie into his embrace, kissing the top of her head, relishing the feel of her body tucked next to his. Today, her long, blonde hair was pulled back in a low ponytail and she wore black pants, paired with black, heeled boots, giving her a sexy teacher look. An ice-blue sweater brought out the blue in her eyes but, more importantly, it pulled tight over her gently protruding stomach. He knew Roscoe had it right... she was a beauty...and she was his and having his baby. The beauty that was now his life overwhelmed him.

Inhaling deeply, relishing in her scent, he asked "How was your day?" He loosened his hold slightly, pulling back to peer into her eyes.

"Great," she replied. "Senior essays are graded and the juniors aced their state tests. My lesson plans are done and I've got all weekend to spend just with you."

His hand dropped to her stomach. "All good?"

Her smile, now glowing, filled her face, warming his heart.

"All snuggled in, safe and sound." Feeling the sudden sting of tears hit her eyes, Rosalie sucked in a shuddering breath. "You know, it's true…some fairy tales do come true."

Zander bent to place a soft kiss on her lips, feeling her body quiver next to his, before pressing her cheek back to his heart. *Yes, there are, princess…yes, there are.*

Six Years Later

Rosalie stopped at the opening of the bedroom and leaned against the doorframe, her gaze lovingly on the occupants inside.

Zander, sitting on the bed, had five-year-old Charity snuggled up close, his arm protectively around her, and three-year-old Evan curled up on the other side, his favorite blanket tucked under his chin, his eyes closed. A book lay open on her husband's lap, his voice ringing out through the room.

" **'And when he saw her looking so lovely in her sleep, he could not turn away his eyes; and presently he stooped and kissed her, and she awaked, and opened her eyes, and looked very kindly on him.'** "

"Oh, Daddy, is that what you thought when you kissed Mommy?" Charity asked.

"Yes, it was exactly what I thought," he answered, smiling down at her. Leaning over, he kissed the top of her head, adding, "And, it's exactly what I think of you too."

She stepped into the room, capturing his attention, his eyes twinkling as they landed on her. She bent to lift Evan, but Zander's hand on her arm stopped her.

"I'll get him," he said, lifting his son to move him over to his toddler bed, kneeling to kiss his chubby cheek as he tucked him in. Turning, he watched as she kneeled at Charity's bed, pulling the covers up around her neck.

He assisted her up, his hand around her waist. As she turned out the light, making sure the nightlight was on, he led her out of the room and down the hall into their bedroom.

An hour later, Zander lay with Rosalie snuggled into his side, her breath deep with sleep. The moonlight sneaked through the blinds, providing a glow to the room, illuminating her face. Pale skin, eyelash crescents on rosy cheeks, and a rosebud mouth. His sleeping beauty.

Closing his eyes, he allowed sleep to come, sweet dreams filling his soul.

Don't miss the next Heroes at Heart
Rafe

If you liked Picking Up the Pieces, check out the other books by me!

Maryann Jordan
Baytown Boys (small town, military romantic suspense)
Coming Home
Just One More Chance
Clues of the Heart
Finding Peace
Picking Up the Pieces
Sunset Flames

Heroes at Heart
Zander

Alvarez Security (military romantic suspense)
Gabe
Tony
Vinny
Jobe
Saints Protection & Investigations
(an elite group, assigned to the cases no one else
wants…or can solve)
Serial Love
Healing Love
Seeing Love
Honor Love
Sacrifice Love
Remember Love
Discover Love
Surviving Love
Celebrating Love
Searching Love (coming 2018)
Sleeper SEAL

Thin Ice

Letters From Home (military romance)

Class of Love

Freedom of Love

Bond of Love

The Love's Series (detectives)

Love's Taming

Love's Tempting

Love's Trusting

The Fairfield Series (small town detectives)

Emma's Home

Laurie's Time

Carol's Image

Fireworks Over Fairfield

Please take the time to leave a review of this book. Feel free to contact me, especially if you enjoyed my book. I love to hear from readers!

Facebook

Email

Website